The Rock of Banished Souls

BOOK 4 OF
THE GAVAN MADDOX
CHRONICLES

ALEX POLAK

Published 2022 by Your Book Angel

Printed in the United States
Edited by Keidi Keating
Layout by Rochelle Mensidor

ISBN: 978-1-7320268-4-1

This one goes out to my readers:

Without you guys, there wouldn't be Gavan.

Note from the Author

This is a work of fiction and no comparison is intended with any person, living or dead.

That being said, many people may find parallels with their lives and, ideally, some sense of hope or inspiration in my writing.

If you would like to talk to others about your and their enjoyment, look for my group on Facebook which I've called 'Dinas Affaraon – Followers of the Gavan Maddox Chronicles'. Come join us, I'd love to hear from you. I once heard another author state that the worst thing a writer can do is not be in contact with or not listen to their readers, and I don't want to make that mistake.

Come and join the family, I'm always about and interacting with the group. The people there are supportive of each other, just like a true family, and we'd love to expand. You'll find out updates about the next release, I do giveaways of signed books with each new release, and I'm always happy to discuss my books.

Hope to see you there soon.

Introduction

The battle was raging all around me. I was exhausted, desperately trying to fend off the attacks of the various magick users and monsters arrayed against us. My wards were failing, my energy all but depleted.

Paladin had done his best to support me, but a troll had grabbed him from behind just moments ago and broken his neck. I had already drained Seren of everything I'd stored, so now all I had was myself.

I heard an explosion to my right and saw a body flying through the air. I glanced over, only to see Gabby and Izzy slam against the wall and drop to the floor. They were charred, clearly hit by a powerful fireball.

I saw wave after wave of Order members overwhelming my allies in turn. Werewolves and werebears, vampires and obeahs, all were buried under the weight of the Order's forces.

I heard a scream and my blood ran cold, my eyes drawn to the sound. I saw a familiar body crumple to the ground, dark hair splayed over the floor and her face. Her once vivacious, laughing eyes now stared glassily up at the ceiling.

I fell to my knees, crying out against fate as I watched almost everyone I cared about dying around me. I couldn't even move, railing against the bonds that held me.

I thrashed against the wet...sheets? I came to my senses, unwinding myself from the sweat-soaked bedding and realising it had just been a nightmare.

Well, shit. So much for a good night's rest!

Chapter 1

I struggled through a few more hours, enjoying further relaxing montages of death, destruction, failure, and loss. By half past two, I simply gave up. Clearly my brain was still far too wired from yesterday's events to let me get any decent rest.

Despite having almost no sleep I felt strangely energised, so I thought doing something physical might burn off the residual adrenaline. Then *maybe* I could steal at least a couple of hours' shut-eye before breakfast. I crept out of bed carefully, trying not to wake the sleeping behemoth that had taken the recently vacated side of my bed.

The sight of his furry bulk, instead of the face I wanted to see, brought tears to my eyes and reinforced the crushing sense of incompetence I'd had since the fight in Edinburgh. I pulled on some workout clothes and, not wanting to wake the rest of the house, teleported myself out into the garden. If that thought surprises you, you've clearly forgotten who I am.

My name is Gavan Maddox. I'm a magick user of indeterminate type, apparently the 'Chosen of Isis' (yes, *that* Isis, the Egyptian goddess). I'd been hired to search for the Veil of Isis, finding more than I'd bargained for in the process. After getting my power unlocked and learning to use it, I'd returned to find my employer was royally pissed about the Veil not being accessible. In frustration, he had tortured his liaison to try to find out more about me and how to get it.

I'd rescued her, plus a couple of other unique employees, from the headquarters of the Order of the Nine Seals under Bolton Castle.

Then we, along with some new allies, had decided to go after the Order directly for all the crap they'd been pulling over the last couple of centuries. We'd gone after the three other sites around the UK and Ireland, leaving Bolton for last (which was supposed to be happening this evening, hence my desire for at least *some* sleep).

The site I was responsible for had been under Edinburgh Castle. It had gone OK, though our plans had been leaked so half our force had been incapacitated as soon as we entered. That led to a few deaths on our side during the battle, then an investigation to find the traitor. A Wiccan, of all things, had been the culprit, at which point I'd had the unenviable task of executing the poor woman who had only been trying to help her niece get away from the Order.

Gee, I wonder why I'd be having trouble sleeping after that?!

I stretched briefly, then started running through my katas. They usually help focus my mind or at least quiet it, but this time the images stubbornly kept running through my head. I even ended up with some overlap from my nightmares, at which point I realised I needed another option.

I went and grabbed one of the bamboo canes I'd used to prop up the blanket for the vampires. I planted it in the edge of the flower bed, since I wasn't stupid enough to make a dirty great hole in Seirina's lawn. I enlarged the cane as I had on the moors, then wrapped some fibrous matting from the greenhouse around it as padding. I then just started beating the living hell out of it.

As my mind came up with each image, I focused it in front of me and punched, kicked, elbowed, kneed, or some combination thereof until it went away. Before I knew it, the sky was lightening and two hours had slipped past. My arms and legs felt like rubber but at least the catharsis felt reasonably effective.

I shrank the bamboo again, putting it and the matting away, then filled in the hole in the flowerbed. I translocated back to my room, pulling off my t-shirt and sweats as I went into the bathroom. I took a quick shower to rinse off the perspiration before clambering back into bed.

I had to roll Paladin over again, since he'd taken advantage of my absence to commandeer the whole of the mattress. His groan and snort brought a smile to my face for the first time since I'd woken up, so I covered myself with the sheet and wrapped an arm around the big furry lump. I drifted back off to sleep, hoping to be favoured with some slightly more pleasant imagery from my subconscious this time.

I woke up to the sound of my phone alarm, realising I'd actually managed to sleep without dreams for a solid couple of hours. I wasn't exactly rested, but at least I wouldn't look like I'd been up all night partying now. I still had some shadows under my eyes when I looked in the mirror, though hopefully they'd fade with a couple of pints of Cafegeddon.

I scrubbed the stale taste out of my mouth and showered again. I couldn't be bothered to shave this morning, so I dressed in jeans and a t-shirt then went downstairs following the smell of coffee. My stomach growled loudly just as I got to the door of the kitchen, drawing a smile and a chuckle from Mrs Wilson.

"Sounds like you're ready for breakfast!" she remarked kindly, setting a big plate of eggs, bacon, and sausages in front of me. I thanked her and reached for the coffee pot. My first mug went down in one go, the slight scorch down my throat adding to the wake-up punch of the caffeine. I refilled my mug and dug into my food.

I was savouring my fried deliciousness when I heard footsteps approaching. I looked towards the door, nodding at Seirina as she entered and rising six inches out of my chair. She shook her head at my outdated chivalry, though I could tell she liked the gesture. I just hoped it would work on Angelica as well.

As soon as I even thought her name, my stomach clenched so tight I thought my breakfast was going to make a surprise reappearance. I swallowed hard, then set my cutlery down carefully while still fighting my rebellious digestive tract. How would she react this morning?

My mind started running through all the things we would need to explain to her. How could we bring her up to speed without at least touching on her torture? I remembered mentioning it in passing in Edinburgh but there had been so much going on, she might not even have noticed. I also recalled something between her and the twins when we rescued her and they had scanned her; something about how 'that wasn't the way it worked' and 'he told her when he was torturing her'.

I had a funny feeling it was something painful and personal, so maybe she was better off having it wiped away. Then again, without all that, why would she fight against the Order? She may not have been completely happy working for them, and now that she was free she would hopefully be much more content, but she wouldn't have the same impetus to join us.

There was also 'us'. I definitely remembered her admitting she'd volunteered to be the liaison to me after seeing my photo in the Order's files. However, things had progressed in a very unique way when she had come to see me at Dinas Affaraon. I didn't really want to have the same argument over unwanted telepathy again, plus I certainly didn't feel like trying the 'XXX defence' with observers on hand. Particularly since the twins would be able to see anything she could.

On the fourth hand (Fifth? Sixth? How many hands was it now, and how many did I get?), with my abilities now, none of them would be able to read my mind unless I specifically allowed it anyway. I put my elbows on the table and my head in my hands, feeling the onset of a migraine making an unwelcome appearance.

"It'll all work out, don't worry," Seirina said, making me lift my head off my hands to look at her. "Her feelings were genuine before. You just need to give her some time to get to know you again."

I wasn't surprised she'd known my train of thought, given her enchantress abilities. She'd read my emotions before so I was quite sure she was doing it now, and I was just as certain my conflicted feelings about Angelica would be easy for her to discern.

"Yeah, as long as we survive taking down the Order," I replied, sick of the platitudes everyone had been inundating me with ever since Angie's mind had been wiped. Why did people think all those trite phrases would make a difference?

"You can't–" Seirina started to say.

"If you say I can't give up, can't lose hope, or anything else along those lines," I interrupted, "I think I'll scream. Possibly followed by punching something."

The shock on her face was a picture.

"I'm only trying to help!" she said, crossing her arms and sitting back in her chair. She huffed, regarding me sullenly from under lowered eyebrows. Fortunately, Mrs Wilson broke the tension by putting Seirina's toast in front of her.

"Sorry," I said. "I've had a long night of my brain showing me all my mistakes, both real and imagined, plus plenty of worst-case scenarios for today. My temper is slightly frayed right now."

Seirina had the good grace to accept my apology, uncrossing her arms and reaching for her mug. I picked up the pot and poured for her, completing my contrition with caffeine. She added milk and sweetener, then sipped.

I picked up my cutlery and finished my breakfast, washing it down with the rest of my second mug of coffee. I refilled it again, at which Mrs Wilson took note of the level in the cafetiere and put the kettle on for another pot.

I sat back in my chair, cradling my mug in my hands and sipping more slowly than I had with my first two. The sugar, fat and caffeine were steadily entering my bloodstream, lifting my mood and preparing me to face the day.

I heard someone coming down the hall, so I lifted out of my seat again as soon as the door opened.

"Oh look, he's standing up for us," said Izzy as the twins came into view.

"Yes, but I don't think we're who he was waiting for," added Gabby, smirking as I sat down with a thump.

"'Morning girls," I said, doing my best to stay up-beat. I was a hair away from feeling embarrassed, though it wasn't like everyone didn't know how I felt about Angie. It was a little late to try and play it cool now.

"'Morning," they chimed out together.

"How are you feeling this morning?" I asked, desperate to turn the focus away from myself and fill the time until Angie got downstairs.

"We're fine, thanks," said Gabby cheerily.

"Yes, we slept great," Izzy agreed.

"Good," I said, "because we need to go through the information Eligos picked up from his raid."

Gabby nodded while Izzy had already started on their coffee. It made me feel slightly schizophrenic when they started doing different things at the same time. How did it work when one was eating and the other was drinking? The mind boggled.

Then all of that went right out of my head as I heard footsteps in the hall again. There was only one person it could be now so I shot to my feet, almost knocking my chair over as I did. I ran a quick hand through my hair, ignoring the soft sniggers from the twins.

"Good morning, Angie," I said as she came through the door. She looked over at me and smiled, and my heart skipped a beat.

Time to make a second first impression (shut up, I know what I mean).

Chapter 2

I stepped to the side and pulled a chair out for Angie, ignoring the tittering from the twins as they put their heads together.

"A true gentleman," Angie said, "how rare these days." She dimpled as she sat down, hovering slightly to allow me to push her chair in for her. I sat back down, reaching for the coffee pot and pouring her a mug-full. I added the amount of milk and sweetener I knew she preferred, handed it to her, and held my breath.

"Oh wow," she said, closing her eyes to savour the taste. "I've never had coffee so smooth before. What is it?"

"My own personal blend, which I've named Cafegeddon," I replied, smiling as I recalled the first time she'd tried it. Her reaction then had been almost identical – which I realised made perfect sense, seeing as she was now almost exactly who she'd been then, thanks to her memory wipe.

"Thankfully," Seirina said, startling us both out of our private little moment, "Gavan brought his coffee with him, and was kind enough to share. Now that I know the recipe, it's my first choice too."

I looked over at her and she gave me a ghost of a wink. I realised she was still on my side, showing my generosity to Angelica. I inclined my head slightly, toasting her with a minimal raise of my coffee mug.

I felt heartened to know I had allies in my quest to win Angie over again. It was a daunting feeling, knowing my efforts over the last couple of months had been wiped away, but at least now I wasn't alone.

I refilled my mug again, finally feeling human after my lack of sleep last night, then sat back in my chair with a sigh. I relaxed as the ladies chatted, enjoying a few moments of peace before we had to start planning for the evening's assault on Bolton Castle.

Once everyone had finished, we adjourned to the study. I pulled the memory sticks Eligos had given me out of my pocket, handed them to Seirina and sat down as she switched on her computer.

Both were filled with personnel files, each one with various tags denoting personal pressure points which could be utilised to force obedience. It was a terrifying insight into the workings of the Order and the mind of its leader. I even saw some files marked as 'failed'. I went to the desk and opened one, seeing it related to a werewolf.

They'd tried to recruit her but she hadn't been interested. Then they'd tried to coerce her and she'd fought back.

So they'd killed her.

I closed that file and scrolled through the list, my anger rising with each new 'failed' file I counted. The number of families who had lost someone was heart-breaking, making me more and more determined to remove this blight from the magickal community.

"Oh my God," whispered Angelica, following the scrolling files from where she was sitting. "I knew they coerced people, if only from my own experience, but I had no idea they went this far!"

The twins had their heads pressed together, hugging themselves, and Seirina had tears streaming down her face. Clearly none of them had known quite how bad things were with the Order, how deeply their operatives had tried to insinuate into the families of anyone they were interested in.

"Seirina, I need you to start going through these lists," I said. "Pull out the names of anyone who was coerced, plus the families of anyone on the 'failed' list. Try and contact them; see if any of them want to join us.

"Since we're not using zombies this time you won't need to do any prep-work before the fight this evening, though we'll definitely want them for next time. I have a feeling the American site is going to be a serious challenge, given the most monstrous Order members have been moving there since it was opened." I cast a sideways glance at Angie but she didn't react, too engrossed in the horror of the lists to give any notice to what I was saying.

Seirina noticed my attention, shrugging as I looked back at her. I wasn't disheartened by the lack of acknowledgement, however. Truth be told, I actually found it encouraging to see how upset Angie was by this evidence of the Order's hideous behaviour. It showed her humanity hadn't been corrupted by working for the scummy little turd at the top.

"I want the three of you to stay here tonight," I said to Angie and the twins, bracing myself for the backlash from attempting to give orders to women (however well-meaning those orders might be).

"Good," said Angie.

I thumped down heavily into my chair, my eyes wide.

"I'm quite happy to sit this one out," she continued. "We can help make phone calls, collate the lists..." Her eyes suddenly unfocused, a shiver running over her shoulders.

I was tempted to look into her mind to see what was upsetting her, though I restrained myself. She would undoubtedly sense me intruding, given her own telepathic abilities, and I didn't want to offend her. I'd prefer her to tell me things because she *wanted* to, not because she felt a need to explain her own thoughts after I'd peeked in uninvited.

"Well, I'll leave you ladies with the important work," I said, hoping to convey my appreciation for their efforts. "Meanwhile, I need to touch base with Summer at Dinas Affaraon."

Seirina rolled her eyes and suppressed a smirk, obviously knowing exactly what I was attempting to do, but she allowed me my subterfuge. After all, she *was* an enchantress. She'd offered her support and advice before; I doubted she'd be upset by my ongoing feelings for Angie.

I took my leave of them, headed back up to my room, and woke G and Pal. I teleported us to my office in the shop and Paladin sniffed around eagerly, intrigued by this new and exciting location. Gauvain and I left him investigating and went out into the main area, hearing Summer rattling around in the kitchen as we exited the office.

I crept in behind her, poking her in the sides and then laughing raucously as she shrieked loudly and jumped about three feet into the air.

"You stupid bastard!" she swore, slapping me on the chest before laughing along with me. "Why do you always take delight in scaring the shit out of me? You really do have a twisted sense of humour. So how's everything going with Angelica? What's going on with the Order? When d'you think you'll be finished with them?"

"I see nothing's changed," I jumped in as she drew breath. "You still ask twenty questions before you get the answer to the first."

"Hey, you're the one who had a mystical awakening, not me," she replied brightly. "I'm still the same old Summer."

"A fact I'm sure Emily appreciates every day," I told her, winking. "And yes, I'll *always* enjoy making you jump. To answer your other questions, we've taken down the Order's satellite offices and we're going after their headquarters this evening. Then we'll attack their final site over in America. So hopefully, we might be finished in a few days." I held my breath, ignoring Gauvain's chuckle in my head.

"Nice try," Summer said, crossing her arms. "I *know* you didn't miss the Angelica question. Come on, give!"

G laughed in my head again and I sighed, acknowledging my delinquency. I filled Summer in on the broad strokes of my relationship with Angie, shielding my ears from the various squeals and squeaks of Summer's joy. Then I watched her face fall as I informed her of the mind-wipe Angelica had suffered, hope making it light up again as I told her of the conversations after.

"At least there's still a chance," Summer reassured me, gathering me up in a hug. I wrapped my arms around her familiar form, drawing comfort from my friend, then released her and stepped back.

"I wanted to check in on you, make sure you were OK," I said, "but now I need to get back. I'll keep you updated as things go on."

She crossed her arms again, tapping her foot and tilting her head as she looked at me.

"I promise," I laughed, holding my hands up defensively. "Daily updates from here on!"

"You'd better," she scolded, "and there better be some good news in there. Otherwise *I'll* kick your ass, never mind the damned Order!"

"Yes, dear." I sighed and rolled my eyes, ducking as she swatted at my head in response to my sarcastic tone. We both laughed again, and I pretended to run away as I went back towards the office. It was nice to enjoy the simple pleasure of catching up with an old friend, especially after the insanity of the last few weeks.

Don't get me wrong, I was grateful my magick had been unlocked. Still, it had complicated my life in ways I never could have imagined before. Yet another case of the eternal truth, 'Be careful what you wish for'.

Paladin bounced over as G and I re-entered the office, almost knocking me over as he rubbed against my side. I laid my hand on his head and teleported us back to my bedroom in Seirina's house.

I opened the window to allow Gauvain outside for a flight. Paladin, on the other hand, jumped up onto the bed and flopped down, laying his head on his paws for a nap like any dog given the opportunity.

As I opened the door, I could hear overlapping voices from downstairs. The ladies were obviously busy contacting potential allies for our fight against the Order.

I set off down to the study to join them.

Chapter 3

I reached the study door, tapping lightly before I walked in. There was no point standing outside waiting for permission, not with three women talking on phones – I'd be lucky if any of them had even heard me!

Seirina gave me a single upward nod when she saw me, waving me to the only unoccupied chair in the room. I sat and waited, losing myself in my reflections. There were so many different things spinning through my head, I started getting dizzy.

There was the Order: The assault on Bolton Castle, discovering the location of the American site, assaulting the American site, and defeating Elrulin somewhere in there.

Then there was Iyrin: What was it? How did I free myself from it? How could I make sure it stayed away from those I cared about?

Alongside those, what about Angie? Should I be trying to get her memories back, or was she better off without the trauma? Could I rekindle our relationship from scratch?

Also, my shop and Summer: Could I put my expansion plans into effect? Would Summer get on well with the twins? Would Angie enjoy working with them as well?

Plus, what about Lucian? What was he really up to with Elrulin? Should I try to defend him to Isis, given what I'd learned about him? Could I ever truly trust him?

Then there was Elrulin himself: Did I stand a chance against him? Should I try to capture him and take him back to Isis, or simply kill him since he'd already been judged by the Aaruan council? How could I counter his Aaruan abilities *and* his new vampiric nature?

I leant forward, put my elbows on my knees and my head in my hands. The whirlwind of thoughts chasing each other through my mind crystallised into one focal idea: I was *SO* screwed!

Then again, as I'd remembered before, when you were hip deep in shit (or possibly deeper in my case) there was no point whining about it. Pick a direction and start walking. I was here, now. Time to deal with it and move forward as best I could.

"Everything OK at your shop?" Seirina's voice cut through the murmur of other voices in the room, raising me out of my self-pitying introspection.

"Yeah, no problems," I replied lightly, then sighed dramatically. "Summer is now demanding daily updates, however, with a requirement of good news included." I cast a quick glance towards where Angelica was sitting, knowing that Seirina would pick up on and understand the gesture. True to form, she gave a gleeful, almost demonic grin as she no doubt contemplated meddling in my love life.

"Well, we'll just have to see what we can do about that then, won't we?" she remarked. The only thing missing was an evil chuckle and her rubbing her hands in anticipation. I smothered the terror that threatened to lift my stomach into my throat at the thought of her getting involved in my relationship with Angie, covering it with an overly exaggerated sigh.

"I think I'd rather proceed at my own pace, if you don't mind," I stated, tilting my head and raising my eyebrows. This time it was a laugh that threatened to break free, given the disappointed huff that Seirina expelled as she sat back with her arms crossed.

"Spoilsport!" she observed tartly, before giving me the ghost of a wink. "Then again, probably for the best." I pretended to wipe my brow in comical relief, noticing as I did that the twins had finished their calls and were listening in to the end of our conversation. I shut up and sat back in my chair, especially as it sounded like Angelica's conversation was also drawing to a close.

"So how's it looking?" I asked, once she'd hung up the phone. "Think we'll get any more to join us?"

"It could take weeks to go through both of these memory sticks, even if we get anyone who's willing to contact friends like a phone tree," Serina said, looking at her screen again. "We'll definitely get more allies. I just don't know if it'll be in time for the assault on the American site. You can forget about Bolton tonight; you've no chance of any new fighters."

"We won't need them tonight," I observed, wanting to reassure them their efforts weren't in vain. "With all of Eligos' forces in one place, plus our own, Bolton should be easy. The only deciding factor will be whether Elrulin is still there. If he is, it'll be me who has to face him anyway. To be honest, I'm not sure if I'd rather get this over with or put off facing him until I've gathered more energy and come up with a viable strategy." My stomach flipped over again as my anxiety about the fight swamped me.

"I don't know that any one person stands a chance against him," Angelica said, wide-eyed. "Everything I've seen or heard about him seems to indicate he's got abilities unlike anything you've ever encountered!"

I realised I hadn't yet told her about my Veil quest and resultant magickal awakening, nor the level of my training. We'd all been so focused on filling her in on her *own* forgotten events, none of us had thought to recap any other pertinent information. I went over the high points for her, Seirina and the twins chipping in occasionally with various factoids they felt I'd skipped – like how I'd met Isis herself, how remarkable my improvement had been, and the fact that Elrulin was from Aaru, so I actually *was* familiar with his abilities (other than the whole soul-eating thing).

Her memory wipe also meant she'd forgotten the revelation regarding Lucian's origins, so she was now just as in the dark as the rest of them. By the end of our little catch-up session, Angie was looking at me with wide eyes and her mouth slightly open.

"So you basically have the powers of a *GOD*?!" she whispered, at which I winced slightly and rubbed the back of my neck.

"Umm, well, maybe a small 'g'," I temporised, not wanting to elevate myself to such lofty heights. Seirina had no such qualms, snorting indelicately at my self-deprecation.

"Says the man who can piss off the Devil and live to tell about it!" she said, tilting her chair and winking at me behind Angie's back. I narrowed my eyes and pursed my lips at her in annoyance that was only partly in jest, though she just laughed softly.

"Regardless, I don't think Elrulin should be underestimated," I told them, trying to get back to the matter in hand. "That's why I'd rather you, Gabby and Izzy stay back this evening." I directed this last comment to Angelica, at which she nodded in understanding. The twins were also relieved at being kept out of harm's way.

"Probably for the best," Izzy remarked.

"Yes, we'd be more of a hindrance than help," Gabby agreed.

"They know where to look for any files now."

"And we're not exactly warriors."

"We're definitely more useful staying away from the fighting."

"And Gavan could always come and get us afterwards if he needs us."

"Great," I interrupted, "so you three can stay here and keep working on the files. Seirina and I will gather the rest and take on the Bolton Castle site this evening. Hopefully we'll find details of the American location, then we can take that down and finally be done with all this. I, for one, can't wait to get back to my regular life, and I'm quite sure Seirina is looking forward to having her house to herself again."

"Well," Seirina replied, "while it has been pleasant having company, I *am* ready for a little peace and quiet again. After all, they do say–"

"Fish and guests begin to stink after three days?" I finished for her, raising my tone at the end to check my interpretation of her thought process. Her subtle grin was all the answer I needed. Although Mrs Wilson was more than capable of caring for a larger group, decades of living alone had no doubt accustomed Seirina to a more peaceful setting than she had been allowed for the past few weeks.

"At the very least," I remarked, "I should be safe to move back to my own home once we've finished the assault on Bolton Castle. After all, I can set up wards the same as we have here and I already have at my shop.

"Tomorrow, if you like, I can introduce you to Summer and we can get you started in the shop," I said to Gabby and Izzy, watching as their faces lit up in anticipation. I turned to Angelica. "I would be more than happy to extend the same offer to you, as well," I told her. "I know you'll be looking for employment now that you've escaped the Order's clutches."

"That's very kind," she replied, sounding a little uncertain, "but your file said your shop is quite small. Would you really have the space and resources to employ all of us *and* your existing staff-member?" she asked.

"Of course, you've forgotten the conversation we had a few days ago!" I slapped my forehead in annoyance. I really had to get used to having conversations over again, otherwise poor Angie would start feeling like an outsider as we discussed ideas we had already established. "My magickal awakening has given me several ideas for expanding my store, not least of which is keeping it open twenty-four hours a day to cater to the magickal community."

Angie's eyebrows raised at my ambitious plans, though the twins' eyes sparkled as they sat forward. They were clearly eager to get their new lives started and I knew Summer would be endlessly fascinated by them. They would also give her help and company when I wasn't there. Furthermore, she'd be able to have a proper holiday – maybe even a honeymoon, if I could finagle things properly with Emily.

Mrs Wilson brought in some tea and sandwiches for lunch, so we chatted about the plans I'd come up with while we ate. Then the ladies returned to the computer files while I went to let Gauvain and Paladin out for a stretch.

The afternoon wore on, and my adrenaline began to rise as I prepared for this evening's assault.

Chapter 4

We decided to have an early dinner, so Seirina and I would be fuelled up and ready for the fight; plus the ladies would be re-energised to continue their efforts. Mrs Wilson made her fabulous lasagne again, one of my favourites, and I indulged in the garlic bread since I didn't have to worry about my breath for kissing now.

As it neared six o'clock, I got ready for my excursion. I belted on my sword, Muharar, and Gauvain entered his claw on the bracelet I had made in Aaru and now wore constantly. Since we'd be inside in close quarters again, he wouldn't have space to fly. Paladin's tail was a blur as he wagged it in anticipation. I went downstairs to await Seirina, preparing to take us to the vantage point where I had parked before my mission to rescue Angelica.

Once Seirina had joined me and we had the others' best wishes I teleported us both, along with Paladin, to the parking area I remembered from that fateful morning so long ago, and yet so recently. I idly recalled snippets of the conversation I'd had with Angie and the twins while I waited for Seirina to text the various faction leaders, asking them for photos for me to use to set up portals. I messaged Lucian to request that he inform Eligos, sending along a picture of where we were.

As the responses began to arrive, I opened gateways to bring our forces through. We greeted each other as friends now, bonds formed through our previous battle together. There was also a new sense of deference towards me, a certain degree of respect I hadn't noticed previously. I hoped it wasn't fear inspired by my role as executioner the night before. The actions I had taken had been abhorrent to me, however necessary they may have been.

The last thing I wanted was to become known in the magickal community as an executioner, someone to be feared. I was trying to *rid* our world of a threat, not replace it. What use would it be to expand my store and cater to the supernatural species if they were all too afraid to come?

I would just have to hope that fighting alongside me tonight and in America would show them they could trust me, prove to them I was still the same man I was before. After all, war required a different mindset and code of conduct. I was sure those who had lived long enough to experience the difference would know that, and maybe help those of the younger generations to see it too.

I felt my cheeks aching with the fixed smile I was putting on as a front. I wanted to appear friendly and approachable, however the rictus look seemed to be more weird than welcoming. It was definitely the younger Wiccans who were shying away, though whether it was my expression or the fact that I'd executed one of their own last night was unclear.

Eligos arrived just as the last group, namely the vampires, were also arriving. I'd brought them last since I didn't have a tent set up like I had on the moors. I now knew they could survive the sun, but I didn't want to make them any less comfortable than they needed to be.

Once I'd closed the portal behind Dominic's group, I went over to Eligos to work with him and get a look inside the site. I knew we needed to head into the top floor meeting room, as we'd originally planned for Edinburgh, but I wanted to make sure I wouldn't be teleporting into the middle of a gathering of some kind.

He immediately agreed with my caution, as I knew he would, reaching out to grasp my wrist as he had done before. Since I knew where Bolton Castle was, I directed him on our psychic flight. We were at the chapel in moments, zipping straight down through the altar into the tunnels. I missed the guard vampires, though I assumed they were back at their vantage points where I had seen them on my rescue mission.

The meeting room was empty, though we went over to the activity notice board to ensure there wasn't something booked for the next couple of hours. The next meeting was scheduled at ten a.m. the following day, so Eligos brought us back to our bodies at the vantage point car park. I thanked him, then went to talk to Aurora.

"Hey," I started, relieved when she, at least, didn't shy away from me. "Where do you want to set up this time? You could stay here, or I could take you to the gardens of Bolton Castle just before we attack; it's entirely up to you."

"I think we'll stay here," she replied after a few moments' consideration. "It's a beautiful area, and you can teleport or portal people here just as easily as to the gardens. Plus, there's less chance of some random straggler stumbling over us and ripping us apart before anyone can get to us."

"Fair enough," I said, wincing a little at the thought of a vampire or some other enemy tearing through the Wiccans. I appreciated their help, despite them not being fighters. They had provided what support they could with the scapulars I had passed out at Edinburgh, and fortunately we hadn't needed their healing expertise for any serious injuries thus far. Still, no need to push our luck if we didn't have to.

"OK," I called out, raising my voice to get everyone's attention, "everyone get ready. I'm going to teleport in, then open a portal for the rest of you. We'll take it floor by floor, working downward.

"Eligos, you and your forces go through the castle itself. Look for any Order offices above ground, either take care of any members you find or drive them down into the tunnels for us to deal with."

Everyone agreed to the plan, then I established the area where I'd open the portal and teleported into the meeting room. It was as empty as I'd seen with Eligos, so I opened the portal to bring everyone in from the vantage point.

They all came through together, acting more as a unified team rather than the disparate factions they had been before the Edinburgh assault. The vampires went straight out to start clearing the offices on this floor, leaving the rest of us to catch up as we could.

To my surprise, the entire floor was deserted. The vampires were coming out of the offices and reporting that the filing cabinets were empty, looking as though everything had already been ransacked. I got a bad feeling, a sense of foreboding about what we would find as we went through the rest of the floors.

Since there was nothing to go through on this floor, Dominic and the other vampires joined us as we went down the stairs to the next level. We burst out from the stairwell in a mad rush, immediately splitting into two groups to go left and right. Once again, every office we came to was vacated; the corridors were deserted and filing cabinets hung open and empty.

We met up on the far side of the level from the stairs, furious at our enemy getting away, yet all somewhat relieved that we weren't having to fight.

"Don't lose focus," I warned everyone. "It would be just like those underhanded assholes to set something like this up, then ambush us as we get complacent. Keep your eyes and ears open." I looked around, getting nods of acknowledgement from everyone.

We went back to the stairs, continuing down through the levels. Each floor told the same story: Empty rooms, files gone, clear evidence of abandonment due to some kind of forewarning. Our initial enthusiastic charge soon slowed to a purposeful stride, though heads were always swivelling to check doors, look round corners, and monitor behind us. No one wanted to be caught in an ambush.

Soon enough, we reached the bottom, coming out into the corridor leading to the cell block vault door. As we approached the door, it swung open and Eligos came out. He had obviously made it through the offices above ground in the castle, then found his way down.

"There is no need to go farther," he informed us, at which my shoulders finally slumped in dejected frustration. "By your appearance, I see you have encountered the same as I. So the Order has clearly become aware of our assaults last night, and thus has abandoned this location as the next logical target."

"Exactly," I agreed. "I don't know if they got some kind of alert from one of the other sites, like a silent alarm or something, or whether someone else among our forces let something slip again." There was angry muttering from behind me at that comment.

"I tend to favour the former explanation," I continued, raising my voice above the swell of discontent. "Especially after having scanned everyone last night. Whatever happened, we need to try and find *something* that can point us towards the location of the American site."

"The archives here are gone," Eligos informed me, "and the offices above have likewise been cleared. How do you intend to locate our quarry? While I can view at a distance, I need a target. I cannot simply search the entire planet, nor even just North America."

"Does anyone have any psychic abilities?" I asked the group. Disappointingly, though unsurprisingly, there were heads shaken.

"Not personally," came Seirina's voice from the back, "but I might know someone who does."

"Fine," I said, a plan forming. "Wait here, I'm just going to take a quick look at Elrulin's office so I can teleport back to it without having to go through the entire base. Then I'll take you all out." I gestured to Eligos and he turned, leading me through the holding cells and past the time suite where I had been questioned.

We went through the archives and at the far side, there was an elevator. This took us up into the castle itself, the doors opening into an opulent office suite. There were scraps of paper on the floor, no doubt dropped during the hurried evacuation, though the offices and cabinets were as denuded as those below.

I took a good look, committing the location to memory, then nodded to Eligos to indicate I was done. We went back down, re-joining the rest of our forces. I opened a portal, leading the way through to the car park where the Wiccans were waiting.

There were a few gasps conveying their surprise at our quick return, possibly indicating to them something may have gone wrong. I explained what we'd discovered while the rest of the group came through. The Wiccans soon became just as disheartened by our frustrated efforts as the rest of us.

"I'll let everyone know once we've located the new site in America," I told them all. "For now, go home and relax. At least we can be happy we've chased the Order out of the country!" There were cheers, though I had a sudden thought.

How had they left so quickly? Did they now have someone who could open portals? If so, we were actually *less* safe than before. That had to be the first thing I looked into.

Chapter 5

I sent everyone away through portals, then took Seirina back to her house where the twins and Angelica were eagerly awaiting our update. They were as surprised as the Wiccans had been at how soon we returned, expressing a combination of relief at our safety and disappointment at how we had been thwarted in our endeavours as we told them what we'd found.

"I need to check something out," I informed them, pulling out my phone. I looked up the airfield or airport closest to Bolton Castle, discovering Manchester is a mere sixteen and a half miles away. I rang the airport, asking about any large group who had booked last minute. Unsurprisingly, they refused to release such information to a civilian. Seirina caught on and motioned me to hang up. I did so, raising a questioning eyebrow at her as I did.

She picked up the phone on her desk, then put it back down and reached for her rolodex. She flipped through, stopping after a few seconds, then picked up her phone again to start dialling.

"Brian?" she said. "It's Seirina. Seirina Cr- Oh, you and your flattery." She chuckled at some comment from the other person, presumably 'Brian'. "Listen, I need a favour. Yes, yes, I'll offset it against your tab. Look, I need to know if any large group suddenly flew out in the last couple of days. No, I'll hang on. I need to know quite quickly."

She sat quietly, tapping her fingers in time to the 'hold' music I could just about hear from the receiver. After a couple of minutes, the music stopped and the voice came back. I still couldn't quite hear what it said, though I got the general idea from Seirina's responses.

"A private charter?" she remarked. "Yes, that's probably it. A *full-size* passenger airliner? How many would that hold? Around four hundred – yeah, that must be them. When did they leave?" She closed her eyes and sighed, sagging back into her chair. "Four pm this afternoon? Thanks Brian. No, I *don't* owe you now, you cheeky sod. You've a way to go to get square! Yeah, you tell her that!" She chuckled again, then thanked her contact and hung up.

"I gathered what you were investigating from your unsuccessful conversation," she told me. "Brian is my contact at Manchester – you pick up a few useful connections when you've been around a couple of centuries or more. As I'm sure you heard, a private group chartered an entire jumbo jet at short notice the day before yesterday.

"Apparently, today was the earliest it could be ready. As you just heard, they left at four o'clock this afternoon, heading to New York. From there, I'm sure they can re-route to anywhere in the US once they've refuelled."

"So we only just missed them?" I said, at which she winced and nodded. "Damn it! If we hadn't had to deal with Fiona after the Edinburgh attack, we'd have been able to get to Bolton last night. If they only booked the plane the day before yesterday, they must have done it after she informed the Scottish group of our assault.

"They probably let Elrulin know, and he must have decided to move everything to the new site in America. If the decision hadn't been for the death penalty last night, I'd kill Fiona right now! Elrulin's going to be dug in like an Alabama tick at that new site now!" I slammed my fist down on Seirina's desk, making the pens rattle as the holder bounced over.

"Hey, don't take it out on my desk!" she scolded, righting the cylinder and returning the pens.

"We don't even know where the damn site *is*!" I complained, thumping heavily down into one of the chairs opposite Seirina. "They've cleared out the files from Bolton. That's why I asked about psychic abilities – maybe someone could read something from Elrulin's office, be able to point us in the right direction at least."

The twins and Angelica were following our conversation but staying quiet, seemingly as lost as me as to what to do next.

"You mean psychometry?" Seirina said. "I thought that's what you meant earlier. In that case, as I said, I know someone who *might* be able to help."

The twins gasped and Angelica let out a soft "oh", all sounding as hopeful as I felt. Now that we knew the Order had escaped by plane, not portals, I could relax about the risk of an unexpected counter-attack for a while. Now I would focus all of my efforts on locating this new American site.

The notion sparked a thought, so I pulled my phone out again and fired off a quick text to Cheveyo. He needed to know what had transpired, and that the Order was now wholly based at their new location on his side of the pond. Hopefully, he and his colleagues could start cobbling together some form of defence until we could locate their base and eradicate the Order completely.

"So who's this helpful soul you know of?" I asked, putting my phone back in my pocket.

"I said he *might* be able to help," Seirina retorted. "I can't guarantee anything when it comes to this particular individual. He may not even open the front door to us, let alone agree to exert himself. Even then, there's no absolute assurance of success. Still, he's the only one I can think of."

So saying, she spun her rolodex again, finally pulling out a card and passing it across to me. The address was in The Shambles, the oldest street in York. The name made me stifle a snort, since I had been expecting another exotic, esoteric name. Instead, the man's name was as traditionally Yorkshire as any I'd seen: Fred Moorhouse.

"I'm sorry, but you want me to go and see a psychic named Fred?" I said, ignoring the suppressed laughter from the twins. "Has he got a flat cap and a whippet, with a bath full of coal?" I riffed the common stereotypical Yorkshireman preconceptions, only to see Seirina's lips thin.

"I wouldn't let him hear you talk like that," she advised curtly. "Remember, *we* need *his* help, not the other way around."

I inclined my head and adjusted my facial expression, recognising the validity of her advice.

"Well I doubt he'll still be open at this time of night," I remarked, glancing at the clock on the wall. "I think the best bet would be to get a good night's sleep, then set off for York first thing in the morning."

For once I was able to get all the women to agree with me, so I decided to quit while I was ahead. I said goodnight and headed upstairs to bed.

When my alarm went off in the morning, I stretched and tried to get some life back into my legs – a Jack Russell the size of a lion is not exactly conducive to efficient blood flow when it lays across you all night. Paladin groaned as he thumped down off the bed. He bowed low as he stretched his front legs, then pushed out his back legs one after the other. After his brief calisthenics he clearly needed another nap, so he dropped where he stood and curled up.

I shook my head in tolerant amusement, then opened the window for Gauvain. He flew out for a stretch, probably to look for any rodents or even a rabbit if he was lucky. I, meanwhile, went into the bathroom to get ready for the day.

I felt somewhat more human after showering and scrubbing the film off my teeth, so I got dressed and headed to the kitchen for breakfast. Cafegeddon and toast completed my morning preparations, so I sat back with a second cup to await my guide. Since Seirina was so unsure if her associate would help us, I figured she'd be the best one to come with me and try to convince him.

I was lost in thought as she came into the room so I barely looked at her, merely grunting a welcome.

"Well, good morning to you too," she said sarcastically, sitting down and pouring herself some coffee.

"Hmm?" I looked up, realising she was looking at me. "Sorry, I was miles away. What did you say?"

"Never mind," she said tolerantly, rolling her eyes. She sipped her coffee and I took a deep breath, preparing to broach my plan with her.

"So this bloke you know," I began, catching her attention. "Any ideas on the best way to gain his interest? Anything that might particularly pique his curiosity?"

She shrugged. "He's not the sort to get involved for the sake of a cause. Unless it's specifically about him, he's a 'live and let live' kind of a guy. You'll probably have to appeal to some other aspect, like his business sense."

"Well, if the Order gets destroyed, I suppose there'll be more freedom within the magickal community to use his services. Maybe that'll be enough of a reason for him to help out," I finished hopefully, at which Seirina tilted her head and shrugged again. "Since you know him, I'd appreciate you coming along to help convince him," I told her.

"Fine," she huffed. "I suppose it won't take long, since we can teleport there."

"Actually," I replied, wincing slightly, "we'll have to drive. I was thinking about it last night. The Shambles is a major tourist attraction, so the chance of us finding a quiet spot to teleport or portal into is slim to non-existent. This is why I still have a car. Don't worry, as soon as we're done I can send you back here via portal, so at least you only have to drive one way."

"Oh joy," she said dryly. "In that case, we'd better get going. I'd rather get there early and avoid too many crowds. Just let me go change. I'll meet you by the front door in ten minutes."

I had a bad feeling, knowing that 'ten minutes' in girl preparation speak can translate to an hour without any trouble at all. Still, if I wanted Seirina's help to convince this individual, I didn't really have much of a choice. I passed Angelica and the twins as I walked down the hall, telling them quickly what Seirina and I had decided and saying goodbye.

I went outside and called Gauvain, reaching up to catch him as he landed. We discussed it and he agreed to come with me. Since Seirina was coming, he agreed to enter his claw for the trip so I went around the house to the car. Paladin had already decided to stay and guard the bedroom, since a lion-sized Jack Russell ambling down The Shambles might be a tad conspicuous.

I unclipped the Isofix system I'd mounted Gauvain's perch on, moving it to the back seat instead. I offered him the option of riding there but he refused, since he said he'd feel out of the loop being behind us.

After I finished prepping the car, I turned back to the house to see Seirina already at the door. She had changed into a flowery summer dress, similar to the one she'd been wearing the first day I'd met her. I turned back to the car and opened the door for her, smiling at her when she thanked me. Then I got into the driver's seat and we set off for York.

Time to get ourselves a psychic.

Chapter 6

Even though we had spent a significant amount of time together over the last few weeks, I suddenly found myself tongue-tied in Seirina's presence. Previously, all of our discussions had been towards a specific aim. Whether that had been Angie's rescue or the later plans for the assault on the Order, we had a specific focus for our interactions.

Now, however, I was faced with a drive of over an hour and all our plans were already set. How does a thirty-odd-year-old magickal newbie make small talk with a necromancer-cum-enchantress with over three centuries of life experience? What was I gonna do, discuss the weather? I shifted uncomfortably in my seat, drawing an amused glance from Seirina.

"OK, you're either trying to work out how to ask me something delicate or you have no idea what to say without the focus of making plans," she said. "Given that you've already asked me to stay out of things between you and Angelica, I'm leaning more towards you being uncomfortable. Let me guess, the whole necromancer thing again?" She turned away, her eyes glistening slightly. "I thought we'd gotten past this over the last few weeks."

I was shocked. I hadn't considered her as having any kind of insecurity. I guess age can bring wisdom, though it can also give you more time to develop neuroses. The surprise of seeing her upset at my perceived discomfort with her gave me the stimulus I needed to overcome my initial hesitance.

"No, it's not that at all!" I reassured her, hating that my uncertainty had made her feel this way. "To be honest, I'm far more intimidated by our age difference than by your abilities. I was actually just wondering what the hell a newcomer to magick with only three decades of life experience could make small talk about with a three-century-old magickal veteran."

Her head snapped round towards me, her eyes drying and a smile threatening the corners of her lips. She leant away slightly, raising an eyebrow and appraising me in an entirely different light.

"So my being a necromancer doesn't bother you?" she asked. The simple fact of her asking the question gave me a glimpse of her own insecurity. How often had she been shunned or rebuffed once people found out about her?

"That's like hating a lion for killing a gazelle," I reasoned, seeing her frown and continuing to explain. "Look, the way I see it is you didn't choose to study necromancy, it's who you are. You've shown me time and again that you're a good person. To be honest, I think your enchantress side has balanced your other aspect, and those powers actually scare me far more than the necromancy."

"Really?" she asked, her frown disappearing and her eyebrows shooting up.

"Yeah, of course. The reason most people are terrified of necromancers is because we're all so scared of death, so anything associated with it automatically becomes dark, unnatural, and freaky. People forget that death is a normal, natural part of life. Yes, loss is sad, but beyond that it's no more scary or dark than the mysteries of birth.

"*Love*, on the other hand, is scary as hell. It totally overrides your intellect, can bring you to the highest joy or the blackest despair, and if you get it wrong, it can utterly destroy your life."

"Huh," she said. "That's the first time anyone's ever said that to me. I'd never even considered it that way myself. You know, you're actually quite clever for a man." She winked at me and gave me a cheeky grin, at which I pretended to be insulted.

"Oh sure, play the X vs Y chromosome card," I huffed, then chuckled. "Well *as* a man I realise just how easy it is to screw things up with a woman. Something you'd say to a guy friend and get a laugh with can fall totally flat or worse if it's said to a woman. Equality of the sexes is a fantastic ideal, and I heartily endorse it, but there's no denying that there are some fundamental differences in how we think."

"True, and not just the age-old perceived differences like sex versus love and all that. I know plenty of women who just enjoy sex for recreation – and no, I won't introduce you!" I had perked up jokingly at her comment about her friends, then sank down into my seat and pouted at her quick rejoinder.

"Spoilsport!" I groused humorously, making her roll her eyes dramatically.

"I'll tell Angie," she threatened, prompting a quick back-pedal on my part.

"Women? What women? Who wants to meet any other women? Not me! You must have misunderstood," I blurted out, making her chuckle again.

"Yeah, that's what I thought." She nodded slyly. At least we weren't sitting in uncomfortable silence any more, though the way this conversation was going, I might have been better off just turning the radio on!

"X chromosomes a billion, Y chromosomes still waiting to score!" I quipped, drawing a full-on belly laugh from the passenger seat. I smiled wryly, shrugging to acknowledge the inequality of our position.

As the miles steadily disappeared behind us, we relaxed into casual conversation. I learned more of Seirina's childhood stories from Scotland, the struggles she'd had growing up. It was interesting to note that despite the centuries between us, the trials and tribulations of childhood were much the same.

It seemed as though kids could be evil little shits with or without technology, with or without magick as the difference to be hated.

I shared some of my less-than-enjoyable back-story as well, each of us commiserating with the other over our unfortunate episodes. As we drew into York, talk turned inevitably to the acquaintances she'd made over the years. The man we were going to meet had apparently quite literally bumped into Seirina when they were both walking along The Shambles a few years ago.

She had been reminiscing over a previous visit with her husband, while Fred had been coming out of his shop. The air of sadness around her had prompted him to read her, which then led them into conversation. They had subsequently exchanged cards in case either of them needed the other's services in the future.

Once we were inside the walled area of the city, I looked for a parking spot. The benefit of coming so early was that I found a space relatively quickly, near a restaurant called The Blue Barbakan. I knew it as I'd taken a date there once, back when it had been The Blue Bicycle. The food had been memorable and excellent, the date was neither. Bitch ate my dessert, as I recall.

As we walked up the road from where I'd parked, we passed a boutique delicatessen and café called The Hairy Fig. I'd returned there many times before, always going away with a lighter wallet and heavier shopping bag. They had wonderful loose teas and coffees (though they couldn't compete with Cafegeddon); various styles of bread; amazing cheeses, meats and pickles; and their hand-made Cornish pasties were unsurpassed.

I made a mental note to stop in on the way back to the car, once I'd finished my dealings with Seirina's psychic.

We crossed a road and reached St Crux, the chapel at the bottom end of The Shambles. They often had stalls outside, though that was usually at the weekends. The café inside was already doing a brisk trade with the early-bird tourists, however.

We headed up the historic cobbled street, glancing in some of the windows as we passed. Seirina's friend had his shop about halfway up on the right side as we were looking, so we came to it soon enough.

The shop window was remarkably unassuming, a simple swath of black velvet with a deck of tarot cards fanned out in an arc. They were face down, though one card had been removed and placed in the centre of the arc face-up. Appropriately enough, it was the Magician. There was also no name, so I could only surmise Seirina's friend wasn't interested in the tourist trade. Clearly, he was more focused and selective than I was in clientele.

When I tried the door, it was locked. There was no bell, no knocker, not even a letterbox slot in the door. How did this guy stay in business? What, did he only unlock when he sensed someone worthwhile was coming?

"Actually, yes," came an upper-class accent, the tone highly reminiscent of Stephen Fry playing Dr Gordon Wyatt in *Bones*. "That's exactly how I find my clientele." The door opened to reveal a slim, sandy-haired man. He was tall yet slightly stooped, as though he spent most of his time hunched over books. He was dressed in beige slacks, loafers, and a white button-down shirt with a Fair Isle sweater over his shoulders, the sleeves knotted in place of a tie.

To complete the clichéd librarian look, he was even wearing a pair of round, steel-framed glasses. I remained cautious, however, refusing to be taken in by his innocuous appearance. I doubted Seirina would have kept his card, and recommended him, if she hadn't been convinced of his abilities.

"So," he continued, looking at both of us. "What brings you to my door this fine day?"

"I thought you just said you sensed worthy customers," I replied cautiously. I didn't want to antagonise him, though I wanted to clarify exactly where we stood. Just how psychic was this guy?

"Fine, I may have gilded the lily somewhat," he admitted. "I know when someone is coming who needs me, but not why. It's more a general 'psychic alert' than a full-on detailing of everyone's business. That sort of reading requires a focal source and much more effort; it's far too hard to maintain all the time."

"OK," I acknowledged. "That makes sense. But you *are* the real deal, yes? You can read items and locations for information?"

"Of course," he said, and Seirina looked at me pityingly.

"Do you really think I'd have brought you all this way if he was a phony?" she asked indignantly. "I know we have a bit of breathing room now, but we still don't need to be wasting time. We need to find out where they've gone before they have too much time to strengthen their position."

Fred looked to and fro between us a couple of times before smiling somewhat crookedly.

"I think you'd better come in," he said, standing back from the door. "It sounds as though we need to have a discussion, and it would appear that it has the potential to be interesting."

Chapter 7

Seirina entered first, giving Fred a small nod of thanks as she passed him. I followed, ducking slightly as the door was lower than average. Clearly it was original, built when people were shorter than today, which fit with the age of The Shambles itself. Seirina introduced me to Fred, who then gestured for us to precede him into the building.

I followed Seirina down the short entrance hallway, then through another low doorway into a room with a round table in the centre. It was covered with a deep blue cloth speckled with golden starbursts, and it was surrounded by antique-looking wooden chairs. I snorted at the clichéd appearance, turning to look at Fred as he came through behind me.

He shrugged easily, no doubt understanding what I was amused by, yet appearing unruffled by my scorn.

"Most people who come to see me are woefully naïve, if not totally ignorant, concerning the magickal world at large," he said, pulling out one of the chairs and folding himself into it. He crossed his legs at the knee and motioned to us to each take a seat ourselves. "As such, they have certain preconceptions and expectations, mostly informed by popular culture such as the cinema, so I've found it easier to pander to them rather than explain an alternative. I've found people to be more relaxed and receptive if those expectations are met, even if only in part."

I nodded, fully agreeing with his sentiment. It was something that was rife in the world – people were far more accepting of things that fit in their nice little boxes, rejecting and persecuting anything out of their experience or understanding. My own childhood mental health label was proof enough of that.

"Fair enough," I allowed, looking around at the rest of the room. It was decorated like a simple sitting room, though with no TV. I spotted a crystal ball on the bookcase, plus another deck of tarot cards, but there was no sign of anything for sale. "Clearly you're not stocked up to open for business. I'm guessing the only thing you sell is your ability?"

"Fortunately, I invested well a number of years ago," he stated, smiling in a quietly self-satisfied way. "The return allows me a comfortable life without need for any other income stream. As a result, I only take on clients if their case holds a degree of interest for me, though I still charge for my services – pocket money, if you will. So I hope you're prepared to meet my price?"

"I hope you can actually help," I riposted, refusing to be intimidated. When it came right down to it, if I was paying for his services then he was an employee. Yes, he had the right to refuse the job. If he took it, however, *I* would be setting the rules not him. I always found it annoying when tradesmen expected everything to revolve around them, rather than turning up when they were supposed to and doing the job they were hired for in a timely fashion.

His eyes narrowed assessingly. He had been treating me as a curiosity, something to distract him from the routine of his day. Now he was looking at me more like someone seeing an advert for a new film that might interest him, though he still wanted to see the trailer before he made up his mind.

I took a deep breath and prepared to make my pitch.

"Have you ever heard of the Order of the Nine Seals?" I asked him. His lips pursed and his brow furrowed in distaste. "I'll take that as a yes. At least you didn't start swearing at me – that's what Seirina did when I asked her the same question." She smiled, cocked her head to the side and shrugged, acknowledging the truth of the story.

"Have you ever had any dealings with them?" I continued.

"Not directly," Fred replied. "Though I've had several clients who asked questions that led to the Order. I've certainly seen the misery they've caused over the years. Why?"

"We've been trying to take them down," I told him. He snorted and started laughing. His mirth died away as he looked over at Seirina and saw she wasn't smiling.

"Wait, you're serious?" His voice went up at least two octaves.

"As a heart attack," I replied. "In fact, we've already assaulted their various sites across the British Isles and chased them across the Atlantic." His mouth dropped open and his eyebrows rose so high it looked almost painful. He glanced over at Seirina in disbelief, only to see her smile and nod in confirmation.

"OK, I'm officially impressed and interested," he said, crossing his arms and leaning back in his chair. "I am, however, somewhat surprised to hear that you've been able to achieve such resounding success thus far. Yours is not a name I've ever heard of in magickal circles before now, nor have any of my previous psychic investigations ever led to you.

"That means either you have no magick of your own, which I discount based on the feeling of your presence here, or you're new to your power. You seem older than usual for an awakening, plus I don't see how you could have learned any significant abilities if you've only just unlocked your magick."

"Well, that's a fairly involved tale," I told him, immediately realising that his curiosity was the key to getting him involved. "If this all works out, maybe I'll tell you about it some time." Seirina nodded slightly and winked at me, clearly catching on to my idea. "For now, we need you to come with us to the Order's main headquarters in Bolton. They've cleared out all their files, so we need you to try and get an impression from the offices or something, try to find out where their new headquarters in America are."

"Well, that sounds interesting and even worthy," he remarked. Then he looked up at the ceiling and steepled his thumbs, appearing to consider something. "OK, I'll do it – for ten thousand pounds." I gasped at the audacity, considering there was no guarantee he'd succeed.

"That's a lot of money," I said, sitting back and crossing my arms. I looked deep into the weave of the table cloth, thinking over the options. "Since we have no assurance of success, how about a compromise: Two thousand up front, then the rest *if* you manage to pick up any useful information for us."

"That sounds fair to me," Seirina agreed, speaking up for the first time since we'd sat down. "A retainer, then the rest on satisfactory completion. Is that acceptable to you, Fred?"

"Oh, very well," he said, huffing slightly as if insulted. Then he grinned. "So, you're new to magick but not a complete fool. Good to know." I chuckled at his typical Yorkshire attitude to money. I'd once heard someone describe Yorkshire men as 'Scotsmen with all the generosity squeezed out of them', and Fred certainly seemed to live up to that reputation.

At least he was being agreeable, as opposed to the stubborn and argumentative clichés that also were portrayed as classically Yorkshire. I thanked the gods for small mercies and moved on with the discussion.

"So can we go now?" I asked, still wanting to get the Order destroyed as soon as possible.

"Do you have the money?" Fred asked in return. I hated people who asked questions in response to other questions, although in this case I guess it was reasonable.

I pulled my phone out of my pocket and opened my mobile banking app, making sure to select the business account for the shop rather than my own personal account. "What are your account details?" I asked, pulling up a transfer window. He gave me the numbers and I sent him two thousand pounds as agreed. Once he'd verified the money, he slapped his hands on the table and pushed himself up out of his chair.

"Right then," he said, rubbing his hands together, "shall we get going?"

"I'm not coming," Seirina told him, standing up herself. "I merely came along to make the introductions. Gavan, whenever you're ready, I'd appreciate you opening a portal for me."

Fred gaped again, looking between us. I winked at him, then turned to Seirina.

"I don't think there's quite enough space in here," I observed, looking around the room. "I think it'd be better if I teleported you. Fred, do me a favour and don't move for a minute. I don't want to pop back and explode you."

I stepped over and held a hand out to Seirina. She put her hand in mine and I focused on her back garden, teleporting us both there. I released her hand, waved brightly, then popped back to Fred's place.

His face was a picture, his jaw low enough that I could see the back of his throat.

"So, you can teleport *and* use portals?" he said incredulously, putting his hands on the table and leaning towards me. "I *definitely* want to hear your story once we're done. You seem to be a total paradox, newly awakened yet comfortable with advanced abilities."

The left side of my mouth pulled up in a half smile, my right eyebrow rising to balance it. I was going for mysterious, though I probably came off more as demented and possibly psychotic. I decided to give up, relaxing back to a neutral expression.

"So do you want to teleport, portal, or drive?" I asked. "Driving will take about an hour and a half – I checked earlier – so if you want to get this over and done with, magickal transport would probably be better."

"No disrespect," he said, straightening up, "but I've only just met you. I definitely want to get there as quickly as we can, though I'd prefer to see where we're going. As such, I think a portal would be preferable."

I shrugged easily, not really bothered by which option he preferred.

"We just need somewhere a little more open, unless you want your furniture shredded by the portal's event horizon," I told him. He looked around in alarm at his cherished possessions.

"This way," he said, gesturing to a door opposite to the one we'd entered through. I followed him through, finding a staircase. We climbed up to the next floor, then up again into the roof space. He had a door that opened onto a small roof terrace, on which there were a few pots of herbs (culinary herbs, not intoxicating ones, just to clarify).

"Oh, this is lovely," I complimented him, breathing in the scents of mint, rosemary, and sage. "Amazingly peaceful, considering you're in the centre of town here. It must be a wonderful place to meditate and clear your head."

"If you call drinking beer and reading a book in a deckchair 'meditating'," he said, chuckling, "then yes, absolutely." I laughed appropriately, then turned to face the open area.

"Shall we?" I asked, opening a portal to the office suite I remembered from Eligos' guided tour. Fred smiled and stepped through, then I followed.

Chapter 8

Fred looked around the office suite assessingly, though he didn't seem to be looking at the décor. Since we were in the outer office, I doubted there would be anything of Elrulin's on any of the desks. This was probably where the secretaries and personal assistants had sat and given Elrulin's attitude, I thought he'd probably treated them more as fixtures and conveniences than actual people.

We went into the largest office, which was the one in the corner, since that would most likely have been Elrulin's. There were the same signs of hurried packing with a few sheets of paper strewn across the floor, though I quickly dropped them after a cursory glance revealed only a random word or two.

Fred immediately walked around the desk and sat in the high-quality, leather executive chair. He rested his hands on the arms, reclined his head against the high back, and closed his eyes. I hoped he was trying to pick something up, rather than just taking a nap on my dime, so I kept quiet and gave him some time.

I went back out into the secretary's area, deciding to check over the other offices again just in case Eligos had missed anything before. Not that I had any definite reason to mistrust him; I had simply realised everyone had their own agendas and allegiances. After Iyrin's revelation about Lucian still being in contact with Elrulin, I had decided to double check everything important and be suspicious of everyone.

I would have to be careful about it, otherwise it would undermine all of my efforts to put our little alliance together, but I refused to be quite as naïve in future. All it would take would be for me to trust the wrong person for a split second for people to die. As the old saying went, 'For want of a nail, a kingdom was lost', and I had no intention of allowing my fledgeling 'kingdom' to fall.

Fortunately for my trust issues, the rest of the offices were as empty as Eligos had said they were. Not particularly helpful, I'll admit, but at least reassuring in terms of confirming the trustworthiness of my most mysterious ally. I'd been harbouring some doubts about him ever since I'd learned of Lucian's perfidy, especially as Eligos had been introduced by the Devil in the first place. I was glad to get some independent confirmation of what he'd told me, since I could at least have a little more faith in his reports in future.

I went back into the corner office to see Fred sitting forward now, his brow furrowed in either concentration or confusion, I wasn't sure which. He looked up as I came in, lifting his hands from the desk where he had been pressing them. He shook his hands vigorously at the wrists, sighed deeply and sat back in the chair again.

"This is very confusing," he said, creasing his brow. "There seem to be dozens, if not hundreds, of different impressions overlapping. All of them are muted, sort of muffled, and there's an undercurrent running through that jumbles them even more."

I felt a chill run down my spine as I realised what he was reading: The evidence of all the different bodies Elrulin had inhabited over the years, all the souls he had snuffed out with as much consideration as I might eat a sandwich. The 'undercurrent' that Fred was feeling must be Elrulin himself, though his impression was no doubt muffled by being inside those stolen forms.

I explained to Fred about Elrulin, how he fed off souls and then rode their bodies, changing every so often as they wore out. The look of horror and distaste on his face was exactly how I had felt when I first learned how Elrulin operated, which at least made me warm up to Fred a little more. It certainly showed he was sympathetic to the idea of Elrulin being the bad guy in this.

"Well that at least explains what I'm feeling," he remarked, wincing and rubbing the back of his neck in a way that was eerily familiar – I did the same thing when I was frustrated. Was he picking *me* up because I was close by? He looked up and cocked his head when he saw me staring at him.

"What?" he asked curiously.

"Sorry," I replied. "It's just you reminded me of me just then. I have that same habit of rubbing my neck. I was just worried my presence might be jumbling things up for you, confusing the issue with yet more layers to pick up." His eyes narrowed slightly, looking at me with a new air of assessment.

"Interesting," he said, drawing the word out slightly. "Not many people would consider that. Most people want to be as close as possible when I'm working, try to be involved in what I read."

"I'm sure that's just because they want to be close to the friend or relative they've asked you to contact for them," I said, thinking through it as I was talking. "So does it impact on you?"

"Not as much as you might think," he replied, shrugging. "It's no different to being in a café with someone. If the next table is close their voices can get a bit louder, though it's still possible to concentrate on what your friend is saying."

"Hmm," I mused, understanding what he was saying in principle. "Fair enough. I'll just try not to think too loudly around you, then."

He smiled and nodded, then stood up from the chair.

"There's no point trying to read anything in here," Fred said, coming around the desk. "All those different bodies are like trying to read a single voice from the middle of the audience at a concert, while standing up on stage."

Now it was my turn to smile, since the imagery was fairly evocative and the difficulty was quite explicit as a result.

"So where else do you want to try?" he asked, as we left the office. I was momentarily surprised at his eagerness to try again, then I remembered he had eight grand riding on his success. I silently congratulated myself on structuring our deal this way, then considered his question.

"If you can't read anything from his stuff," I said, "what other options do we have? I'm not exactly an expert on all this."

"Well what I've been attempting is called psychometry," he said, falling into a lecturing tone. "It's a technique of reading the energy field of an object, allowing the practitioner to obtain knowledge of the history of that item. Lots of people know of this technique, even if they don't know what it's called, since it's the most common psychic skill used when people are looking for contact with loved ones.

"There's another type of reading, one that relates more to locations than items. It's the same theory that explains hauntings as an impression of emotional or traumatic events. Have you ever heard of stone tapes?"

I shook my head, though the name seemed to convey pretty much what he meant.

"No, but I guess it means an event gets recorded on a rock?" I said.

"Basically," he replied. "I've found it works best with intensely emotional situations, plus the older and more natural the rock, the cleaner the recording seems to be. It also makes it easier if the event is more recent, since things seem to lose clarity over time. Hauntings only remain clear because of the powerful trauma associated with the event."

What he said made sense, so I tried to think where would be the best place to try and pick up some useful information. It needed to be somewhere the Order would have had important discussions, somewhere Elrulin might have gathered them to give them instructions...

I remembered the surprise birthday party the Edinburgh branch had held for Alison, the one that had degenerated into an all-out food fight. The top floor meeting room was the only place I could think of where that kind of gathering might take place. I opened a portal to the meeting room here; easy enough to do since I'd already done it once for our assault. We stepped through and Fred looked around.

"Hmm, maybe..." Fred trailed off as he traced his fingers across the wall. He stopped, closing his eyes and breathing deeply as he tried to detect something. After a few moments, his eyes snapped open and he shook his head. "No, I'm sorry. There's nothing in here. The walls are too processed and artificial, plus there's not been enough emotion or trauma in here to imprint anything."

As he said that, an image came into my mind. Somewhere I'd been where trauma was a regular occurrence. A place where the walls were rough and unfinished, located in the deepest bowels of this underground base.

The cells.

I told Fred my idea and his eyes lit up like a kid at Christmas. We headed for the stairs, deciding to walk instead of using a portal. Fred said the less energy thrown around to disrupt any recordings, the more likely he would be to pick up some clear information.

Once we reached the bottom of the staircase, we stepped out into the hallway and headed around towards the giant steel vault door. The door stood wide open, just as we'd left it after our abortive assault mission.

We went through, past the guard station inside, and into the main cell area. As soon as he saw the rock walls, Fred became far more animated and enthusiastic. He lifted both hands as if pressing them against a window, then closed his eyes. He stepped slowly along the corridor between the cells, murmuring to himself as he tried to sense something.

He started going into one cell after another, standing still for a moment then shaking his head and coming back out. I was becoming despondent as the number of remaining cells slowly dwindled, six left, then five, four...

As he stepped into the next cell, with only three left after, Fred suddenly opened his eyes and looked at me, smiling so big I thought his face would crack.

"I've got something!" he whispered, his face shining with excitement. "Just give me a moment to see what I can pick up. I *might* be able to play the conversation so you can hear it, or I may just have to tell you what I can hear."

"What if I link minds with you?" I asked excitedly. "That way you can just focus on the recording and not waste your energy on trying to play it out loud for me."

Fred looked at me and nodded, his lower lip protruding slightly as he considered my proposal.

"That could actually work," he said. "Just don't distract me. I need to focus, and this takes quite a bit out of me." I nodded, and we got started.

I put my hand on his shoulder, linking to him mentally. I also fed him a slow stream of energy to try to take some of the strain for him. It was an interesting experience, allowing me to detect what he was doing to pick up the psychic vibrations.

At first it was like a staticky radio, then it became clearer as Fred homed in on the source. It was an Order member threatening a prisoner, telling them to cooperate.

"Either you tell us now, or we take you with us to America," said one voice, clearly the Order member.

"So what?" replied the other. "One cell's pretty much the same as another."

"Oh, you have no idea," taunted the Order member. "Our American site has a whole new level of power you wouldn't believe. Believe me, you *really* don't want to be put in the holding area over there.

"No one escapes from The Rock of Banished Souls!"

Chapter 9

A thrill of excitement and anticipation ran through me as we heard the echo of the name spoken by the Order's jailer. I had been surprised to note the Order member hadn't sounded like Stheno – though I guess even monsters must get a day off. I suddenly wondered if they had a union, then mentally shook myself to get back on track.

"The Rock of Banished Souls," I repeated out loud, separating my mind from Fred's now that we'd heard what I needed. "Between the way he said it and the name itself, it sounds like some kind of supernatural prison. Have you ever heard of it before?" Unfortunately, but perhaps unsurprisingly, Fred shook his head.

"Nope, I'm afraid not," he said, shrugging. "Then again, I've never really looked into American legends. There's more than enough history and mythology overlap here in good old England for me. That's one of the main reasons I chose to live in York – it's steeped in lore."

I nodded absently, only half listening to his explanation. My mind had started spinning along different tangents as soon as he'd said no. Was this 'Banished Souls' place an existing legend? Was it something ancient, maybe even Native American? In which case, might Cheveyo have heard of it? Banished Souls sounded spiritual, so would Sovereign know about it? Was it something new Elrulin had created; in which case, how would we locate it? Or had he simply renamed some existing location to suit his own purpose, which again would make it seriously challenging – if not downright impossible – to track down.

"Well at least I have a name, however obscure, to start on," I said, thinking out loud to myself as much as telling Fred. "Thanks for your help, Fred. I'll take us back to your place." So saying, I laid my hand on his shoulder and teleported us, forgetting his preference for portals in my distracted state of mind.

"Gah!" he exclaimed, stumbling slightly and shaking off my hand. "That's seriously disorienting if you're not ready for it! You could have warned me!"

"Oh gods, sorry Fred!" I gasped, putting my hand over my open mouth briefly as I realised what I'd done. "I totally didn't think! I was so wrapped up in musing over what we heard, I forgot all about opening a portal. I just brought us here the way I'd have done it if I was with Seirina. Really, I'm so sorry!"

He waved off my effusive apology with a grin. "It's OK, no harm done," he said genially. "I can see it's much quicker, so I understand you using it normally. Plus, after what we heard, I'm not surprised you were distracted. Just warn me next time, will you?" He chuckled to show there were no hard feelings, so I joined in with relief.

"Oh, that reminds me," I said, pulling my phone out of my pocket. "You certainly fulfilled your end of the arrangement." I opened my banking app and sent the other eight thousand to the same account as before. "There, ten thousand, paid in full." He nodded appreciatively, then led the way back down through his home.

"I have to say, I'm glad Seirina introduced us," he remarked as we reached the sitting room. "This has been very interesting, and I can sense there's a lot more to come in your future – if you survive this, of course."

"Umm, thanks, I think," I replied, raising one eyebrow and dropping the other for a moment. "It was good to meet you too. Interesting to watch you work, as well. Maybe we'll meet again some time." I held my hand out and he grasped it immediately, wrapping his other hand around it warmly.

"Count on it," he said, winking.

I suddenly wondered if he'd read me at some point. Did he now know what was coming in my future? I *almost* asked him, then thought better of it. I had quite enough to be going on with right now. I'd worry about the future if the present didn't kill me!

I accepted the business card Fred held out to me with thanks, then turned and left. Even though Seirina and I had arrived early, it was now lunchtime and my stomach was rumbling. The Shambles was as busy as ever, so I threaded my way down past the tourists and made my way back to the car.

I mentally discussed what I'd learned with Gauvain, who'd deliberately kept quiet during our little excursion. He hadn't wanted to distract Fred, so he also hadn't joined our link to hear the stone tape recording. He agreed with my concern over the difficulties of finding the location of the Order's new base, even *with* the name, though he was positive we'd manage somehow.

His optimism lifted my spirits, so as we neared the car I ducked into the Hairy Fig. I bought some seeded rye bread, a selection of meats, cheeses, and seafood, and half a dozen of their awesome Cornish pasties. The owner remembered me from previous visits, so we chatted amiably as she gathered everything together and rang it up.

I left and walked back to the car, put the bags in the back and moved Gauvain's perch back to the front seat. He immediately erupted from the claw on my wrist, landing on the branch and stretching.

Oh, that's better, he said. *I do so prefer being out and in full form.*

I smiled and shook my head, now used to hearing the same old thing every time he was in the claw for any appreciable period. I got my phone out and wrote a text to Cheveyo and Sovereign, telling them the name we'd discovered and asking if they'd ever heard of it. I sent it off, realising they'd probably still be asleep but at least they'd see it when they woke up.

I spent the drive back chatting with Gauvain, remarking on the scenery as he obviously hadn't seen it on the way *to* York (a fact he was quick to point out). I would have stopped somewhere to let him stretch his wings, but I knew Seirina would be waiting to hear what Fred had discovered and I didn't want to keep her waiting.

As we drew near, I could sense Paladin again and I could tell he was excited to see us. We drew up to the gate and I pressed the intercom button, smiling as I informed Mrs Wilson that I'd returned with treats for lunch. I parked in my accustomed spot and got out. G soared up for a stretch, while I gazed around at the garden and house I'd become attached to during the weeks of this little campaign.

My musings were interrupted by a huge furry missile knocking me off my feet and landing on top of me. I managed to react quickly enough to slow my fall and cushion my landing, though not quickly enough to avoid the bath of dog slobber I was deluged with in welcome.

Hiya! he thought loudly, making Gauvain chuckle in our shared mind-space as he stayed safely up out of the way. *So did you find anything? Do you know where we have to go?*

"Pbth, gack, gah!" I spluttered, trying to hold Pal far enough off my face to breathe. He finally backed off sufficiently for me to sit up and wipe my face, though his tail was still blurring back and forth. "Good grief, Pal, did you really have to try and drown me?"

You've been gone for ages! he complained. *I'm just glad to see you back.* His tail slowed down and drooped a little, immediately making me feel like the biggest, most ungrateful shit in existence.

"Sorry," I said, hugging his neck. "You're absolutely right, and I'm glad to see you too. You'll hear what we found when I tell Seirina." As soon as I'd hugged him, his tail had picked back up and his whole body was wiggling in excitement. I was reminded again of all my previous pets. This world would be so much better if everyone were as honest, trusting, and loving as dogs.

I stood up and dusted myself off, both from the gravel and the new showering of dog hair I'd received. Pal bounced around me, particularly interested in the contents of the shopping bags as I retrieved them from the back of the car. I had to hold them above my head and threaten him with sleeping outside to get him to keep his nose out long enough to carry them in.

"You don't even *need* to eat," I complained as we neared the front door, where Mrs Wilson had been watching and waiting. "Why are you so interested?" Gauvain alighted on my shoulder just before I reached the door, rubbing his face against my cheek in a slightly more dignified greeting than his oversized brother.

Why do you like the smell of flowers or perfume? Pal countered, reminding me yet again of how much more than just a giant dog he was.

"Fair enough," I conceded. "Just don't drool all over it. *We* would still like to enjoy it, preferably without a dog slobber gravy."

"Oh, gross." Seirina laughed, coming to the door of her study. "I was looking forward to lunch until I heard *that*!"

"Don't worry," I reassured her with a grin. "I have defended the sanctity of our victuals with alacrity and determination, succeeding with aplomb." I put on my poshest voice to sell the whole 'knightly duty' gag. I was rewarded by the long-suffering eye rolls and head shakes I had sought from both Seirina and Mrs Wilson.

"Why are you such a goof?" Seirina sighed, smiling again as I shrugged.

"Probably because he's a man," came another voice from the kitchen, and Angie poked her head out of the door. "Come on, we've been sitting in here since you told Mrs Wilson you had a special lunch. We're hungry!"

"As you wish," I said, making Seirina smile as she caught the reference.

I walked in, saying hello to Gabby and Izzy, and set my bags on the kitchen work top. I unloaded the various tubs and bags of goodies, everyone remarking on their personal favourites from the selection.

Mrs Wilson soon helped me lay it all out on platters, in dishes, and on a chopping board, then everyone set to with gusto. After smelling the bread and pasties in the car on the ride back, my already rumbling stomach had started to think my throat had been cut so I dug in just as eagerly.

I could tell everyone liked it, since there was precisely zero conversation leaving only the sound of cutlery and eating.

After a while, once everyone had eaten enough, there were sighs of contentment and I sat back in my chair.

"Well, that was lovely," Angie said, wiping her mouth primly and setting her napkin down. "Now how about you stop keeping us in suspense and tell us what you found out?"

Chapter 10

"I see," I observed. "So once again I'm relegated to the role of storyteller?" Everyone in the kitchen either rolled their eyes, sighed, or shook their heads – or some combination thereof. I smothered my grin at the success of my levity-inducing indignation and crossed my arms, attempting to maintain the humour for a bit longer.

"OK, enough you big drama queen," Seirina said to general agreement, at which my façade broke and I had to laugh. I held both hands up in front of me, partly in surrender and partly to ward off the various looks of disappointment, impatience, and resigned tolerance.

"Alright, I'll tell you," I said, chuckling. "Enough with the laser eyes of death!" I got the desired amusement, then sat back in my chair with a sigh of contentment at my full stomach. "So where should I begin?"

"Seirina already filled us in on the trip to York," Izzy informed me.

"And the discussion with Mr Moorhouse," added Gabby.

"So there's no need to go over all that."

"You can just get on with what you found."

"Or more importantly," chimed in Angelica, "what Mr Moorhouse picked up from his efforts on your behalf." She smiled at me as she said it, so I knew she wasn't disparaging my efforts thus far; she just wanted to get to the meat of the story.

I took a quick sip of my water, then started the tale. The disappointed looks on their faces as I informed them of Fred's initial failure were hard to look at, though I knew they wouldn't last. Seirina looked the most disturbed when I recounted what he'd said about the layered sensations on Elrulin's desk, the compounded impressions of the various bodies Elrulin had stolen over the years. I knew she was remembering her husband, which made me almost regret telling her.

She lost her faraway stare and focused on me when I paused, swallowing my sympathy past the lump in my throat. She smiled softly and nodded ever so slightly, acknowledging my feelings. Then she gave me a rolling motion with her finger, telling me to get on with the story. I took a deep breath and picked up the thread again.

They all looked intrigued when I mentioned Fred's idea about stone tapes, then disheartened again when I described the failure of his efforts in the meeting room. They started peppering me with questions, asking whether we'd actually found anything useful. The where, how, and when. I stopped and crossed my arms until the barrage of questions abated, raising an eyebrow while I waited.

It didn't take them long to pick up on the fact that I wasn't going to just answer their questions, so they settled down and stared at me impatiently until I started talking again. I told them of Fred's comment about older, unworked stone and strong emotions being the best to get a 'recording' from, watching their faces light up as I revealed my idea of trying the cells.

"Ooh, yeah, the walls there are barely even smoothed," remembered Gabby.

"And the prisoners would certainly have strong emotions," added Izzy.

Angelica looked interested but no more than that, which surprised me. I had thought she might be worried we had picked something up from when she was held captive, then cursed myself for an idiot when I remembered: Her memory wipe meant she didn't recall her experience there, including my ham-fisted chivalry when I rushed in to save her and got myself captured.

Once again, I was faced with the painful dichotomy: Glad she no longer had the pain of her torture and interrogation at Elrulin's hands, yet devastated at the loss of the relationship we'd started to build. I consoled myself, as I had before, with the knowledge of her interest in me regardless, and the idea of rebuilding our bond without the overlay of her pain. You know, being a decent guy really sucked sometimes!

I finally revealed the details of the recording Fred had found, watching their faces for any sign of recognition when I mentioned the Rock of Banished Souls. Much to my disappointment, none of them showed any evidence of having heard the name before. Despite this, they all seemed heartened by knowing we had somewhere to start our search.

Seirina commended me on my foresight when I told them I'd already texted our American allies, appearing hopeful of a positive response from the shaman or the obeah. The others echoed her sentiment, then I stood up and stretched.

"There's not much we can do now until we locate this 'Banished Souls' place," I said. "We should take a break, get some rest, then we can start researching the name.

"Seirina, I've got one piece of good news for you," I continued with a sly grin, watching as she perked up. "Now that we've chased the Order out of the country, I'm going to move back to my own place. It's about time I gave Summer some time off. She's been running the shop single-handed while I've been doing all this, and I'm sure she could do with some down time."

Seirina closed her eyes, rested her head back and sighed deeply. "Oh, thank the gods," she breathed dramatically. "Peace and quiet again!" The rest of us burst out laughing at her overblown response.

"Oh, now who's the drama queen?" I teased, watching as she opened her eyes again and sat up. "And here I thought you liked me!"

Seirina glared down her nose at me in mock disgust. "Remember when we said how 'fish and guests start to stink after three days'?" she asked tartly. "Well just think how long you've been here, then you'll understand how I feel right now!"

I winced as I understood just how much I'd imposed on her, quite how much I'd disrupted her life. "I'm sorry," I said sincerely, my stomach twisting in sudden anxiety. "I really do appreciate everything you've done for me – for all of us. None of this would have been possible without your help. Hell, Angie would still be Elrulin's prisoner if you hadn't told me how to find them. I don't think I'll ever be able to repay you–"

"Just remember to save Elrulin for me and we'll call it even," Seirina interrupted, tilting her head and giving me an evil grin. The twins and

Angie joined in as she chuckled, while I wiped my brow in exaggerated relief.

"Phew," I said. Then I raised an eyebrow at Seirina. "You might have to settle for a *piece* of Elrulin. There's no *way* I'm letting you have him all to yourself. Tell you what: I'll kick his ass, then leave him just alive enough for you to finish him off."

"Deal," Serina said, giving such a savage grin that even I was momentarily taken aback. It showed just how much hatred she was harbouring over all the years with her husband that Elrulin had taken from her. I only hoped this would balance the scales for her, easing the pain she still felt. Holding such a powerful grudge could only sour life for her, which I was quite sure wouldn't have been her husband's wish.

"How about we agree to talk a couple of times per week," I suggested, looking around at all of them. "That way we can update each other on how our searches are going. Of course," I amended, "if anyone discovers what or where this soul thing actually is, don't wait for your regularly scheduled call. Pick up the phone straight away."

Everyone agreed and we all hugged, saying our goodbyes as we prepared to go our own separate ways – at least for now. The twins and Angie said they were going to stay in Seirina's safe house until they'd saved up enough to get their own place. They hadn't had to worry about it before, as the Order had provided them with housing.

"If it would be easier," I said, "don't forget I offered you the flat above my shop. You wouldn't have to commute for work, and the building has wards as good as this place."

The twins' eyes lit up in excitement at my reminder, while Angie smiled hugely and a tear trickled down her cheek. I pulled a clean handkerchief out and passed it to her, Seirina smiling at my old-fashioned gesture.

"Do you rem…" I started, then caught myself with a pang of regret. I had been about to ask if Angie remembered how to get to Dinas Affaraon, before *I* remembered she hadn't been since her memory was erased. "Do you remember the address from the file?" I hurried to cover my lapse, relieved when no one seemed to pick up on it.

"Absolutely," Angie said. "I've been looking forward to seeing it for the first time – again." I grinned in return, glad she was comfortable enough with what had happened to her to make jokes about it now.

"How will you get there? For that matter, how have you been getting back and forth from where you've been staying?" I asked curiously.

"We've been using taxis," Angie said, as if it were the most obvious thing in the world – which I suppose it would have been, had I bothered to apply even an ounce of common sense.

"Of course," I said, inclining my head. "Here, use my car to get your things. I can collect it from the shop. I'll teleport home, then do the same to get to work in the morning." I pulled my car keys out from my pocket as I spoke, proffering them to Angie.

"Thanks," she said, accepting them. "That will certainly make things easier for us."

"Yes, absolutely," said Izzy.

"It'll definitely be better than struggling with, and paying for, taxis," Gabby chimed in.

"Very generous," tacked on Seirina, at which point I looked up at the ceiling in despair.

"Wonderful, now you're *all* joining in!" I complained. "I can't *wait* for Summer and Emily to meet you all. Then I can suffer through a *six* part harmony. Deep joy."

They shared a communal laugh while I simply crossed my left arm in front of me, rested my right elbow on the back of my left hand and put my right hand to my forehead. I closed my eyes and sighed.

I was *so* screwed. Again.

Chapter 11

I informed G and Pal that we were relocating as I packed up my things, making sure not to forget my Cafegeddon supply now that Seirina's own orders had arrived. Gauvain was pleased to be going back, no doubt since he'd have his nice perches and be admired in the shop again. Paladin had only been to the shop once; then again, he was happy as long as he was with me, so didn't really get overly interested. I'd ordered a couple of dog beds for him, the biggest I could find, so that he'd have one at home and one in the shop office.

I cleaned up the paper from under G's perch and took it down to the rubbish, along with the perch itself. I disassembled the makeshift stand, putting the branches on the compost heap at the bottom of the garden. Then I grabbed my bag, said goodbye to Seirina, and thanked Mrs Wilson for looking after me.

I teleported straight to Dinas Affaraon, making sure to clarify I meant the shop and not the city in my mind, leaving Pal and my bag in the office when I arrived. He curled up for a nap (big surprise) while I went out into the main area with G. I was surprised to not see Summer, then I heard her come out of the store room.

"Boo!" I said, even startling Gauvain enough that he flew off my shoulder to his perch by the counter.

"Shit!" Summer swore, jumping but managing to hold onto the box of scented candles she was carrying. No doubt she was in the process of restocking while it was quiet. "Gods, why are you such a pillock sometimes? Remind me again why I put up with you?"

I guffawed. "It's a gift, and because you love me," I replied, earning myself a particularly old-fashioned look followed by an eye roll and head shake.

"Maybe, but you definitely make it hard sometimes," she informed me, at which I smirked.

"That's what she said," I riffed, getting a smile in response.

"If you'd have made me drop these," she told me, nodding to the box of candles. "I'd have made you clear them up. And I'd've kicked your butt while you did." She grinned cheekily. "I've missed you, you great doofus. Are you done with the Order now? Are you finally back to do some *real* work?"

"Well, we've chased them across the Atlantic," I said. "But they've set up shop at their new location in the US. We've discovered a name for where they've gone – 'The Rock of Banished Souls' – but we have no idea where or what it is. Until we do, we're basically in a holding pattern while we research the name."

"So you *are* back for a while then," she said, to which I nodded.

"Also, since they're across the pond now, you and Emily can get back to your own place," I told her, which made her face light up. "In fact, could you ask Emily to get your stuff together and head home as soon as she can, please? I hate to put pressure on you, but Angie and the twins I rescued from the Order are going to use the flat now. It'll mean they're on hand for working here, so we can start mapping out some plans I've had for expansion."

"Ooh, that sounds exciting," she replied. "I'll ring her now, just let me put this box down."

"Here, I'll take it," I said, grabbing the box. "I'll fill the shelves up while you ring Emily." I walked over to the candles, setting the box on the floor and opening it. I filled up the spaces, listening to Summer's side of her conversation with Emily.

I marvelled, as I had done many times over the years, at my good fortune in finding someone like her. The only thing that ever really annoyed me about her was when she put herself down. She had a tendency to downplay her own intelligence sometimes, plus she would disparage her appearance. I had lost count of the number of times I'd had to tell her off for being like that, usually mentioning Emily's love as proof that she really was as good as I said.

She hung up the phone, smiling at me as she did. "She'll be out in about an hour. She said she'll strip the bed and put the sheets in the wash before she goes," Summer told me. "I'll give her a ring when we're getting ready to close, so she can come back and pick me up. We only brought the one car when we knew we were staying here," she explained.

"What would I do without you?" I asked, as I often did.

"Oh, you always get soppy at times like this," she joked, brushing off my compliments as usual. "You're such a marshmallow. Any softer and you wouldn't have a skeleton!"

"That wouldn't bother you," I said. "You've never been interested in bone...ers!"

"You always have to lower the tone, don't you?" she said through her laughter, shaking her head.

"Says the woman who spent two days, and I quote, 'staying in and getting sweaty' last time she had any time off," I observed, at which she shrugged and laughed even harder.

"What can I say?" she asked, once she had her breath back. "We're just slaves to the rhythm of the night!" She burst out laughing again and I joined in, glad to be able to enjoy some simple, light-hearted banter again. The last few weeks had been a real strain on my nerves, so it was nice to get back to a degree of normality.

"For now," I said with my own head shake, "how about we get back to the rhythm of the *day?*"

"Spoilsport," she said with a mock pout, then grinned and bounced off back to the store room.

We spent the next few hours restocking the shelves, interspersed with dealing with the occasional customer. A couple of pendants, a diary, and someone who seemed to be restocking themselves as she bought six assorted candles and a box of each scent of incense sticks.

As it neared five o'clock, the girls drew up and I directed them to my usual parking spot. I went out and helped them carry their bags up to the flat, then showed them around. We made up the bed that Emily had stripped – what a shocker, she and Summer had been sharing instead of using both bedrooms.

Angie handed me back my car keys and our fingers brushed as she did so. I felt a *frisson* of electricity run up my arm, though I could tell it was all me. Each time I saw her, I missed what we had had before. I had to hold myself back from grabbing her, kissing her, then dragging her into the bedroom and barricading the door for the next few days.

Some of that longing must have shown in my expression, as she flushed and looked down for a split second. Then my heart skipped about a dozen beats when she looked up at me from under her brow and ran the tip of her tongue over her lower lip. My body tightened in response, my shorts growing uncomfortably restrictive all of a sudden, and this time it was my turn to flush.

"Umm, yeah, so, well," I stammered. "I, uh, guess you know, um, where everything is now, er, so I'll, you know, let you all get settled. I'll, er, see you tomorrow." I turned and calmly left the flat – OK, I ran out of there like all the hounds of hell were at my heels.

Hey, at least I'm honest right?

I went downstairs and shot into the shop with my heart now running a mile a minute, then screeched to a stop in front of Summer. She was standing in the middle of the space, her arms crossed and an intense scowl on her face. I could sense the disappointment radiating off her in waves.

"What the hell are you doing down here?" she asked, shocking me into dumbfounded silence. What had I done wrong this time?

"Umm, working?" I said, confused. "The girls are upstairs, unpacking and getting settled. I told them I'd see them tomorrow, then we can show them how everything works here and get them started."

"After everything you've told me about Angelica," she said, tapping her foot loudly. "Now that she's upstairs in your bed... OK, *one* of your beds," she amended when my eyebrows shot up and my jaw dropped down. "*This* is when you chose to come back down here?! Is my gayness rubbing off on you or something?"

My nervous laughter was a little louder than I intended, though the release made me feel better. I calmed down quickly, taking a deep breath and hugging my friend.

"No, your 'gayness' is not rubbing off on me." I replied, rolling my eyes. "I'm still just as into women as you are. But Angie's been through a hell of a lot recently and I don't want to pressure her or scare her off.

"Technically, as far as she remembers at least, we've never even been out on a date. Just because I remember every curve of her body, every spot that…" I trailed off, my mind racing down warm, dark, secret pathways that I had absolutely no intention of sharing with Summer.

"I know, sweetie," she commiserated, uncrossing her arms and stepping over to wrap me in a sympathetic hug – at least as high as she could reach. "I could see from that first visit how attracted to her you were. Now you've – how do I say this delicately?"

"Since when have you worried about delicacy," I asked, "especially around me?"

She smiled, acknowledging the point.

"Fine, now that you've touched and tasted the prize," she continued, though even I winced at the level of bluntness she reached with that one. "Why aren't you up there, showing her the 'amenities' and helping her 'get comfortable'?" she asked, her inflection telling me *exactly* what those amenities were supposed to include.

"So your suggestion for reassuring her as she sets out on an entirely new path in life is a rousing game of 'hide the sausage'?!" I asked incredulously, making her snort in amusement now that it was my turn to be indelicate.

"Well you could always try and make everything better by playing 'doctor'," she said suggestively.

"Dance the horizontal tango?" I asked, trying to one-up her.

"Make the beast with two backs," she responded, getting into the swing of the game.

"Take her for a ride on the pink pony," I suggested.

"Ride her tunnel of love," she said, laughing again.

Oh for the love of the gods, Gauvain said, clearly transmitting his thoughts to both of us since Summer looked over at him at the same time I did. *You two are as bad as each other.*

Summer and I snickered like naughty school children, while G shrieked and flapped his wings in disgust.

"Come on," I said, "let's lock up and go home. Tomorrow's gonna be a busy day."

Chapter 12

W e shut up the shop for the night, our routine honed over years of practice. I almost forgot to grab my bag and collect Paladin from the office (seriously, how do you *forget* a Jack Russell the size of a lion?) but Gauvain reminded me at the last minute. I swear, some days I'd lose my head if it wasn't attached.

Emily was waiting outside in her car for Summer, so I waved as I walked past. Her eyes were huge as she looked at Paladin, no doubt amazed by the reality despite what Summer might have already told her. They drove off while I loaded everyone into my car. Then we finally headed for home.

The flat smelled a little musty, what with no one having been there in weeks, so I opened the windows and set a couple of fans going. As soon as he saw my bed, Paladin immediately jumped up and lay down. He stared at me with a big doggy grin on his face and his tail thumping the mattress loudly, almost daring me to tell him he couldn't sleep there.

"You needn't get *too* comfortable, furball," I said, crossing my arms with a mock scowl. "As soon as your dog beds arrive, you're sleeping in them." His tail continued to pound the mattress regardless, so I smiled and shook my head in resignation.

You know you like snuggling up at night, he said happily. *I don't see the problem.*

Face it, Gav, Gauvain chimed in, *you're not going to win this, so you may as well just enjoy the company.*

"Oh great," I said, trying desperately to sound grumpy and failing dismally. "Gang up on the poor defenceless hairless ape!" We all shared a mental laugh, then I went to get G and myself some dinner out of the freezer.

I spent the rest of the evening doing simple chores – laundry, dusting since it hadn't been done in weeks due to my absence, along with checking over my ready bag to make sure it was reset for wherever I might need to go next. Gauvain made the point that since I didn't need to use the airlines anymore, I wouldn't have to worry about security going through my things. As a result, I included a couple of folding knives for back-up. I would also be able to take Muharar, though that wouldn't fit in the bag.

I debated where to keep my sword now I was home, wandering between rooms. I eventually settled on leaning it against the end of the couch for now, while resolving to look for a proper tabletop sword stand or wall hanging in the near future.

After all the excitement of the day, I wasn't surprised to feel completely exhausted by nine o'clock, so I grabbed a quick shower and went to bed. G was back on his perch in the bedroom, while I was left to wrestle for some space on the bed.

When I woke up the next morning, I felt a momentary stab of confusion at my surroundings before the events of yesterday reasserted themselves in my memory. I'd clearly been away too long and had started to get *far* too comfortable at Seirina's house, if my own bedroom confused me. I would miss Mrs Wilson's calm efficiency getting all the laundry and cooking done, but it was nice to be back in my own place.

I got up and stretched, putting on my running gear and getting ready to head out for my morning run for the first time in ages. Since we didn't have to worry about Order surveillance now, both G and Pal elected to join me. Gauvain flew out of the open kitchen window while Paladin thumped down the stairs behind me.

I set off on my usual course, noting all the plants that had shot up and spread out since I'd last seen them. It was remarkably therapeutic to be back on my old stomping grounds, and I finished my run feeling more relaxed than I had for a long time.

I jumped in the shower and got myself ready for the day, chatting idly with G as he sat on the shower rail preening in the mist. I thought about teleporting to work, then reconsidered. The shutters had to be opened from the outside, plus the alarm was on, so I couldn't just pop into the office. I also couldn't just appear on the street with G and Pal, since there was no way of knowing if some random pedestrian might be walking by right where I landed. It would be bad enough if someone in a car was passing at just the wrong time.

I resigned myself to continuing to use the car for the time being, though if my plans for the shop went well, eventually things would change. We all went down to the car and piled in, setting off to see what surprises the day had in store for us. That was when I remembered Angie and the twins would be starting today, at which point my calm and relaxed demeanour made a quick exit.

Summer on her own I could deal with – just. Summer with back-up was going to be a whole different experience. Summer with back-up from the twins was even worse. Summer colluding with a woman she *knew* I had feelings for was worse still. All of them together could potentially be fatal – at least to my self-image and what remaining shred of dignity I had been vainly clinging to.

I momentarily debated turning around and going back home to bed but, fortunately or unfortunately, I had just reached the one-way system in the town centre. I was stuck going forward and of course, just my luck, Summer was parking as I arrived. Once again, I was up that well-known creek in a leaky canoe.

"Morning, Gav," Summer called as we both got out of our cars. "Morning, G; morning, Pal." Paladin bounced over and said hello in his typically boisterous manner, while G maintained his dignity and simply said hello mentally.

We opened the first shutters and Summer went to start the Cafegeddon while I finished with the security system. Gauvain flew to his perch by the counter, his favourite spot in the shop, while Pal traipsed into the office for another world-class nap. Still, I didn't begrudge him since he was continuing to feed energy into Seren whenever we were near each other.

"I see you've officially changed the morning greeting," I said to Summer as I went into the kitchen. "No more asking if I've had any luck." She turned and looked at me with her eyebrows raised and her lips pursed to the left.

"You had your bloody luck in Tibet," she replied tartly, then her eyes twinkled. "Plus I'm well aware you went home last night instead of upstairs, so you didn't get lucky that way either!" I sniggered immaturely along with her, then sighed regretfully.

"You know why I couldn't," I said.

She patted my arm consolingly.

"Hey, she'll be working here full time now." I could already hear the cogs turning in her devious little mind.

"*Summer,*" I said, drawing her name out warningly. "You keep your plans to yourself. I want this to happen naturally, if it's going to. I mean it, no meddling!" I scowled at her as hard as I could, since she'd started grinning halfway through my tirade. I shook my head in despair, knowing she'd do as she pleased regardless of what I said.

I reached past her to the coffee pot as it beeped, desperately needing caffeine if I was going to make it through the next few hours. Summer held out her cup expectantly and I looked from it to her face slowly, narrowing my eyes in mock threat.

"OK, OK," she said. "You're on your own. Just give with the coffee already!" As I poured for her I heard her mumbling under her breath, quite certain she was equivocating on her surrender. I couldn't make out what she said, though I knew it didn't bode well for my chances of non-interference.

At that moment, I heard a knock at the door. Since we didn't open for another twenty minutes I thought it was probably our new staff members, so I went out to let them in. Angelica stood behind the twins, who waved at me through the glass, their faces lit up with huge smiles. Clearly they were excited to get started, an impression they confirmed with the way they burst in once I unlocked the door.

"Morning, Gavan!" Izzy said brightly, as they grabbed me for a hug.

"Morning, *boss!*" stressed Gabby, casting a quick glare at her sister. Izzy covered her mouth fleetingly.

"Sorry, that's what I meant. Morning, boss," she said, looking back at Gabby guiltily.

"We have to make sure we don't get overly familiar now we're his employees," Gabby said.

"Oh yes, we must show proper respect."

"This is the workplace now."

"And he's the boss."

"Though I doubt he'll treat us like our last boss did!"

"Oh, definitely not."

"Still, proper workplace decorum must be maintained."

"The correct relationship is key."

"Oh, you don't have to worry about that," came Summer's voice from behind me. She'd clearly come out of the kitchen to meet our new recruits, and I could see she deliberately didn't react to the twins' appearance. I was glad I'd told her about them, so she had been forewarned. "We work better as friends than as boss and employee. You should hear some of the names we call each other when we get going sometimes."

"Summer..." I objected lamely, but she just ploughed on ahead and ignored me.

"Besides, he needs keeping in his place so he doesn't get too big for his boots," she continued. "After all, he's only a man. He needs a good woman to keep him in line." She directed that last comment with a wink to Angelica, who had followed the twins in but hadn't been able to get a word in yet. She grinned cheekily at Summer's suggestion, however, which made my heart start doing loops and my stomach tie itself into a pretzel.

"Oh, men definitely benefit from a strong hand," she replied, at which Summer's smile threatened to split her face open.

"Well, I'll have to let you provide that," Summer said quickly. "I've never been one for driving stick, and I'm quite happy with Emily."

"So when is one of you going to propose then?" I jumped in, desperately trying to turn the conversation away from firm hands on my stick. Thankfully, the twins immediately jumped on the new topic.

"Ooh, are you going to?" asked Gabby breathlessly.

"I love wedding dresses!" added Izzy.

"I hate you, Gav," Summer deadpanned at me, at which we all shared a laugh.

"OK, time to start the day!" I said, clapping my hands together and rubbing them.

Chapter 13

I spent the next hour or so showing Angie, Gabby, and Izzy around the shop. I explained about the various items we had and told them about the different types of books, from pedestrian to arcane. Then Summer took them through the computer system, showing them how the sales system worked and how to place special orders for people.

I also showed them the kitchen and facilities, telling them I kept things stocked and to help themselves – except for the coffee. They could use the machine, but no bogarting the beans to take home. They laughed at my pretended strictness, though Summer gave them a cautionary head shake to let them know I was serious about the beans.

I showed them briefly around my office but explained that anything in there could only be dealt with by me. If a customer wanted anything from my personal collection, I had to be involved. I also told them about trusting their instincts regarding customers. Given their telepathic capabilities, if they were even the slightest bit dubious about someone's intentions or motives, they had the right – even the *responsibility* – not to sell to them.

All of them stood a little taller when I expressed my faith in their abilities and perceptions. Summer gave me a subtle nod of approval as she saw them relax and settle into being here. I was pleased they seemed to be comfortable and hoped they'd find a real home with us, much as Summer had.

I also told them about booking appointments for anyone wanting to commission me to find a specific item. Angelica smiled, realising I was referencing how we had originally met – not that she could remember it. I let them know the best and worst times to book for, how long to give per appointment, made sure they knew to notify me and, most importantly, enter it into the computer scheduler.

We decided to spend the rest of the morning continuing what Summer had been doing when I got back yesterday: restocking the shelves. We generally tended to do it during the week since it was quieter than the weekends. There were a few jokes about the stockroom being private, mostly from Summer, until finally I glowered at her.

"OK, enough, we get it," I said. "It's very amusing, but there'll be no funny business on work time, thank you very much."

"I don't know whether to call you a spoilsport or a coward," Summer replied grumpily, crossing her arms.

"And I don't know whether to be disappointed or relieved," came a voice from behind me. I spun to see Angie exiting the stock room with a box of backflow incense cones. "On the one hand, it's nice to know this is a safe space. On the other…" She looked me up and down suggestively.

Summer gave her a beaming grin and went to stand next to her, both staring at me for a moment. Then they looked at each other knowingly, then Angie continued over to the incense stand.

Oh yes, you are DEFINITELY in over your head, Gauvain remarked, shuffling along his perch to get a drink. *I shall be intrigued to watch as the situation unfolds.*

"Oh, great," I said quietly. "Now everyone thinks they're Dr Phil."

Now that everyone seemed to be settling into their respective roles, I chose to head to my office and continue researching this whole 'Banished Soul' deal. G flew to my shoulder as I walked towards the door, landing just as I turned to Summer.

"I'll be in here if anyone needs me," I said, getting a quick nod and a waving gesture in response. Knowing I was dismissed, I rolled my eyes and went into my sanctuary. Pal lifted his head as I came in, thumping his tail a few times. He closed his eyes and relaxed again after I'd stroked his head as I passed.

G hopped from my shoulder to his perch as I went to sit in my chair. I stretched and sighed deeply, then sat forward and reached for my Surface. I checked my emails to see if Seirina had sent me anything she'd found but, unsurprisingly, there was nothing. I emptied the spam folder of the usual dating/hook-up site invites and Viagra offers, then got to work.

When I searched for 'The Rock of Banished Souls', the top result I got was a song by someone called Banished (I'd never heard of them but I guessed they must be a rock band) called *Inherit His Soul*. There were a few other entries for their music, then something from the *Inheritance Cycle* fandom about 'the vault of souls'.

I sighed, accepting it wasn't going to be as easy as that. I'd expected as much, though one can always hope. Clearly, my initial thought had been right: Elrulin had either renamed a location or created something new. Given his habit here of locating his bases under historical sites, I was leaning towards the former possibility.

My main problem was that America was a relatively young country. England was millennia old, while America was only just two centuries. If you measured a country's age by centuries, comparing those to a person's years of life, most European countries were in their twenties or more. America, however, was just in its 'terrible twos'. Maybe that was why other countries tended to regard Americans' attitudes as loud and demanding, just like a toddler: Their country was essentially just that (not that I ever told my American friends that – I'm a comedian, not a moron).

However, that meant there were no sites even *approaching* the age of the sites in England, Scotland, and Ireland. Some of the ones Elrulin had hidden under over here had been historical monuments before Columbus even set sail.

I sat back and tried to recall what I knew of American history, trying to identify any prominent locations. The problem was, history lessons in England tended to include all the European events from hundreds, if not thousands, of years. The battle of Hastings was in 1066, for Christ's sake. That was over four centuries before Columbus, who had set off with the *Niña, Pinta,* and *Santa Maria* in 1492. As a result we had a lot more to learn, so American history was nowhere near as rigorously taught as it was to US schoolchildren.

As I was reflecting, I had a sudden thought: Plymouth Rock! The initial landing site of the first settlers on the Mayflower. People who had either left or been kicked out of their origin countries – essentially, *Banished Souls*! Quite literally, a true *Rock of Banished Souls*! Could it really be that easy? I crossed my fingers and dove back into the internet to see what I could dig up.

Aside from learning that there was a chicken breed called Plymouth Rock – interesting but hardly relevant – I found plenty of easily accessible information on the historical locale. I discovered it was now actually in two pieces after it broke in 1774 when people attempted to haul it to the Plymouth town square. Half stayed where it was, half went to the town. That piece was then moved to a museum in 1834, then back to join the other half in 1880. Apparently, only a third of the real rock is now underneath a granite copy, the rest having been taken by various people over the years.

There wasn't anything big enough at that site in Plymouth to cover a large base, though I learned a forty-pound chunk now resided in a church in Brooklyn Heights, New York. It wasn't exactly a castle but then, America didn't really *have* castles like that. Churches frequently had underground tunnels such as catacombs, as I'd already discovered under the chapel at Bolton, so it was a distinct option.

Although I was excited by the possibility of having discovered the Order's new location, I was also cautious that this had seemed too simple. It had only taken a little thought and extrapolation to come up with Plymouth Rock, and there were other locations that could just as easily fit the bill.

Ellis Island, for example, was where a huge number of immigrants had first set foot on American soil. The Statue of Liberty: One of America's most beloved and recognizable monuments, symbolizing their independence and freedom. The Lincoln Memorial, Bunker Hill Monument, the Alamo... There were arguments for each. I was able to discount the White House and the Capitol Building, since they were far too highly monitored and trafficked to be accessible to the Order (thank the gods).

My initial surge of excitement abated somewhat as I realised the scope of the problem again. As young as America was, it was still a vast country with plenty of sites spread out across it. I still had high hopes for my initial idea, since it seemed to fit so exactly with the name I'd learned, but I couldn't pin everything on that one possibility.

I barely noticed time slipping by as I lost myself in research, until I was startled by the sound of the door opening. I looked up to see Angelica walk in with a wrapped baguette from the sandwich shop over the road. I glanced at the clock on my screen, shocked to see it was already quarter to two. My stomach let out a loud gurgle, letting me know it was definitely time for a break, at which Angie smiled and held out the roll.

"Sounds like I'm just in time," she said. "Your stomach was clearly about to go hunting without you soon." I laughed, taking my lunch from her and looking to see what filling it was. "Summer said you like their chicken tikka but they were all out, so I got you brie and cranberry since she mentioned that too."

"This is great, thanks," I said, taking a huge bite and swallowing after only a couple of chews. "Oh wow, I didn't realise quite how hungry I was!" I practically inhaled the rest of the sandwich, Angie turning and leaving as I was on my third big mouthful.

I gave G a piece of the brie, then put the last chunk in my mouth with a satisfied sigh. I threw the wrapper in the bin and stood up, stretching the kinks out of my neck and shoulders. I went out into the shop, smiling at my 'harem' on my way to the kitchen. I reached into the fridge, grabbing a can of Pepsi Max and popping the top. I chugged the entire thing, my throat almost hissing as the moisture hit it since I'd not even had a drink since my coffee when we opened the shop.

I belched loudly as I walked out again, all four heads turning towards me. The twins were laughing, Angie's mouth was wide open at the sheer volume I'd achieved, while Summer waved a hand in front of her nose.

"Wow, so refined," she said sarcastically. "Thanks for sharing, Gav. I think you could get a few more decibels if you reach from your boots, maybe signal ships at sea." Angie joined in the mirth at that and I swept a deep bow.

"Too kind, ma'am," I said pompously. "Now, shall we get back to work?"

Chapter 14

I grabbed another can from the fridge and went back into my office. I decided to start making a list of possible sites, with pros and cons of each. Thanks to the wonders of modern technology, I was able to quickly look up information on each site, though of course the Order could easily have altered their chosen site using magick. That meant the *location* was more important than any existing infrastructure.

I moved the church in New York down the list somewhat, since there would be little to no privacy. I remembered a comment about the new American site being popular with the more monstrous Order members since they didn't have to hide. That could potentially be as a result of the extent of the underground network at the new site, though somehow I doubted it.

I concluded that an island would definitely be the best type of location, since the Order could control the entire thing. Then, as advertised, no one would need to hide. I started looking at Ellis Island and Liberty Island. I became confused for a moment, as the information on Ellis Island stated it was part of the Statue of Liberty National Monument. Then I read further and understood – they *were* two separate islands, just close together and served by the same ferry.

However since the islands *were* so close together, large monsters such as trolls out in the open could be seen from the other island. It didn't matter which of the two islands was used, the other would be a security risk. I doubted even the Order had enough money to obtain the relevant access to *two* such well-known historical sites.

All of which meant that my research from this morning was about as much use as an unwaxed paper teapot. Well maybe not quite that bad, since it at least eliminated some potential locations. That wasn't as much help as it might have been, given the scope of the problem, as I'd realised earlier. Still, even a tiny amount of progress was better than no progress at all. I printed my list out and put it in a folder, then stuck it in a drawer and closed it in disgust.

I sat back in my chair and reached up with both arms, stretching to work out the inevitable kinks from sitting hunched over my computer for hours. I got up and decided to go help in the shop for a while, maybe clear my head and see if any other bright ideas came to me. G hopped to my shoulder as I passed, wanting to come with me.

I saw Angelica helping a young woman with the scented candles, overhearing them talking about their favourite scents. I smiled at her tactic, realising that the more they talked the more the young lady was likely to buy. It was a technique I'd used many times myself and it was pleasing to see Angie use it so instinctively. She was naturally approachable – probably why the Order had used her as a liaison, quite apart from her telepathic powers – and I could already tell she'd be an asset to the business.

The twins were behind the counter, polishing some of the pendants from the display case and subtly being in position to ring up sales. Again, a useful trick as it meant the customer didn't have to wait to pay so didn't reconsider their purchases. I sensed Summer's teachings, as it was her favourite spot when we were working together. I smiled at them, receiving a subtle nod from Gabby while Izzy continued to focus on the jewellery.

Gauvain fluttered over to his perch by the counter, drawing a surprised gasp from the customer. I spotted a laminated notice on the front of the counter that I'd missed earlier. Summer had obviously run with the suggestion I'd made, since the placard politely but clearly told people not to touch G unless someone was with them. It also plainly informed them of our lack of liability for bitten fingers should they ignore the advice, which made me grin.

In today's society of 'sue everyone for anything you can', you had to cover yourself as much as possible. I mean seriously, some of the warning signs you saw around today were verging on the ridiculous. Sometimes I really wished we could follow the Facebook meme – remove all the safety warnings and just let Darwinism weed out the stupid ones.

I heard the toilet flush and the sink running, then Summer came through from the back.

"Typical," she said. "I can't even have a pee without it being public knowledge." I laughed at her dramatic tone, watching as she failed to maintain her 'irritation'.

"Give it rest, you drama queen," I said, laughing along with the twins.

"Hey, at least I'm royalty," she snarked, making me roll my eyes.

"Moving on," I said, slightly exasperated. "So how are they doing? Any problems?"

"Oh, definitely," she said. "They're terrible...ly hard workers. They're awful...ly good with the customers. They're horrendous...ly efficient. Fire them all immediately – before you realise you don't need me anymore."

The girls were all chuckling, getting louder with each description, along with the candle shopper. I tilted my head and raised one eyebrow in tolerant amusement, pretending to consider my options.

"Too late," I said eventually. "You're fired. Get out. Actually, you can stay to the end of the day, then I don't want to see you back here – for two whole weeks." I laughed at the growing horror on the twins' faces, then even harder as they realised the joke. "My way of saying thanks for minding the store while I've been off gallivanting recently."

Summer beamed, grabbing me tight and squeezing as hard as she could.

"Just don't spend the *whole* fortnight in bed," I requested. "Or the pair of you will drop dead of exhaustion, dehydration, and pleasure overload." All four of my employees gave almost identical head shakes, at which I realised something once again. "I really need more guys around."

"Umm..." came a hesitant voice from near the door. "Can I just get these three candles please?" We all spun to see the young lady Angie had been helping looking between each of us.

"My apologies, miss," I said, recovering quickly. "We forgot you were here. Please, step over to the counter, and we'll get you sorted out. I tell you what, I'll even give you the three candles for the price of two, to make up for our lack of professionalism."

"Actually, I thought it was hysterical," she said cheekily. "Though far be it from me to turn down a deal."

I smiled at her, nodding to the twins at the register. They clearly had their glamour working again, since I could only see them separately if I really concentrated. This was another reason I wanted to get my expansion plans underway: If everything worked out how I wanted, they wouldn't have to hide like that.

I watched approvingly as the twins wrapped the candles in tissue paper and placed them in one of our logo-embossed paper bags. The girl thanked us again and left, looking over the shelves briefly as she passed them. Hopefully she'd come back, maybe with friends next time.

"That's right, sweetie, two whole weeks!" I heard Summer say, turning to see her talking on her mobile phone. It didn't take a genius to figure out she was talking to Emily and, judging by the squealing from the phone, they were equally excited to have some free time together. I was glad to be able to do something like this for them now, since Summer was always left running the store whenever I went off on a commission or to a sale.

With our new staff, she could *finally* have some well-earned time off. As I listened to my best friend making her plans, I abruptly realised it would leave me alone with Angie and the twins for two weeks. I looked over at Summer and she must have seen the panic in my eyes. She gave me one of the evilest grins I'd ever seen on her face, finishing her call and putting her phone in her pocket with a flourish.

"No take-backs," she said, pointing at me gleefully. "I earned it, you know it, so I'm taking it!"

"Don't worry," I reassured her. "I wouldn't do that to you. I know how much you've done, and you know – or at least I hope you do – how much I appreciate you. Still, just don't go trying to 'extend' your little vacation. Otherwise I'll come into your bedroom and drag you out by your hair, no matter who or what you're in the middle of."

"I love it when you get all butch and authoritarian," she said, pretending to simper and swoon.

"So masterful," agreed Izzy.

"Such a commanding presence," chimed in Gabby.

"Makes a girl weak at the knees," Angie joked.

"Total panty-wetter," added Summer.

"OK, that's *quite* enough," I said, cringing. "I can see I grossly underestimated how bad this was going to become, quite how evil you'd all get once you got together. I may have to rethink my staffing choices if this continues…" I threatened – only partly in jest. I could feel a trickle of sweat edging its way down the back of my neck as I faced four women who had formed into a unified front in less than one day.

"Right, like you've never threatened *that* before," Summer said, deadpan. "Lemme guess, next you'll try and pull the 'boss' card, right?"

"Anyone would think you know me," I said. At this point, Angie, Izzy, and Gabby were watching the back and forth between us like a tennis match – much like the rest of us normally watched the twins when they had one of their 'duologues'.

"What, like maybe we've been working together for the last decade?" Summer suggested.

"Maybe even had dinner a few times?"

"Celebrated birthdays together?"

"Had holiday seasons together?"

"Relentlessly meddled in each other's love lives?"

"Yeah, when *are* you going to propose?" I finished with a *coup de grace* I knew would strike home, laughing as I saw the twins' faces light up in anticipation while Summer just glowered. "Hey, you kept asking me about my magick and now I have it. So I figure if I keep asking you about getting married, eventually I'll get to walk you down the aisle."

"I swear, I will make your life a living hell if you try it!" Summer promised, and this was one threat I knew for a fact she'd follow through on. I decided discretion might just be the better part of valour at this point.

"Have a nice holiday," I said, hands up and backing away to general amusement.

Another day, another female victory.

Chapter 15

The next two weeks were, to my surprise, excessively normal. Apparently, without Summer there to stir the pot and teach them bad habits like taking the piss out of their boss, the twins and Angie reverted to a state of previously unknown (at least to me) highly efficient professionalism. The shelves were restocked, customers helped, records kept, and orders placed. Within two days of Summer going on her break, they seemed to have running the store down to a fine art. I was about as essential to the day-to-day operations as teats on a bull, which allowed me to catch up with the bookkeeping accumulated from all the time I was away.

Once I had the accounts straight – which was quite enjoyable, since the Order's spying and fact-finding had led to them spending time and plenty of money here – I was able to start thinking about my expansion plans. Since I already had advertising in place and a bit of a reputation (although not magickal just yet, more to do with my commissions), I wanted to stay here rather than find a whole new location. There was also the fact that I'd spent a fair amount of time and energy setting up the wards protecting the place, so it was already a safe space.

Now I just needed to learn how to put my idea into effect. I already knew part of it, so I needed to discover how to adapt what I knew to achieve what I wanted. It was pretty much the reverse of an earlier mistake, so I knew it had to be *possible*, and there were enough examples of my idea in legend and fiction that I knew it must have even been done before. It would just take a little experimentation and practice to be able to do what I wanted with my abilities. I also had to figure out exactly where in the shop to put the new area.

Considering how I wanted to arrange things, I didn't need people to have to squeeze through some tiny gap to get there. I was sitting at my desk on Wednesday of the second week, drawing up a floor plan of the shop on squared paper, when my phone rang. I put down my ruler and hit the answer button without looking, putting it on speakerphone in case I needed to write anything down.

"Dinas Affaraon, Gavan Maddox, how can I help you?"

"Oh, I don't know," came a familiar voice. "I can think of a book I'd quite like to take a peek at."

"Seirina," I said genially, sitting back and arching my shoulders backwards to stretch them. "I was planning on checking in with you tomorrow, just like last week. Mondays and Thursdays, remember? So have you heard something in the last couple of days? Or has Iyrin finally got off its skeletal ass and been useful at last?" I could feel the watcher's irritation as a tremor through our link briefly, then it faded away again. The lack of any ongoing excitement told me it was being as much use as always – sod all with a side of nothing.

"No, Iyrin has been about as forthcoming as ever," she said, confirming my interpretation of our link. "I got an email from Sovereign this morning. She's been through every lore book she has, spoken to every obeah and practitioner she knows. She's spoken to Cheveyo and apparently he's spoken to every tribal elder *he* knows. *No one* has ever heard about, read about, or even seen hints of any 'Rock of Banished Souls'."

"Shit!" I swore, thumping my fist on the arm of the chair. "So that puts us right back at square boned!"

"Not quite," she said. "We still have the name, and we still have the Order out of this country and across the ocean. That means we have time and space to research in peace, plus the right thread to try and unpick. Just because we didn't get an easy answer, doesn't mean we won't get there eventually. We just need to look in other places."

"Yeah, I've had a few ideas about that," I replied, pulling up my list and attaching it to an email for her. "I've kinda discounted them as valid sites, but you could send it to Sovereign and Cheveyo for them to check out. No point missing something obvious."

"See, that's progress," she told me, clearly trying to reassure me. "Even eliminating sites gets us slightly closer. We may have to gradually work through hundreds of locations, but we'll get there eventually."

I took a deep breath and nodded, even though she couldn't see me. "Thanks," I said. "I'm calm again now. Sorry, just got frustrated and disheartened for a second. Don't worry, I'm good."

"I wouldn't go quite *that* far," she said with a chuckle. "Fair to middling, maybe."

"Bite me," I grumbled good naturedly.

"That's Angie's job, isn't it?" she teased, which made my shoulders tighten. "Or haven't you got that far yet?"

"We've been a bit busy with the shop," I evaded. "I haven't even asked her out yet. Last time, we were kind of pushed together artificially. Between her coming to the shop twice, then me rescuing her from the Order, we never got to know each other in any normal kind of way. She said she was attracted to my picture in the Order's file but I want to see if she even likes the everyday version of me, not the 'knight in shining armour' I played when I charged into Bolton Castle. Or in my case, more a shite in tarnished armour."

"Oh for heaven's sake," she scolded me with an exasperated sigh. "If you don't pull your head out of your ass, and get out of your own damned way, I'll put my foot up there *with* your head and see if I can't yank the stick out at the same time."

"Well that's a vivid, varied, and extremely colourful combination of imagery," I said, wincing at the picture she'd painted. "Thanks for the pep talk. I'll take it under advisement." I could hear her frustration down the line. "Anyway, I have work to do – on several topics, now that our colleagues haven't found anything. I'll catch up with you next week. Monday, as usual. Bye!"

"Gavan..." she started to call out, but I hung up. I put my elbows on the desk and my head in my hands. Why did everything have to go tits up? The only thing that went right recently was my search for the Veil, though even *that* came with consequences. Yeah, great, it unlocked my magick. Even boosted my power to super-human, god-given levels (thank you Isis). On the flip side, I now had superhuman enemies of varying levels of power. I was apparently even 'destined' to fight in some kind of apocalyptic battle at some indeterminate point in the future. The one thing I'd wanted my whole life and it came with so many strings, I could knit a blanket big enough to cover Europe.

So now where did I look for the next clue? I already knew there was nothing about the Rock of Banished Souls in any of my current library. I remembered Lucian mentioning a pair of twins down south, which in turn triggered a memory of a bookshop I'd used before for some rare, esoteric volumes. Maybe they could find me some literature on ancient, alternative American history.

The shop was called The Bookworm and it was situated on a pier in a small village called Redsea, down in Cornwall. It was run by a family called Davis, who had apparently been there for years. I decided to take Gauvain with me for a little jaunt, since I thought he'd enjoy the sea air. He might even catch himself a fish. Pal could stay and guard the shop, since a lion-sized dog was, as ever, not exactly inconspicuous.

I let the girls know I would be stepping out for a bit and was rewarded with beaming smiles. The fact that I trusted them enough to leave them alone in my beloved shop seemed to make them immensely proud, if the braced posture, raised chins, and squared shoulders were anything to go by.

I said goodbye and teleported myself and G down to Redsea. I chose a landing site underneath the main pier so I'd be out of sight of anyone in the area. I breathed in the smell of seaweed, since it was low tide, and promptly covered my nose and mouth. I dashed out along the sand, away from the green-encrusted pilings that were turning my stomach. Gauvain spiralled up into the sunshine with a loud screech, drawing the admiring glances of several nearby tourists who were sunbathing.

I walked up the beach towards the coastal road, then turned towards the top of the pier. The inland end of the pier was a traditional arcade, much as you might find at Blackpool. There was a merry-go-round, ring-toss, skittles, shooting gallery, dozens more game booths, plus multiple food carts selling everything from ice cream to hot dogs to popcorn. Then, about halfway out along the walkway, there was a metal fence with a turnstile in it, manned by a mature man in uniform – a true armed forces veteran, if his bearing was anything to go by.

Beyond the fence, the pier changed dramatically. There were high-end shops that would have looked more at home in Beverly Hills than Cornwall. There was a jewellery shop that I could barely afford to look in the window of, even *after* getting my Order retainer. There was a bakery that smelled like heaven – the kind of smell that would make a cartoon character float in there drawn by the waves of scent pulled by his nose. Another shop that seemed to change hands every couple of years as I'd seen from my previous visits, which currently looked as though it was a high-end hairdresser, with the traditional black-and-chrome chairs and hairstyle pictures. The fourth shop, balancing the pattern of two on each side, was of course, The Bookworm.

The entire end of the pier was taken up by a shop called Arodnesse. It was apparently owned, along with the rest of the pier, by the two remaining members of the oldest family in the area: Scarlett and Schofield Godolphin. I didn't know much about them, I'd just heard of them from Mr Davis when I'd been in The Bookworm. Their shop looked very stark, done up in Art Deco black and silver with an arched entrance.

The top floor had a curved roof and the windows were curtained, as if the owners used it as living quarters. On the right of the ground floor, it looked like a traditional tourist seaside shop with sticks of rock, buckets-and-spades, sunglasses, postcards, and trinkets. On the left, it looked like an antique glass and jewellery shop, the window showing only one or two pieces that were never the same each time I came down here. The dichotomy between the two sides was jarring, yet somehow fit perfectly. I had never gone in as I had seen a huge spotted cat in there once, and I'd never been a fan.

I strolled along the boards, holding my arm out for Gauvain as he flew down to me. He told me he'd caught a small mackerel for himself, eating it before he'd re-joined me. As I neared the bookshop my gaze was arrested by a truly unique woman, fitting the description that Mr Davis had once given me of Miss Scarlett Godolphin. She was reasonably tall for a woman, just a couple of inches shy of six feet, athletic but not over-muscled, with her hair split down the centre. Her right side was pink, the left brunette, yet she didn't seem to be a punk. As I drew closer, I noticed her eyes were also different colours – blue on the pink hair side, hazel green under the brunette. That meant, unless she was wearing a single coloured contact, she had at least a degree of chimerism. She raised a hand in a vaguely dismissive wave in my direction, spending more time looking at Gauvain and only sparing the briefest of glances for me before turning and going into her shop.

I shrugged, pushing the enigmatic heiress out of my mind to focus on the larger concerns of tracking down the Order. Gauvain hopped from my shoulder to the nearby railing, since a bookshop wasn't really the best place for dust and feathers, and I stepped over to my destination.

I pushed open the door to The Bookworm, inhaling the welcome musty smell of old books. I closed my eyes and revelled in the scent, hearing a raspy chuckle as I did so.

"Now that's the face of a man who truly loves books," Mr Davis said. He had a wonderfully rasping voice due to an accident during a tonsillectomy when he was a child. It had damaged his vocal cords, giving him a voice any Hollywood producer would have instantly cast as an ancient librarian in a haunted house. I loved the guy, and we'd spent many an hour discussing old volumes.

"So what can I do for you today, young Mr Maddox?" he rasped.

Chapter 16

"Mr Davis," I said happily, stepping over to him and shaking his hand. "It's good to see you. How have you been? How's business?" No matter how many times I'd told him, he refused to call me by my first name. He was truly old-school, calling all his customers 'sir' or 'miss' if they were new to his shop, or by their surname if they were repeat customers. As such, I chose to respect his choice and addressed him the same way.

"I've been very well, thank you," he said cheerfully. "My nephew just got accepted to university to study law."

"Oh, pass on my congratulations," I said sincerely. "Which university?"

"Cambridge," he said proudly. "He says he wants to go into corporate law, rather than criminal."

"Sensible choice," I remarked. "More money, less chance of getting on the wrong side of someone nasty. I wish him luck."

"Thank you. So, now that the pleasantries are observed, how can I help?"

I smiled genially. I'd learned never to rush him, as he would view skipping polite conversation as the height of rudeness. If you allowed him a few words of idle chat, however, he could be a more valuable resource than all the books in his shop.

"I'm looking for some lesser-known or alternative histories of America," I said, seeing his eyes light up. The more obscure or challenging a request, the more he liked it. He loved to trawl the world for unique books, uncovering snippets of information no one had heard of in centuries. I liked to think of him as an information archaeologist, the Indiana Jones of books.

"Oh really?" he said, his tone reflecting the interest his eyes had already betrayed. "Anything in particular? Are we talking the truth about what happened to the Native Americans? The real story of slavery? Or, given your *particular* interests, the truth about the Salem witch trials?"

"I'm looking for a particular location," I said. "I've got a name, but all my research so far has turned up exactly nothing. Even a Native American shaman and a New Orleans voodoo priestess couldn't find anything."

"Oh, a *real* challenge," he exclaimed, rubbing his hands together excitedly. "So what's the name of this elusive spot?"

"The Rock of Banished Souls," I told him. "It's the name of the new location for a group I'm trying to help shut down. They're bad news, so keep your search to yourself. If you even *think* someone's become interested in you because of your enquiries, stop straight away and call me."

"Indeed?" he asked, turning serious. "Well you know me, I stick to old books. I stay away from the internet, so it's only people in the know who even come to my shop. Still, I appreciate your honesty about the risk. I'll let you know as soon as I find anything."

"Thank you, Mr Davis," I said. I looked around his store fondly, then closed my eyes. I created some wards for him, protecting the store against magickal or mundane damage, plus a basic layer of protection for him personally. Hopefully it wouldn't be needed, though now I had the ability I'd kick myself if I didn't use it to protect my friends and they got hurt.

"Look after yourself," I said in farewell. "And again, my congratulations and best wishes to your nephew." He gave me a slight bow as I turned to leave, though I could tell by his eyes he was already racing along various threads of thought to try and find what I'd asked for.

I walked out and closed the door quietly behind me, Gauvain immediately swept over to my shoulder again when he saw me. I leant against the railing for a few minutes, closing my eyes and turning my face up to the sun. I breathed in the fresh air, the tang of salt and ozone so unique to the seaside refreshing like nothing else could. I already felt better, knowing Mr Davis was now on the search. It meant I could let him get on with it while I shifted my focus back to my shop. My expansion plans were finally taking shape; I just needed to perfect the required technique.

I took one final deep inhalation of ionised salt air, then teleported myself and G back to Dinas Affaraon. We reappeared in my office, Paladin lifting his head and thumping his tail a couple of times in welcome. Gauvain hopped off my shoulder onto his perch, grabbing a quick drink and then setting to for a good preen to get the sea salt and fish oils out of his feathers.

I stepped out into the shop to let the girls know I had returned, pleased to see everything running as smoothly as ever. The twins were just taking payment for what looked like one of the 'spell book' diaries; Angie was just coming out of the kitchen with some cans of soda. She put one on the counter for the twins – I guessed they'd share – and popped the top on her own. I watched, mesmerised, as she tilted her head back and her throat pulsed when she swallowed. I shook my head and looked away, feeling my cheeks get hot and not wanting to be caught staring.

I stepped around the counter and went into the stockroom, closing the door and taking a deep breath to steady myself. I needed to stop acting like a moony schoolboy and start acting like a friend and colleague, otherwise I'd scare her away by behaving more like a stalker. I looked around, noting that Summer's increased sales meant we were starting to run low on a few things. We had enough to be going on with; we just might need to increase our next order a little.

Then I considered my plans. If I was going to expand and diversify, it might make it easier if the stock *was* running down, since there'd be less to shift around to accommodate the changes. Once the new configuration was set, we could order whatever we needed for the new areas in addition to refilling the routine stock.

I decided to practice this weekend and then, if it worked, I could make the changes on Monday when we were closed. I deliberately hadn't told anyone what I was planning, just in case I couldn't pull it off. I'd look like a proper chump if I bragged about achieving all these wonderful things, only to fail dismally when push came to shove. I took a second assessment of the stockroom, then stepped out and visually assessed the outer area. Since the wall with the stockroom door in it wasn't load-bearing, I could take that section...

I wandered back into the shop, my chin on my chest and my arms crossed, muttering under my breath as I worked out the finer details of my plan. I was so sunk in my own little world, I almost walked right into Gabby and Izzy as they were rounding the end of the counter.

"Oop, sorry girls," I said, slowing my momentum just in time to halt myself on my tiptoes and sidestep around them.

"That's OK," Izzy said with a smile.

"No harm done," Gabby added.

"Though it might be a good idea to walk, then think."

"Rather than trying to do both at the same time."

"There are quite a few breakable items in here."

"And some of them are really quite expensive."

"There's also a standing shop rule regarding damages."

"Namely, 'if you break it, you bought it'."

"It's even written on a notice."

"Yes, it's displayed on top of that case over there." They pointed to my prominently displayed placard and I momentarily felt guilty – before I remembered something.

"I'd be worried by that if I didn't already own everything in here," I said as I laughed. "I was so deep in my own world there, you actually had me going for a minute. Nice job!"

"Well if we're working here," came Angie's voice, making me turn to see her standing by the dreamcatchers, "we're going to make sure it runs as smoothly and correctly as possible. Even if that means we have to keep the boss in line occasionally, too."

"I'm glad you're settling in nicely," I said, looking between them all. "I'm also glad to hear you remember just who the boss is. It's hard enough when Summer refuses to let me be in charge of my own store, I don't need you three following her bad example." The chuckles that followed my little speech were relaxed, so I could tell they were definitely feeling comfortable with where they were and what they were doing.

I was glad I'd helped them start to build a life for themselves outside of the Order. They had been through enough hardships at Elrulin's hands for any five lifetimes, so they deserved the chance to be happy and free. I shook my head, pretending to be exasperated at them, then flounced dramatically back to my office. I couldn't keep a straight face by the time I got there, so I joined my staff in another gut-busting round of laughter.

"You girls are doing a fantastic job," I told them, once I could breathe again. "Keep up the good work. I'll be in here if you need me." I went back into my office and sat down at my desk with a big ol' shit-eating grin, putting my hands behind my head and my feet up on the desk. I stared up at the ceiling and relived the last five minutes, relishing every second of joyous mirth on Angie's face.

I realise you are currently in an excellent mood, Gauvain said cautiously. *And I truly do not wish to rain on your well-earned parade. However may I recommend a degree of caution, combined with a healthy measure of circumspection regarding Angelica?*

"I'm not exactly planning on introducing her to Willie, the one-eyed trouser snake," I said, rolling my eyes. "That doesn't mean I have to be a mealy-mouthed surly asshole, either. I've been having a laugh with Summer at work for over a decade. We work better as friends than we do as employer and employee. I'm *trying* to allow the girls the same courtesy. They spent years as Elrulin's bitches, now they deserve to know what a pleasant working environment is like."

Fair enough, he replied. *I simply wish to help you avoid causing yourself pain and disappointment if things do not go the way you hope.*

"And I appreciate it, buddy," I told him. "Now, any ideas on how to make this idea of mine a reality?"

Chapter 17

Over the weekend, whenever I had a free moment at work, I tried different ways to achieve what I wanted. Eventually, rather than trying to add an extra stage to something I could already do, I recalled what Danu had said to me before I completed my training. Instead of planning each step of the process in exacting detail, I considered what I wanted to achieve as an end result. After all, it had worked when I wanted to block cell phone signals for our Edinburgh assault.

I was at home on Saturday evening when I first managed my goal. I practiced more on Sunday, until finally I was certain I could do what I wanted. I had already asked Angie and the twins to have a day out on Monday, just in case I made a lot of noise. If all went perfectly that shouldn't happen, but when did anything ever go exactly according to plan these days? Edinburgh had been messed up by Fiona trying to protect her niece, Bolton by the Order buggering off to America before we got there. Hopefully, the third time would be the charm.

I'd been captured during my rescue attempt. Then once Angie and I had begun a relationship, her memory was wiped away. I might be the chosen of Isis, but I was beginning to suspect *that* honour came with a curse from several other gods. Either that, or my good luck in having my magick unlocked was leading to plenty of bad luck in order to balance the karmic scales. Maybe I'd just broken a few mirrors recently and didn't know it – an entire factory's worth, if I had to guess. And I hadn't even made it to the apocalyptic battle I'd envisioned when I was in Aaru yet.

Boy, don't you just *love* a healthy dose of anxiety?

After the last customers left on Sunday evening, I wished the girls good night and told them to have a nice day off. All my practicing had used up a significant amount of the energy in Seren, even with Paladin continuing to feed a steady stream through me into the gem. I hoped my plan wouldn't take more than one or two tries, otherwise I might have to give up on my ideas for a while until I could rebuild my energy stores. I decided to have a quiet night in, watching a film or two, probably get some Chinese take-away for dinner. I could use the food and rest to funnel more power into my heart-stone, building up as much as possible for my efforts tomorrow.

By the time I went to bed, I was full to bursting with chow mein, spring rolls, and soup. I lay back in bed, closed my eyes and funnelled my own energy into Seren. The extra food I'd eaten allowed me to replenish my energy even as I fed it into my ring, until at last I was exhausted despite my dinner. I drifted off to sleep thinking of my shop, which inevitably led me to dreams of Angelica. I slept well and deeply, waking up with a smile on my face and a tent in my sheets.

I went for a long run, followed by a cold shower, but I couldn't shake the sense of desire I felt. I *was* able to push it further back in my mind so I could at least get my jeans on, though I figured I was going to need either a DVD or some time alone with my phone this evening to be able to think straight tomorrow. Still, at least I had something to focus on for today to keep my mind off of 'other pursuits'.

I went to the shop with G and Pal, only opening the shutter over the front door halfway so people didn't start thinking we were open. I went back behind the counter and G flew off my shoulder. Rather than his perch by the computer, he went to the one halfway down the shop. Not that he didn't trust me (or so he said), he just wanted to be away from any dust I might generate. I told him I'd be using magick, not a sledgehammer, but he insisted. Dick.

I stepped into the stockroom and assessed things. I moved the boxes away from the back wall, stacking them up along the walls nearer the front to give myself a clear field to work. Then I raised my hands and closed my eyes. I reached for the power in Seren, the power being fed from Paladin, and my own innate energy, weaving them together to create a single cohesive stream. Then I focussed it on the rear wall of the room, piercing the dimensions to create a bubble. It was similar to creating the time bubbles Lucian had taught me about, though this time I was adjusting the three regular dimensions, not time.

I'd gotten the idea from the Tardis, the mill in *Constantine*, Mary Poppins' carpet bag, and all the other fictional uses of the idea. I *pushed* the back wall, expanding and lengthening the room. I added in various other features as I went, since I doubted the one staff bathroom would be enough for all the customers once the new features were up and running. I finished pushing once the space was the size of a reasonable nightclub. Since I had also learned the structure of the walls, I was able to pull together materials to create partitions to section the space off for different purposes.

One of the rooms at the new rear was for storage and was twice the size of the old stockroom. I used magick to shift the boxes from where they were into the new area, then turned my attention to the front of the old stockroom. I carefully took down the door, along with the sections of wall between the body of the shop and the new space. That allowed me to expand the access to the area, though it was still restricted by having to get past the counter. That would enable us to control who could get back there.

I decided against doing any more with the new space, since I had absolutely no doubt that any decorations or floor plans I chose would be deemed ugly or ineffective once the 'Oestrogen Assembly' got involved. I had already made some lists of uses for our 'new' premises, so we could discuss them as a group, then plan decorations and furniture together. This would also mean we weren't tripping over each other in the cramped quarters of the old shop floor, plus enable me to develop other services, making it worthwhile to keep the place open twenty-four hours per day.

The wards I had set up to keep Summer safe while I was away were already in place, since the area was technically still within the walls of the shop. As a result, this place could act as a safe zone for anyone who came in. I could advertise it within the magickal community as a location for different factions to meet and hammer out peace treaties. It could be a sanctuary for anyone on the run. Plus it could simply be a place where the general magickal community at large could meet, talk, and get to know one another. Who knew, maybe a little socialising could strengthen bonds and break down old walls and prejudices. This place could be like a magickal Baskin Robbins – thirty-one flavours in beautiful harmony, with more welcome all the time.

By this point I was exhausted by the expenditure of energy, along with the need to move all the stock. I made sure everything was tidied up, then got G and Pal together to head home. I made myself a couple of sandwiches for a late lunch, together with some crisps and a cold can of Tango. I wolfed it down, having already given G some chicken for his own lunch, then went to take a shower and wash the sweat off.

I watched a few episodes of Supernatural, including one of my favourites – the one where Sam and Dean end up in the 'real world' playing Jared and Jensen playing Sam and Dean. The acting was so hammy it was hysterical, and I kept having to rewind sections to hear the dialogue I missed due to laughing. Gauvain gave up in disgust and simply started preening. Paladin followed his usual pattern of heavy napping.

I did a little more research on the internet during the evening, trying to find out anything about the 'Banished Souls'. I was as spectacularly unsuccessful as I had been up to this point, so I ended up searching random things as the mood took me. I eventually got to looking on Wikipedia for more information on Egyptian mythology, to see if I could identify anything that might give me a clue to this monster battle I was supposed to be in. That was a big, fat, hairy, stinking failure too. My luck was holding at about the same shitty level, so I eventually gave up and went to bed.

Tuesday morning rolled around and I followed my usual workday routine, savouring the normality after all those weeks at Seirina's place. I enjoyed having Paladin and Gauvain along with me for my morning run, and they loved getting out to stretch. Fortunately, since they were magickal beings, they didn't *need* to get out and about the same way regular animals did. They still enjoyed it, however, and Gauvain did still need to eat. Once we'd finished our exercise and I'd had my shower, we all piled into the car and I drove us to the remodelled and enlarged Dinas Affaraon.

I was there before Summer this time, so I started unlocking and raising the door shutter. As I picked out the key to the front door itself from among my keyring, I heard the familiar cheery voice of my friend.

"Top o' the mornin' to ya," Summer called out, using quite possibly the worst Irish accent I'd ever heard.

"Oh, dear gods," I said, rolling my eyes. "What the hell was that supposed to be? You auditioning for the role of leprechaun in some cheesy B movie or something?"

"No," she replied, laughing. "I'm just happy I found the pot of gold several times over the last couple of weeks."

"Oh no," I cried out, slapping my hands over my ears. "Lalalalala-I-don't-need-to-be-hearing-this! Leave Emily's golden pot at home in your bedroom where it belongs, thank you very much."

"Oh wow," she said. "You mean I finally out-cringed the mighty Maddox? This is a true 'dear diary' moment!"

"No," I replied, grinning. "I just know that if I let you overshare, you'll demand reciprocity and want to know all the details about me and Angie from before her mind-wipe. Since I have no intention of divulging, how about you take down the rest of the shutters while I start the coffee?"

"Really?" she asked, surprised. "Normally we do it the other way around." She looked at me curiously but I held my tongue, wanting to surprise her and the others all at the same time.

"Hey, they say a change is as good as a rest," I said, shrugging. "You've just had two weeks rest, so I thought I'd have a change this morning."

"You know, I can always tell when you're up to something," she said, narrowing her eyes as she contemplated just what I might be trying to pull. "Still, I'll let it go as thanks for my two weeks off."

"Oh, too kind," I said, leaving her at the windows while I went in to turn on the coffee machine. As I came out of the kitchen, Angie and the twins were just coming down the stairs and saying good morning to Summer. I stood in the middle of the shop and waited for them all to come inside. The girls helped Summer raise the last of the shutters, then they all trooped in.

"Morning boss," Angie said, echoed by the twins. As they drew level with me and saw the changes behind me, all of them stopped short and stared with their mouths open.

"Welcome to the new and improved Dinas Affaraon!" I exclaimed, sweeping my hand towards the open space behind the counter.

Chapter 18

"What the...?"

"When the...?"

"How the...?"

The stunned voices overlapped each other as the girls all gazed at the huge open space where the stockroom used to stand. Summer stared back at me for a moment before stepping around everyone else and heading to the archway I had designed where the old walls no longer stood. She kept her eyes on me until she drew level, then looked into the new area.

The twins and Angelica followed her silently, their eyes in constant motion as they tried to take in everything about my creation. When she reached the centre of the space, Summer opened her arms wide and turned in a couple of slow circles, looking up and around. I had given the room a high, vaulted ceiling, like an old ballroom in an ancient castle, so the acoustics were phenomenal. I couldn't wait for someone to say something in the centre, since there was an echo point right at the centre of the dome in the ceiling. I had, however, left it plain for now. I hadn't wanted to put a mural up there until we'd decided on a theme. There was no point recreating the Sistine Chapel ceiling if we were going to go with a more modern style for the rest.

"So, what do you think?" I asked, seeing they were all together in the right spot. "Think we can do something with it?"

"It's amazing... zing... zing... zing!" Summer's awed voice reverberated around the room, just as I'd hoped, making all of them stare around with their eyes wide.

"That's so cool... ool... ool... ool!" Angie exclaimed breathlessly. They all laughed, which made the echoes overlap and build until it sounded like an entire room full of people at a Lee Evans evening.

I beckoned them away from the echo point so we could talk without reverb, then led them around to see the new facilities. There was great approval of the bathrooms, which I had modelled after a high-class hotel, with marble counters (I had got the structure from some of the decorative orbs we had for sale) and plenty of space. The new storage area drew Summer's simultaneous joy and dismay, since we now had a better lit and more spacious room, but that just meant increased stock to keep track of.

I showed them the end of the hall where I'd created a slightly raised stage, in case we wanted to have performers or events. The other end had an area which I thought could have a bar, and there was a new, larger kitchen behind it. I had, however, kept our little kitchenette in the shop to use for coffee and drinks, so whoever was in the shop wouldn't have to traipse all the way back here to get refreshments. The echo point would only work with the place empty like this, so if we put tables and chairs in, it would be safe. Clearing the furniture for parties and such, however, would reactivate all its humorous possibilities.

"How in the world did you create this?" Summer asked, astounded by everything she saw. "The outside of the building hasn't changed, I saw that from where I parked, yet this space is bigger than the entire footprint of what we had! I don't get it, how is this possible?"

"I got the idea when I learned how to create time distortion fields," I explained. "That, plus the example of things like the Tardis, made me consider if I could make a bubble that distorted *space* instead of *time*. It took me a bit of practice, and quite a lot of energy, but I finally managed it. I created a bubble at the back of the old stockroom, then took down the door and front walls. I replaced them with the archway, and here we are. I deliberately left it plain, since I knew you'd criticise any decorating choices I made."

I said the last comment sarcastically and they all laughed as planned. It broke the amazed silence that had developed when they saw the new area, allowing them to relax.

"OK, let's get the shop opened," I continued. "We can have a meeting at lunch time, go over some ideas for this, so have a think this morning about some decorative suggestions. Until then, I'll just drape a wall covering over the arch so the public don't notice the change."

We all adjourned back to the shop, where I suited words to action and hung a blue and gold zodiac wall hanging over the new archway. Summer went straight for the kitchenette, grabbing the mugs and the coffee pot to share out the caffeine. The twins fired up the computer, while Angie went to the shop safe for the cash drawer for the till. I had a small lockbox under the counter for the float we kept, since I didn't want everyone having access to the safe in my office. I had too much personal and/or dangerous stuff in there for universal access to be a good idea.

We had a pretty routine Tuesday morning, only one customer who just bought an incense waterfall and some backflow cones. We were able to restock from the weekend rush, which also gave the girls a chance to look at the new space as they went back and forth to the new store room. I could tell they were coming up with some decorating ideas, since they were muttering about colours, furniture, and designs together. I had my own thoughts, so I just left them to it. I was sure I'd hear their conclusions soon enough.

I offered to spring for lunch for everyone, so I went over to Subway and got one of their mixed platters and some cookies. I returned to the shop and we put up a notice on the door to say we were closed for a lunch meeting. I took the food through to the new room, so we could look at the space to visualise our ideas as we discussed them.

Summer suggested lots of gilt furniture with velvet, much to my surprise. Her reasoning was to make it look more old-fashioned, even antiquated, since magick users lived so long (I'd told her about that after Seirina had enlightened me). She thought it would make the area more appealing, make them feel more at home. It was an interesting notion, one that bore consideration, but we agreed to hear all the ideas before making a final decision.

The twins suggested making the place more like the nightclub it had the space to be. They argued it would allow for greater versatility of the location, since there would be significant areas of open space. It would also make for easier cleaning up, whereas velvet was a nightmare to get stains out of. Again a valid suggestion, though I wasn't sure lasers and a mirror ball were *quite* what I'd envisioned. Still, I refused to dismiss any idea out of hand.

Angelica's idea, to my surprise, was at the opposite end of the spectrum from Summer's. She thought the space would look best done up as modern as possible, all polished steel and chrome with black leather. She winked at me as she mentioned the leather. Summer caught it and sniggered. I sighed, giving a small shake of my head, though I didn't hate the idea. I quite liked modern minimalism as a decorating choice for a loft or an apartment, though I thought it might look a bit extreme in such a large space.

My own idea was to set the space up more like a coffee shop/restaurant. It could be like a social club, serve food and drinks, and still be converted for meetings or conventions with a minimum of fuss. That would also give us the greatest range of uses, making the idea of twenty-four-hour opening much more viable. I knew I'd had the advantage of thinking about my plans for several weeks, so my ideas were more developed. I didn't want to force my vision on everyone else without at least talking everything through, however, since I needed their help to actually make this work. That meant I needed them on board with the final decision regarding exactly how we were going to move forward.

We all reviewed the different ideas but, much as I'd hoped, since my idea was the most fleshed out and adaptable, the girls agreed to go with my suggestion. Then the discussion turned to what kinds of tables and chairs, whether we needed some sofas against the walls, what kinds of menu items we needed, the patterns on the tablecloths, crockery, and silverware – at this point, I could feel my testicles climbing back inside and turning to ovaries, with a uterus trying to form alongside them.

I told them to keep going, and to make plenty of notes for me on what they thought might fit best, while I went to open up for the afternoon. I dropped the wall covering into place once I'd gone through to the shop, heaving a sigh of relief when I was out of sight of the decorating committee. I walked over to the door, unlocked it and took down the notice.

I stepped out into the street, taking a deep breath of fresh car exhaust and pollution. Nothing like the sweet smell of stale city air to clear your head. I *really* needed to get the new facilities up and running, so I could get some guys around here. Not that I had anything against women – in fact, in certain situations I found them exceptionally enjoyable – but the oestrogen around here was currently '*Three feet high and rising*', just like the song said.

I could hear Gauvain laughing in my head, so I mentally stuck my tongue out at him and told him to shut up. Immature, I know, but I didn't care. I chuckled along after a moment, recognising the stupidity of my anxiety. After all, if you wanted tasteful decorations, there were worse things than a group of women working together on an idea they agreed with.

I just felt like I could do with a nice, calm, relaxed evening of blood and guts and explosions. Yup, I could definitely feel a night of *Call of Duty* coming on. Maybe some pizza and beer to go with it. I worked out and lived healthily; a little indulgence now and then wasn't going to kill me. And even if it wanted to, it would have to get in line behind Elrulin, the rest of the Order, apparently a laundry list of monsters and evil assholes slated for the big face-off I'd foreseen, and no doubt several dozen miscreants between here and there. Possibly even the Devil himself, unless Isis decided to go soft on him and let him back into Aaru – yeah, right, I'll hold my breath on *that* one, shall I?

I polluted my lungs with another breath of foul air, then headed back inside. I could hear the *kaffeeklatsch* in the back still going on, so I grabbed a can of soda from the fridge and sat on the stool behind the counter. Since we didn't have any customers, I used the computer to go online and look at newer models. I decided to go with an all-in-one system, one with the hard drive and disc reader etc. all built into the monitor. That would take up less space on the countertop. I found one on sale at the local PC World, so I paid for it on the company card and arranged to have it delivered tomorrow.

With that organised, I settled in to wait through another slow weekday afternoon.

Chapter 19

T he rest of the week was spent setting up the new computer – me
– and getting fabric swatches, crockery, and cutlery samples, and
compiling menu suggestions – the ladies. It was wonderful to be
so involved in my own idea (shut up G, of *course* I'm not sarcastic; why
would I be?) and see it start coming together. At least they let me review
the options and have *some* say in which ones we chose. I felt so honoured.

I gradually reconciled myself to the situation, realising they'd be
the ones doing most of the work in this new area so they may as well
be happy there. It was especially important for Angelica and the twins,
since they were able to build something for themselves from the ground
up. They had been stuck in the Order for so long, doing *what* they were
told *when* they were told, it was good for them to finally have some
independence. I held onto that thought, using it to balance my feelings
of exclusion.

We used the money the Order had paid as my retainer to get things
set up. There were some steps we needed to go through, such as hygiene
certification and a liquor license, though we also had to consider how
we would pass future inspections. I didn't think the city officials would
understand us having a selection of blood types on hand for service at the
bar, nor how the area fit inside the building in the first place.

I made some enquiries (OK I talked to Seirina, it still counts) and
found there were a number of 'magick aware' people in several city
departments, including food safety. Apparently this was a pattern in all

major cities, to help keep the magickal community below the radar. They were often people who had only minor magickal abilities, just enough to 'qualify' them for the extended life and knowledge of the wider world. They hid their delayed aging by switching cities periodically, usually coordinating with each other so their positions would simply be traded. It made sense, explaining how this 'subculture' could stay hidden while still being a part of the world.

It was also useful, since it would give me a network through which I could let the magickal community know once the new area was up and running. That would give us a ready-made customer base, who we could then also promote our other potential services to. It would be mostly word of mouth advertising but hopefully, with the magickal world being so insular and close-knit, that would be enough. I would make sure all our allies knew about it as well, and they could then disseminate the information through their individual communities. That should allow us a grand opening that would be hard to beat.

Using the contact numbers I had been given by Seirina, we were able to schedule the requisite visits and inspections over the following weeks, so we moved forward with getting everything in place. We ordered tables and chairs, plates, glassware, cutlery, pots and pans. Some of the deliveries were scheduled for late in the evening to avoid too much attention. Even so, some of the delivery men seemed curious how so much stuff could fit into such a small shop. Mostly they were pacified by the obvious explanations – it's for convenience, it'll be used elsewhere. I even gave one the explanation of setting up a marquee in the car park for a wedding.

Only one refused to be placated, so for that one I was forced to enter his mind and alter his memory slightly. I just made him think he'd seen a larger building as the drop-off destination, though even that small manipulation felt distasteful. I welcomed the sensation as proof that I was unlikely to ever become comfortable manipulating people for my own ends, then went back to hauling supplies through the store. Even with magick, lots of stuff is lots of stuff.

I kept searching for anything on the Order's new location, with no success. I also received emails from Sovereign and Cheveyo telling me they'd looked into my list of possible sites. They, too, had found absolutely nothing. It was disheartening, though I still felt reassured knowing the Order was on the other side of the ocean. Seirina had put the word out to keep watch for any signs of them sneaking back here, plus the Americans were now alerted to be on guard over there. The more eyes we had looking for the Order, the less likely they were to be able to start recruiting again. We might also get a clue as to their location.

Knowing all that, I was happier to continue getting Dinas Affaraon in shape for its expanded opening. We kept the menu relatively small, choosing to do a few things really well rather than having a huge number of things done just average. That would also help keep our supply requirements lower, reduce our wastage, and improve profitability. Yeah, I know, boring business stuff, but important considerations if this was going to be a success.

With a little magickal help to get things in place and prepared, we were ready to go within six weeks. I had an almost constant itch at the back of my mind, worrying about the Order, but otherwise things were going swimmingly. With all the organisational issues, I hadn't had time to do much other than work and sleep. Nor had the girls, so the only one who'd had anything of a personal life had been Summer. Even on Mondays, when we were closed, we'd been using the time to get more done on the 'back room'. We also decided on a rota for keeping the place running twenty-four/seven, for which we agreed we'd need more staff. We sent out recruitment notices through the magickal community, obviously, and had plenty of applicants which allowed us to select the best candidates.

When the time finally came for the great unveiling we had a staff of almost twenty, structured so that Summer was the managing director second only to me as the owner. The twins and Angelica were shift managers, and we had people responsible for the bar, the kitchen, and everything else relevant to such an undertaking. Since this was something of a gamble, I had elected to structure things as a profit-sharing enterprise. That would give everyone an incentive to stay honest and monitor everyone else, plus work to make things as successful as they could. The better the place did, the more we all made. Hopefully, the through traffic would increase the shop's sales as well.

I contacted the different faction leaders a week before the date we set for our opening, letting them know what we'd created and when it would be up and running. They spread the word further, so on opening night we had a list of two hundred people planning to attend. I didn't want it to be a black tie event, since the whole idea was for it to be a place for relaxation as well as socialising, but everyone still came dressed up. I think they were all trying to upstage each other, to make their faction look good.

We had drinks, canapés, and live music provided by a Wiccan band Aurora had recommended. Despite people turning up in suits and fine dresses, the presence of sofas and the encouragement to use them soon had people kicking off their shoes, loosening their ties, and letting down their instinctual barriers. Soon enough there were Wiccans dancing with vampires, weres getting groovy with magick users... I even saw Kazemde share a kiss with the female vampire who had been at Edinburgh with us.

Only once, very early on, was there any sign of aggression. A were and a vampire had snarled at each other as they went through the archway together. That limited unfriendly act had been suffucient for the wards to activate and zap them both hard enough to make their hair sizzle. I'd reiterated the warning they'd already had, following which the rest of the evening had gone off without a hitch.

I was ecstatic, this event marking a new beginning for my life's work and a new sense of freedom for those working with me. I had desperately hoped Summer might use the opportunity of a fancy party to propose to Emily, or vice versa, but neither one had stepped up. I swear, one of these days I was just going to bring them together and stick a matched pair of rings between them with a card that said, 'Will you?'. They might be pissed for a moment, but I knew they both wanted it. They were just afraid, but I'd be damned before I let that rob them of their life together. I could even create the diamonds and gold myself for the rings. Sod it, if they didn't do it by Valentine's Day, I *was* going to do it for them.

The morning after, there were more than a few sore heads. As part of the new equipment and supplies, I had bought an industrial-sized coffee machine and several large bags of the three coffee beans to make up my blend. I was therefore able to make a huge pot of Cafegeddon, which was emptied so fast I made two more during the morning. We were feeling somewhere close to normal by lunch, which was a good thing since we had customers.

There was a group sitting on some of the sofas, chatting over coffee, tea, and hot chocolate; several people coming in for soup or sandwiches; and even more customers than on a normal weekend milling around the shop. If things continued like this, not only would we recoup our investment and stay afloat, but we could also end up making this more profitable than I'd even dared to dream.

I had already taken bookings for dinners, reservations to use the space for business meetings between various factions, and a couple of early birds wanting to use the space for weddings. There were even a couple of requests from overseas ambassadors of foreign magickal councils to come and meet here as a safe, neutral site. Stories about the wards keeping the peace last night had spread rapidly, since someone had apparently caught the zap on video. That had been shared and sent around, becoming a magickal viral clip. I was beyond pleased, since it was more free advertising and of a level you just couldn't buy.

The staff were all just as happy, working hard to get things into a routine. I was giving them space to set their shift patterns how they preferred, as long as all the relevant duties were covered. I was loving the increased shop traffic, since several of them were interested in the books. I was taking the time to deal with those enquiries, letting Summer handle the others. There were a few requests for volumes we didn't have, which gave me an excuse to call The Bookworm and talk to Mr Davis. He was, as ever, happy to help out with esoteric volumes. He usually sent them up by courier if the request was urgent, though sometimes he asked someone to bring them if he knew they were heading up this way.

As the week went on, the shop traffic continued and the 'back room' picked up even more. I thought about calling the area *Cell y Dewiniaid*, since that was apparently the 'Grove of the Magicians' near to Dinas Emrys, which was the newer name for Dinas Affaraon. However, I didn't want people shortening it to 'The Cell', since that had some fairly negative connotations. Instead, I chose to call it The Sanctuary.

It fit with the wards, plus encouraged the impression of it being a safe space for meetings or dates or even just to relax. I used magick to emboss the name above the archway, and the customers admired it when they came. It gave me a warm feeling when I looked at it, and the staff loved it too.

It quickly became exactly what I had named it, in so many ways for so many people. The only issue I had to consider was the non-magick crowd. I didn't want mundanes walking back to The Sanctuary by mistake, so I had to come up with something to stop them. I came up with a glamour which worked on non-magickal folk but had no effect on anyone with magick in their blood. I had a notice on the 'door' which read 'staff only' to explain why some people went back there and 'disappeared'.

So life went on, and the search for the Order continued.

Chapter 20

Autumn was setting in by the time I heard from Mr Davis again. He had located a couple of books he thought might be useful, so I took a morning to go down to see him. I arrived under the pier as I had before, though thankfully this time it was only just after high tide so the seaweed was still mostly covered. Despite the progress of the seasons, the warmth of summer still lingered. There were still those who enjoyed the beach, though now that the schools had restarted there was far less shrieking. I won't say none since couples flirting still flicked cold water at each other, and young men delighted in the cries of those they pursued.

I made my way up the beach again, finding the first half of the pier far less raucous without the youngsters running around. I made my way along, buying myself a hotdog for a snack and giving the end of the sausage to Gauvain. He had decided against fishing this time, choosing instead to enjoy basking in the sunshine while riding on my shoulder.

I reached the turnstile, nodding to the gatekeeper as I passed. He braced smartly and nodded back as I did, seeming to recognise me from before. Although he was simply monitoring a turnstile on a pier in a seaside town, he looked like the sort of man who took pride in his position and would show the same diligence here as he would at the most contested checkpoint or at-risk embassy door. The sort of man you could search for for over a decade and not find, though if you were lucky enough to find one you should never let him go. Apparently the Godolphins, who owned this pier and allegedly much of the town, felt the same way. The mere fact of their excellent judgement of character and valuing of a good man recommended them to me, so I made a mental note to come back and meet them formally when I had more time.

For now, I had to focus on my quest. I arrived at the entrance to The Bookworm, where G flew up to perch on the roof. I opened the door and walked in, taking a moment to let my eyes adjust from the bright morning sunlight outside. A few motes of dust danced in the sunbeams over my shoulder and through the front window, combining with the scent of books to create one of my favourite places. It almost made me regret my choice to be more eclectic in my own shop, since the smell of the incense and candles always eclipsed that of the volumes on my shelves.

I closed my eyes and took a deep breath, as I always did here, to imprint the moment in my memory. As I opened them, I saw Mr Davis come out from the back and catch sight of me.

"Mr Maddox, good morning!" he said brightly. "I didn't hear you come in. I really must get one of those bells, like you have at your shop."

"Ah, but you have that fine gentleman guarding access to this area of the pier," I replied. "You don't need to worry about people just wandering in." He chuckled, nodding to acknowledge my point, but I continued the small talk as I knew he would want to. "If you do, though, make sure to put a metal strike-plate on the door. Otherwise, the metal of the bell will wear away the wood of the door until eventually the damp would get in and damage all these fine volumes."

"Ah, that would indeed be a tragedy," he mused. "Perhaps I shall simply continue to rely on the presence of a good man, allowing me to enjoy my peace and my books."

"I can certainly think of worse fates," I agreed, ready to move ahead with the purpose of my visit. "Speaking of your books, I understand you've located some volumes that might be of help in my search? Have you actually come across any mention of a 'Rock of Banished Souls'?"

"Unfortunately not," he replied, which made my heart sink. Then it lifted a little as he continued. "I have found several passages referencing areas where the Native Americans believed evil spirits dwelled, or where evil men were sent. Perhaps one of them will suggest itself to you as the location you seek. At the very least, they may allow you to exclude some more places."

"One can only hope," I said. I had known the search wouldn't be easy, though I had hoped for a little more success. Still, as my father often said, 'we live in hope, and die in despair'. I just had to hope the second part might be a fair way off yet.

I took the two books Mr Davis had for me, paying for them out of my own pocket since they would be going into my personal collection regardless of whether they gave me the Order's location. I bid him good day and left the shop, turning my face up to the sun and breathing in the sea air. Gauvain joined me, nibbling my ear and preening my hair.

I looked over at Arodnesse, seeing the same large spotted cat meander past the window. It looked over at me and G, seeming to assess whether it could get out to snack on the big white bird. I gave it the stink eye, then teleported us back to my office. Paladin, as ever, lifted his head and gave a few thumps of his tail. Then he re-established his link to feed power into Seren, put his head down and went back to sleep.

G hopped onto his perch, had a few sips of water and started preening. I put the books on my desk and went out to check on things. Everything was running as smoothly as ever, so I said hi to Summer then grabbed a drink and went back into the office. I sat down in my chair and pulled the new volumes towards me.

The one on top seemed to be a general history of some of the Native American tribes, including some of their myths and legends, though I had no way of validating any of the information. I'd need to contact Cheveyo for any kind of corroboration, though how much he knew about the other tribes was anybody's guess. Maybe his contacts could help, but that would mean lugging the book around for various people to look through their individual sections. The downside was there didn't seem to be too much on the spiritual side, nothing about souls or the afterlife as far as I could tell. I set that book aside for future reference – no information was totally useless, after all – and opened the other.

I could immediately tell this one was closer to the mark of what I wanted. It was far more about the mythologies of various tribes: their beliefs, gods, and customs. Since I had no idea which tribe's area the Order had taken up residence in, I couldn't exactly skip to the relevant chapter. I was going to have to read the entire thing and see what possibilities I could dig up. I opened a drawer and got a fresh pad of foolscap, then grabbed a pen, ready to take some notes. I turned to the first chapter and started reading.

By the end of the day, I'd only made it through three chapters. I already had two sides of notes regarding various spiritual sites, though nothing that screamed 'bingo' to me. The only thing screaming was my head, since the print was small enough to make me squint. I pulled a box of Migraleve out of my desk, dry-swallowing a couple of tablets since I had long-since finished my can of soda. I cracked my back and neck, feeling the tension after hours of sitting, then stood up and stretched. I got another couple of creaks, then walked around my desk.

I couldn't exactly say I'd worked until closing time any more, since we didn't *have* one now, but I'd definitely earned my dinner today. I put the first book on my shelf, along with some of my other historical reference volumes, and locked the other in my safe along with the notes I'd made from it. Given the importance of the information I was looking for, I didn't want to risk it going for a walk. I doubted it would, since the wards should prevent thievery, but for every lock there was a key somewhere. For every barrier, there was some kind of work-around. I may not know it, it may take years to dig past, but I knew nothing was truly impenetrable. So, the more layers of security the better. Plus, no one else even knew I *had* the book other than Mr Davis, so out of sight was hopefully out of mind.

Since I had nothing waiting for me at home, I decided to step into The Sanctuary for dinner and a drink. Of course, being the owner meant I didn't need to pay but I refused to abuse the system. I'd already established the rule that staff got a twenty percent discount, so I was happy to pay as well. It meant the staff wouldn't resent me for taking from their profit-sharing scheme, since they saw I held myself to the same standards I asked of them. I also made sure to tip, even though it wasn't as expected here as it was in America. I flattered myself that the staff all seemed happy here, and thus far (touch wood) there hadn't been any complaints from staff or customers.

I had the lasagne and garlic bread, and some raw mince for Gauvain. I got a beer to go with it and just enjoyed the atmosphere. It was fun to people-watch, even more so with the wide variety of people types in here. I amused myself, trying to guess whether someone was a witch, a were, a vampire, or whatever else. Unless they chose to display their unique attributes, they all looked like average people. It was why I hadn't known what Seirina was until I'd read her mind. I did wonder if it was possible to tell by reading their energy, or their aura, or something along those lines, since it could come in useful in the future. I'd have to keep working on it, though, since I certainly didn't detect any obvious 'tells' this evening.

Once I'd finished dinner, I gathered up Paladin and Gauvain and went home. I was currently re-watching *Bones*, starting from season one, and I was up to the episode with the girl in the refrigerator. I set the disc running and dropped heavily onto the sofa, kicking off my shoes and stroking Pal's head when he climbed up to join me. I fell asleep, waking up as the disc warning screen was showing. I transferred from sofa to bed, quickly dropping back to sleep after fighting to hang onto the covers as Paladin lay down and squirmed into a comfortable position.

The book I had been reading seemed to have seeped into my subconscious, as I was having dreams of skinwalkers, tribal dances, and vision quests. The vision quests then merged into more normal dreams – flying, weird and random images and non-sequential ideas. I was still hoping to find something useful in the book I'd got from Mr Davis, though I didn't fancy having weird dreams every night while I searched. Maybe it was just my subconscious sifting through the information to try and locate the Order, which would make sense – though my dreams certainly didn't yet.

Now that the shop was open all the time, as planned, I could teleport back and forth to my office. It meant I could get up later, since I wouldn't have to fight the traffic any more, and I could enjoy a more leisurely run. My hours were now much more flexible, since as long as I put in the time it didn't matter when. I could also safely take time away from the shop without having to put all the responsibility on Summer. My plans to get her and Emily married and off on a honeymoon were also far more feasible, especially since she'd be getting a better income now with the improved profits of the shop.

I teleported the three of us to my office, leaving G and Pal in there while I went out to get some Cafegeddon. I said good morning to everyone, checking everything was running smoothly as usual. Then I came back in and opened the safe, retrieving the book and my notes and sitting back at the desk.

Time for more research.

Chapter 21

As I looked at my notes from yesterday, I realised just how many pages I'd end up with by the end of the book. Given the fact that the Order's location could be related to something in the first chapter as easily as the last, it would make sense to start checking out the locations I'd already identified. I dug out the email addresses for Cheveyo and Sovereign, which Seirina had already provided, then sent them the file with the notes I'd made. I asked them to start looking into some of the information, along with telling them I'd send daily messages with any new ideas I gleaned from the book.

From what I could tell, the volume seemed to track the movement of the invading settlers across the continent. It started with the legends and mythologies of the tribes around Boston and New York, gradually progressing west across the lands. While the legends were interesting, many of the tribes in the central regions didn't have many tales of rocks or mountains, since the land there was mostly flat. There were occasional mentions of deep chasms, or bottomless pits, so I couldn't just skip over them.

The days passed as I read, only occasional interruptions occurring from the staff either asking questions of their own or relaying customer enquiries. I had two appointments for special commissions, neither of which were especially interesting nor taxing. One I didn't even have to move for, as it was just to locate a rare book which I was able to track down with a single call to The Bookworm. Mr Davis knew of it and was able to provide my customer with the contact details of the current owner. They reached an agreement, I got my finder's fee, and then I went back to work.

The second was someone who wanted a pair of crystals enchanted with a protection ward. She was a soldier's wife who wanted to make them into his and hers necklaces before he left for the Middle East. I was able to attach a ward to some crystal necklaces we already had in stock without any trouble, since it was reminiscent of the one Angelica had left me before my search for the Veil. I gave them to the twins for her to pick up the following day, and I once again went back to work.

It was as the chapters of the book reached farther west that I started seeing more promising leads, due to the presence of the Rocky Mountains. The very name of the range promised a greater number of possibilities, so I slowed down and found I was taking more copious notes. I began identifying almost a full page of locations to check from each chapter, which I knew would mean more work for the Americans. Still, they didn't want the Order over there any more than we wanted them back here, so they were happy to continue the hunt.

Since the distances in America were so significant, I gradually grew farther and farther ahead of the searchers. They were soon pages of notes behind me, which gave me a chance to take a day off here and there to aid in the day-to-day running of the store. I used the opportunity to work with the chefs one day, learning from their expertise. I was a decent cook but I'd never been to culinary school, so I didn't kid myself that I was on their level. The only things I offered were my chilli recipe, honed over a couple of decades of practice, and my salted caramel brownies.

Those two reminded me of working in Poppy's shop in Aaru, which made me wonder how she and Roman were doing. I lost myself in my reverie, which in turn led me to set my sleeve on fire in my distraction. I swore loudly, shoving my arm under the tap to put the fire out and healing the mild burn with magick. The chef sniggered slightly and shook his head, which I joined in with once I'd sorted myself out.

We managed to improve my chilli with the addition of some extra cumin, and my brownies with home-made caramel instead of the shop-bought version I normally used. Poppy had made her own as well; I'd just never bothered since I usually made them for other people. I normally just used Rolos in the centre, with a little salt sprinkled on, then a salted caramel sauce or icing on top. Still, he was a chef so I was happy to let him do it from scratch.

As I reached the last few chapters, I finally arrived at the west coast of the US. I found that a tribe called the Ohlone people had lived in the region which was now referred to as the San Francisco Bay Area. There had been an island in the bay they had avoided at all costs for thousands of years, according to the information in the book. They had used it as a burial ground at one time, then the belief developed regarding evil spirits occupying the land. They used to send their worst criminals there to fend for themselves. The book even remarked that early Spanish explorers had seen lights coming from the place, so had noted it on their charts as a bad place, steering clear of it.

Eventually a fort was built there, as it was a strategic point to guard the bay, then the fort became a prison. Even today, with the prison closed down it was still famous – or, at least, infamous and notorious – for the diabolical conditions and the terrible crimes committed to earn a place there. Many people weren't aware that towards the end of its time it was actually a requested transfer by some criminals, as the conditions were significantly improved and the cells were single-occupancy.

As I'd previously considered about Ellis and Liberty Islands, the isolation would make it ideal as a secluded base. The legends of hauntings and evil spirits would enable more obviously monstrous Order members greater freedom, plus the visitors would provide an additional source of income and prey for the Order. Everything about the legends surrounding the place resonated more strongly the further I read. I wrote it in capital letters, bold, italics, underlined, and highlighted in my notes, suggesting to Cheveyo to drop everything and check this place before any others.

I couldn't believe I hadn't thought of it before, looking back. For the love of Isis, the place was even known far and wide as The Rock! The Americans had sent their unwanted there for centuries, first the Native Americans had done so and then the invaders had followed suit. Criminals and evil spirits, any unwanted beings had been quite literally banished there by any who dwelt in the area. My skin was tingling with the rightness of my discovery, and I breathed the word aloud like a revelation.

"Alcatraz!"

As well as messaging Cheveyo, I was so certain of my discovery I sent messages to Seirina and the faction leaders about my thoughts. I quickly received texts and emails agreeing with my interpretation, promising to begin alerting their forces to be ready once we had confirmation from America. I refused to put *all* of my eggs in the one basket, however, so I checked the rest of the book for any other possibilities and sent my final notes to Cheveyo and Sovereign. I had a funny feeling they wouldn't need to search them, though.

I shut down my computer and went out into the shop, since it was barely lunchtime. I was so pleased by my research, I had a giant grin on my face all afternoon. Everyone noticed and commented, including Angelica. I was so happy with myself, I invited her out for dinner before I even considered what I was doing. We still hadn't been out on a date since her memory wipe, as we'd been so busy setting up the new aspects of Dinas Affaraon and The Sanctuary, though we'd remained friendly.

I had been more unavailable than normal recently as well, what with my research into possible Order locations. I knew Summer, despite her promises of non-interference, would have been dropping hints, suggestions, and innuendos to Angie while they were working. I was also aware the twins would have been doing the same. Despite that, Angelica was an attractive young woman working with a number of young men. I was fully aware she had been asked out at least twice, my guts clenching each time I had heard about it, though to the best of my knowledge she had declined both invitations.

Happily she agreed to *my* invitation, which led to a number of mutters of 'Well it's about damned time!' from Summer, the twins, and several other members of staff who were aware of our situation. I turned to the ring leader and stuck my tongue out at her, making everyone laugh while Summer herself grabbed me for a hug.

"You'd better not mess this up," she whispered in my ear. "Or I'm gonna mess *you* up. She's been through enough recently." She let me go, leant back and gave me a full-on hairy eyeball, raised eyebrow, crossed arms and all. I lifted both hands in front of me, stepping back from her fierce gaze. I pulled her aside, speaking in an angry whisper.

"After all this, you *really* think I want to screw this up?" I asked incredulously. "How long have I been looking for someone? How many dates have I been on – illiterate troglodytes included, thank you very much – up to now? After *finally* managing to get together, she gets her memory wiped and yet you think I have any desire for this not to go right?"

"OK, OK, I get it," she admitted. "You want it to go well. So what's the big plan?"

This was the point at which my brain shut down, my mouth went dry, and I started hyperventilating and sweating profusely. I hadn't actually thought of a plan before I asked Angie out, so I was completely unprepared. Summer, familiar with my behaviour from our years together and fully aware of my anxiety, just rolled her eyes.

"Oh, that's just brilliant," she said. "You ask out a girl you actually care about on the spur of the moment with absolutely no clue where to take her, no reservations made, no idea what you're going to wear... You are, without doubt, the most gormless plonker in existence! Did you even decide what day you were going out, perhaps giving us a chance to plan, or did you say tonight?"

"Umm..." I thought back to what I'd said, suddenly realising exactly how I'd phrased it. I sighed with relief as I answered, "I just asked if she'd like to have dinner one evening; I never actually specified when."

"Well thank the gods for that," she said. "Now we've got a chance to come up with a better plan than jumping out of a plane without a parachute. Tomorrow, Emily and I are taking you clothes shopping."

"Err, I've been dressing myself since I was thirty," I joked. "I think I can manage to pull together an outfit without supervision!"

"Perhaps if you were going bowling," she replied dryly. "Or out for beer and wings. If you're planning something a touch more elegant and refined..."

"Hey!" I objected, slightly louder than planned and drawing everyone's attention momentarily. I lowered my voice and continued. "I took your friend out for sushi in a nice restaurant, remember? Quit acting like I've never been on a date before!"

"An ordinary date, yes," she allowed. "A date with the woman you're in love with and have been crushing on since the first time you saw her, not so much."

At her reminder of the significance of this little enterprise, my mouth once again achieved the rough consistency of the Sahara.

"Yeah, so, shopping then," I said, swallowing.

Chapter 22

The following morning, having arranged with the twins to run things for this shift, and after my morning run and shower, I got dressed and braced myself for the trial ahead. Dealing with Summer and Emily together was often bad enough, but when they had free rein to use me as a Ken doll to play real life dress-up, I could imagine a strong desire to take a power drill to my own temple by lunch time. I decided to take a couple of headache pills now, to stave off the inevitable migraine, washing them down with milk.

I couldn't face food this morning, since my stomach was clenched tight enough to almost be seen through my shirt, plus I even decided to skip my Cafegeddon to prevent the caffeine from making me vibrate. I was meeting the girls in town, so I apologised to Paladin for leaving him behind. A lion-sized Jack Russel might cause a little bit of a stir wandering through the city centre. Gauvain elected to stay home with him rather than be in his claw, so I walked down to the garage like a man heading to the gallows.

I had to drive, since there wasn't really anywhere for me to teleport to. I supposed I could land at the store, then walk around to meet the girls, but I knew I'd end up getting caught up in something. Plus, it was nice to drive once in a while. I'd bought the new car, I might as well *use* the damned thing occasionally. I buckled myself in, started the engine and set off. I had the radio on for some background noise and true to my luck, all the songs were about relationships, love, and heartbreak. I quickly gave up and switched over to a CD.

I finally made it through the rush-hour traffic and found a parking spot in the shopping centre multi-storey car park. I locked up and stood next to the car for a couple of seconds, trying to calm my racing heart. I went to take a couple of deep breaths, only to have an old Land Rover that looked like it had seen better days twenty years ago drive past spewing black exhaust. I doubled over, coughing hard enough to bring up a lung, and tried not to view it as an omen.

As I walked down the stairs from the level I'd parked on, I was so wrapped up in my own head I almost walked into an extremely attractive young woman. She looked familiar, though my distraction meant I couldn't place her. I apologised politely but vaguely, seeing a smile out of the corner of my eye as I continued on down. I reached the upper shopping floor and came out of the stairwell, turning to hold the door for the young lady I'd almost mown down. I couldn't see her so put her out of my mind, focusing back on my upcoming Herculean labour.

I spotted Summer waving from a table in the nearby food court, immediately seeing the back of Emily's head opposite her. Emily turned and smiled as I made my way over to them, more restrained than her effervescent partner as per usual. Seeing them together always made me smile, regardless of my current anxiety, and as I reached them I kissed them each on the cheek. Summer nearly throttled me with her hug but I escaped otherwise mostly unscathed, except for having to wipe a little lipstick off my own cheek. Emily winked at me mischievously, since Summer never went in for much in the way of makeup, so it was obviously hers.

They finished their drinks and took their paper cups over to the rubbish, then came around the barrier to join me. They flanked me, one taking each hand, as if they were simultaneously leading me, protecting me, and (probably most accurately) trying to stop me running away. They clearly had a plan in mind, since they dragged me directly to their chosen store. We went to the menswear section and I was flung unceremoniously onto a stool while my 'style gurus' began searching the clothing racks.

I could already tell this wasn't going to be cheap, since they were looking at the high-end suits. I sighed in resignation, already imagining the shriek from my bank account, and waited for my orders. Summer pulled three different suits out, having checked my size first, and held them up for inspection. Emily refused the brown immediately, going with classic black and a deep navy blue. At least the shirt selection was easy, since the unanimous decision (or at least, unanimous between the only two opinions that apparently counted) was for a classic white with subtle vertical stripes.

I was yanked to my feet by Summer, had the two suit options thrust into my hands, and shoved into the changing room. I tried the black first, going with what I thought of as the safer option. I went out and was directed to turn, bend, twist, and pose by Emily as she checked from all angles. Then I was pushed back to change to the blue. When I came out this time, I knew this was going to be the final choice. Both Summer and Emily went quiet for a moment, staring, then they looked at each other and Emily fanned herself dramatically.

"Wow," she said quietly. "If I was into guys, I'd be dragging you into that room and locking the door! That's *definitely* the one. Don't you think so, sweetie?" she added, turning to Summer.

"Huh?" Summer said, shaking her head as if to clear it. "Oh, yeah, right. Definitely the blue." She looked over at Emily with a gleam in her eye. "You know, with the right pair of heels, that would look *amazing* on you!"

Emily blushed, looking at me with a totally different expression on her face. I could tell I was no longer the focus of their attention so I tried to sidle away. I made it about six inches before Summer grabbed me by the ear, even though she had to stand on tiptoes to reach. The pain immediately bent me over as she dragged down on the delicate tissue, making me wince and stopping my retreat.

"Oh no you don't," she scolded. "Get over here. It may be the right choice but it needs some minor alterations." She called over the assistant who got to work pinning and measuring. The trousers needed to come up by about half an inch to break perfectly, apparently, the shoulders needed easing by a quarter of an inch, and the waist of the jacket needed to come in by two thirds of an inch. The man with the pins (I refuse to say gentleman, since gentle he certainly was not) promised the changes were minor and could be done by tomorrow.

"That'll be fine, thank you," Summer said to him. Then she turned to me and continued. "Right, get back in there and change. We'll get the shirt and you can pay, then it's shoes."

"Yes, mother," I said snarkily, sounding like a grumpy child shopping for school uniforms. I retreated quickly when she spun to glare at me, fearing she was about to whack me over the knuckles or something. I got back into my jeans and placed the suit back on the hanger, being careful not to loosen the pins, then exited the changing area and handed it to the assistant. He pulled the price tag off, handing it to me so it could be scanned, and then he safety-pinned a job ticket to the jacket. He gave me the other side so I could also pay for the alterations, then carried the suit through to the back.

Emily had already picked up a shirt, holding it up for approval. Summer nodded so I didn't argue, I just took it along with the tickets to the register. I handed over my debit card, putting in my PIN when requested and trying desperately not to look at the numbers. How the hell could a few bits of cloth be so expensive? Even if they *did* apparently make women weak at the knees, and want to drag me off to... Yeah, OK, they were worth it.

With a slightly better attitude, having envisioned Angelica reacting the same way Summer and Emily had, I followed them to the shoe shop three doors down. We went in and I sat down as instructed, waiting while my self-appointed personal shoppers chose a few options. I preferred a slip-on to lace-ups, simply for the tidier appearance, so rejected two of their choices. Seeing my increased interest and acceptance of the situation, they let me have a little more input and I chose to try a very simple pair first.

The sales assistant brought out the right size but I found them to be a little tight, since my feet were wider due to mostly being in sneakers. Emily offered another style with a subtle line around the toe, since they came from a range purported to be for wider feet. They were pretty nice, so I shrugged and nodded in acceptance. The assistant brought out the right size and I slipped them on, stood up and walked around a little. They were OK, though while I was up I saw another style from the same range and picked it up. When I went back over to where I had been sitting, Summer huffed and put her hands on her hips.

"And they say women can't make up their minds," she groused. "I thought you wanted slip-ons. I believe those are called 'laces'," she said, pointing at the offending strings on the shoe I was carrying.

"Oh, quit being a baby," I said, laughing as she pouted. Emily, on the other hand, sidled up next to her and squeezed her butt.

"You *know* what that look does to me," she whispered to Summer, at which the pout disappeared and there was mutual smouldering.

"Oh, for the love of..." I said, sighing. "Must you two *always* embarrass me in public?" I went to a stool farther away and sat down to try on the shoes which the assistant, who had quickly scurried off when we were pretending to argue, had just brought out.

Thankfully these shoes earned approval from both me, in terms of comfort, and the girls in terms of appearance. I left the lovebirds flirting with each other and went to pay, smiling at the sales assistant as she looked awkwardly away from them.

"Lovers, huh?" I sympathised with her. "What are you gonna do? Anyway, shall we run these through the till? I'd like to get out of here before they start pawing at each other...again!" She jumped slightly, then turned and hurried over to the register.

I paid for the shoes, taking the bag from the helpful young lady with thanks. I walked over to Summer and Emily who, I was glad to see, had simply sat down on the bench and waited. They stood as I reached them, each taking a side once again, though this time putting their arms through mine. We walked out arm in arm and in step, laughing together as we turned it into a production of taking our steps diagonally so it looked like we were interweaving our legs.

We managed it for four whole steps before we tangled, laughing harder as we gave up. I thanked the girls, promising them I would actually return for my suit the following day. (What, they thought I'd pay that much and *not* collect it?) Then Emily had another thought.

"By the way, where are you actually going to take the lovely Angelica on this big date?" she asked, looking up at me and tilting her head slightly.

"Well I was thinking of Number 8, in Selby," I told them, naming a very nice restaurant I knew they'd also been to on their own romantic occasions.

"Ooh, good choice," agreed Summer. "I love their food, and it's a lovely intimate atmosphere. Just ask for one of their more secluded tables." She winked as she gave her advice, making Emily laugh and swat her hand.

"Oh, you're terrible!" she mock-scolded Summer.

"Like you weren't thinking the same thing!" Summer retorted, while I just shook my head and kept walking.

"Hey, how about we come too. Make it a double—" Summer started, at which I cut her off sharply.

"Over. My. Dead. Body." I told them firmly. "You two can stay home and eat pizza or something, just stay the hell away from that restaurant." I saw the devious looks in their eyes, so I clarified my point. "I swear, you turn up and I'll teleport you both to the middle of the Arctic Circle!"

I stomped away, listening to the giggles behind me. Fuck my life!

Chapter 23

I drove home, windows down and music blaring to try and drown out the echoing threat of Summer and Emily turning up on my date. Fortunately I hadn't set a date yet, so maybe I could book the restaurant for a day when they weren't available. Then again I'd been pretty emphatic with them, so they'd probably listen. I snorted in doubt at my own reassurance, though it did *occasionally* happen – once or twice per year, maybe.

When I got home I carried the bags upstairs and put everything away. Gauvain and Paladin were happy to see me and I spent a few minutes stroking feathers and hugging a big fuzzy neck. Then I teleported us all to the office at the shop, ready to get on with the rest of the day. Paladin flopped down onto his bed, elegant as a sack of potatoes, while G stayed on my shoulder. We went out into the shop which was where G abandoned me for his perch by the counter, ready to be admired while keeping an eye on things.

When I'd installed the new computer, I'd upgraded to a digital bookkeeping program which worked with the register and stock record to streamline everything. It meant I didn't have to sit and do the books every week or month, plus it made sure we didn't run out of anything. I still liked to look through it every so often, mostly to see how we were doing, and since we'd finished shopping faster than expected I decided to do it this morning.

I was shocked by just how much turnover had increased since the grand reopening. The switch to twenty-four-hour operation, plus the addition of The Sanctuary with all its services, had more than quadrupled the previous average weekly takings. Even with my commission work added to the takings from before, this new level of income would more than triple the annual income for the shop as a whole. If my special requests increased commensurately, I could end up making enough money to finally start collecting some of the rare and unique volumes I'd always coveted from Mr Davis.

I sat back in the chair behind the shop computer screen, putting my hands behind my head and looking up at the ceiling with a smile on my face. I remembered talking to Angie about wanting to collect more valuable and rare books when she'd first turned up. The thought of possibly earning as much as a hundred million pounds for my search had been intoxicating, to say the least. Losing out on that had been extremely disappointing, though I'd found something I would have given all that and more to obtain on my search.

Theoretically, given my new abilities, I supposed I could create wealth to replace it. After all, diamonds were just carbon atoms in the correct lattice, so I could buy a ten pound bag of charcoal and end up with *billions* in diamonds. I didn't really think that was especially ethical, however, nor the reason Isis had helped me unlock my power. Making rings for Summer and Emily was different, since it wasn't for me and would give joy. Simply making money, well... There was a reason it was said that the love of money is a root of all kinds of evil. I was better off placing my affection somewhere less dangerous.

Making money from my business was something I had been doing anyway, so using my magick to expand the business merely helped me create jobs for others. That, in turn, gave a living and sense of belonging to lots of people, along with creating a safe space for the magickal community. Overall I felt this was a fair exchange, so using the money I earned here was fair game for my collection. After all, I'd been living within my means beforehand, so anything extra was gravy.

Talking of gravy, back to my date with Angelica. When? And, more to the point, where? I'd considered Number 8 in Selby but now, knowing Summer and Emily frequented it and had the potential to turn up, maybe I should think of another option. The problem with *that* was I didn't know many really good restaurants. Not unless I went farther afield, like Leeds or maybe York. I tended to prefer York, so I started thinking of what nice places there were.

There were some fish restaurants, a couple of nice Italian places... Then I remembered a review I'd read online. It was for The Grand Hotel, which was the only five-star hotel around. They had a restaurant where you could get a chef's tasting menu. It was about eight courses, and they did wine pairings with each course. I'd always wanted to try it but I'd never found a good reason. It wasn't exactly a ten-pound all-you-can-eat buffet, after all. Dinner with Angelica, on the other hand? Now *that* was a reason to push the boat out a little.

I rang and spoke to the receptionist at the hotel, who informed me the restaurant was closed on Sundays and Mondays. That would be great, since I could book a Friday evening. Then I could book the weekend off in case things went really badly – or really well – and I didn't feel like being here. I was told that Fridays and Saturdays were the busiest days, so advance booking would be required. The earliest Friday I could book was two weeks from the coming Friday, giving me plenty of prep time. I booked for seven p.m., thanked the young lady, and hung up.

I went onto the rota system and slated both Angie and myself to be off work for that Friday and Saturday. I knew Summer would notice, though since I'd mentioned another restaurant she'd be at the wrong place if she tried to crash our date. The thought put an evil grin on my face, imagining her turning up with Emily to spy on us and finding us nowhere in sight.

"What's got you looking like the cat that got the cream?" Angie asked, making me jump as she came up behind me.

"Oh, just making a few plans," I said, waggling my eyebrows. "So about that dinner... How about two weeks from Friday? Dinner at seven, I'll pick you up here at five so we can get there in good time and have a drink first, OK?"

Her mouth opened in surprise before she caught herself. Then her eyes sparkled, her cheeks dimpled as her smile almost split her face in two, and if she'd nodded any harder she might have sprained something.

"I'll take that as a 'yes' then, shall I?" I said, smiling big enough to match her.

"Oh, definitely!" she replied breathlessly. Then her eyes widened. "What should I wear? Is this a 'pizza and beer' sort of date, a 'nice restaurant' meal, or an 'oh my gods, break out your best dress' kind of thing?"

I winked, then raised a hand. I put up one finger, and her smile wavered a little. I raised a second, at which her happiness was evident as she nodded and started to turn away. Then I cleared my throat and put a third finger up beside the others, watching as the shock set in. Her eyebrows raised, her jaw dropped, and her head tilted slightly as she silently questioned if I was serious. When I nodded to confirm, wiggling my three fingers ever so slightly in emphasis, she swallowed.

"I guess I'd better go shopping then," she whispered. "A new dress, new shoes..." She leant in close, dropping her voice to a throaty whisper that made my underwear suddenly feel far too tight. "Maybe even some new lingerie."

Now it was my turn to swallow convulsively, my mind already wandering through the possibilities of La Perla and Agent Provocateur. Angie pinched my cheek lightly, raised her eyebrows suggestively a couple of times, then bounced away happily. I followed her with my eyes as she made her way over to the twins. She spoke to them quietly, and that immediately led to squealing and hugging. I shook my head to clear it of the erotic imagery currently sashaying seductively through my mind, turning my thoughts back to work.

Since I had my personal issues kind of sorted, or at least scheduled for progress, it was time to get back to the more important subject: Tracking down the Order. I opened my email but there was no news yet from Cheveyo. I decided to go into my office and see what I could dig up in the way of useful spells or abilities. I was reminded again of Danu's distaste for spell books, though I'd already found useful techniques such as the glamour I'd used on Gauvain. Maybe I could dig up some interesting battle magick. Hell, I'd even take *Harry Potter*'s 'Avada Kedavra'. Funnily enough, I discovered *that* was actually a real curse. It was apparently based on an Aramaic spell which translated to 'let the thing be destroyed', and it was the basis for 'abracadabra'.

I guess maybe Rowling did her research better than most people realised. Maybe she even knew something about real magick. I didn't have time to go hunting her down to find out, however. Though it did make me consider just how many 'fantasy' authors of note – Tolkien, Jim Butcher, Orlando Sanchez, John Logsdon, and Christopher Paolini to name just a few – might be either 'in the know' or even truly magickal themselves. Maybe I'd have to go to one of these so-called 'author conventions' one day and investigate to see if they were really just coven meetings.

That was for another time, though. Right now I just needed weapons. I began pulling out volumes, starting with the *Key of Solomon*, and trawling through them for any techniques that might make for a good offence. I already had my wards and shields for defence, so it was more a case of thinking about new ways to attack. I wanted things that could attack as many as possible as quickly as possible, to try and minimise the casualties on our side.

There was a cool idea I came up with about creating a vacuum to suffocate whole groups, though that would only work indoors. That led to trying the opposite, increasing the pressure in an area. It was hard to maintain, though when it was let go it could create some interesting pressure equalisation effects (such as significant, even debilitating, cramps and headaches). Effective for groups, though only the first was a guaranteed kill. The second could kill, with a ruptured aneurysm or something, but there was no certainty.

I already had fireballs and electroballs (I decided 'arcballs' sounded better), plus plasma, all of which were great for precision work. I came up with another idea of creating poison gas clouds, though that took a lot of energy unless I was close enough to gas myself as well. I read up on breaking opposing shields, looking for faster methods than opening myself to magick and feeling around for how they were constructed. That took way too long in the heat of battle, plus left me exposed to attack. I discovered a way to create a pinpoint attack of energy, practically only a single atom wide at the tip, which could be driven into a shield like a wedge and then expanded to pop the shield.

I realised it would also work on bodies, though it would be extremely messy. I did consider the whole 'turn them into frogs' thing, or rats or slugs or whatever, though with how much energy and concentration my *own* transmogrification took, I doubted it would be much good as a battle strategy. Maybe one-to-one, but not full-scale war.

I also considered the pre-prepared idea of enchanting some kind of item with a particular spell to throw, though that would take practice and I didn't have the time right now. Definitely something to put a pin in for later, though.

As the afternoon drew on, Summer stuck her head into the office with a grin on her face.

"Do I take it, by the matching days off in a couple of weeks, that you've finally set a date for your date?" she asked with a grin.

"Yes, Little Miss Nosey," I said, sitting back and cracking my spine. "So don't even *think* about booking yourself off to try and trail us."

"The thought never crossed my mind," she said, trying to sound innocent and failing utterly. She ducked back out of the office and I smiled to myself.

Thank Isis I had had the idea to switch locations.

Chapter 24

As the next couple of days went by, having collected my adjusted suit and stored it safely at home, I continued practising the new magicks I'd found while almost obsessively checking my email every hour on the hour. I was desperate to hear from Cheveyo or Sovereign about the sites I'd sent them, though I realised they did have their regular lives to lead. It was still frustrating, as I wanted to get this damned chapter of my life closed, locked, and with the key thrown away. I was tired of having the threat of the Order hanging over my head, even though it had only been a few months. I realised then just how bad it must have been for someone like Seirina, having had that for *centuries*. That reminded me, it was check-in time. I picked up the phone and selected her number.

"Seirina Crow, aye, wha' d'ye want?" Clearly she hadn't checked the caller ID since she'd put on her Scottish accent again. I laughed, remembering the first day I'd met her in person.

"Knock it off, you big faker, it's me," I said genially, hearing a laugh at the other end of the line. "How're you doing? How's things?"

"Oh hi, Gavan," she said lightly. "Sorry, I was concentrating on something for a client so I just hit the speaker button. Yeah, things are back to normal, thanks. No one hanging around or anything. Yes, the wards are still up, before you ask. I decided you were right, I'm going to keep them. Like you said, better safe than sorry."

"Oh good," I replied, leaning back in my chair and putting my feet up on the corner of the desk. "I'm glad you've come 'round. Just think of it like an alarm and home security system." I heard a distracted "hmm" and realised she was focused again. "Glad to hear you're busy again too. I'll let you get on, I was just checking in. No news yet from the States; I'll let you know as soon as I hear anything."

"Mmhmm, yeah, right," she said distractedly, making me chuckle softly.

"Yeah, so my third eye is coming in nicely. I've instituted topless waitresses in The Sanctuary for 'Men's Monday', and male strippers for 'Women's Wednesday'," I ad-libbed, smiling hugely.

"Yeah great, sounds... Wait, what?" she suddenly caught herself, making me laugh out loud. "Oh fuck off, you prat!" she swore, laughing. "Yeah, OK, I'm distracted, sorry."

"No worries, I'll let you get back to it," I said, still laughing. "Bye!" I heard her farewell and hung up, smiling. It was the simple things in life you treasured, winding up a friend definitely being one of those things.

I was ready for a break so I dropped my feet off the desk, stood up and went out into the shop. As I came out, I heard a raised voice along with a shriek from Gauvain.

"Look, I said I want two and I need them today!" Just the comment and tone of voice told me it was an overly self-important and entitled woman, the sort often referred to as a 'Karen'. My heart sank and I closed my eyes, since these were the customers everyone in any kind of service industry hates and I was just waiting for the fateful words to come spilling out of her mouth. I made myself a bet, smiling as I heard the inevitable phrase before I reached a count of ten. "I want to talk to the manager!"

I looked over at the counter, seeing it was Sophie serving today. She was one of our newer hires but was very pleasant and knowledgeable. She was a nineteen-year-old Wiccan, working here to help her pay for college where she was studying botany. She was also doing some online studies in Wicca, so when she worked here she usually sat in The Sanctuary working on her computer during her breaks. She was one of the sweetest people you could hope to meet, though I could see this particular customer was pushing her buttons hard enough to bring a flush to her cheeks. Fortunately I saw Summer hurrying over, so I just leant against my door frame to enjoy the fireworks and be on hand in case I was needed.

"What seems to be the problem?" Summer asked pleasantly as she arrived.

"This stupid girl refuses to sell me two of these, and she's trying to overcharge me! I want the manager, now!" stormed the customer. By this time, her voice had drawn all the attention from The Sanctuary so everyone in there was watching avidly. Since they were hidden by the glamour it was like a reality show in real life, or more accurately like watching a car crash in slow motion.

"Well, I am the manager for this shift ma'am," Summer replied calmly. "However, I'd be grateful if you would refrain from abusing the staff. This young lady is certainly *not* stupid – she's at the top of her university class – and the prices for the items are clearly displayed." I saw Sophie look gratefully at Summer for the support, then she caught sight of me so I smiled at her as well.

"Well then, this whole store is a scam and a rip-off! You can buy a caduceus lapel pin for five or six pounds online. I've seen them!" shouted the woman. Now I understood her problem. The caduceus brooch we had in the display case was quite large for a pin, about two and a half inches tall, and was solid gold with a ruby at the top. As a result, it was over six *hundred* pounds, not a cheap six pound piece of tin. Summer was valiantly trying to explain to the woman, but she was having none of it and was becoming louder and progressively ruder. I heard G calling her a series of choice names in my head, so I had to struggle not to laugh.

"Look you fat, useless bitch," the increasingly loud woman replied, which was when I stood up off the door frame and started walking. "Either you sell me that pin for what I've said, and get another by this afternoon, or–"

"Out!" I said firmly, cutting her off. She stopped mid-tirade, turning to see me just behind her shoulder.

"No one was talking to you," said the woman tartly, turning back to Summer. "I'm dealing with your manager, though she's fucking useless, too!" I hate bullies, and I wasn't going to let her get away with this behaviour.

"OK, firstly," I began, drawing her attention back to me. "you are being extremely rude, which isn't tolerated in this store."

"I don't–" she started but I cut her off, working up a head of steam and seeing Summer grinning as she realised. She put her hand on Sophie's arm and drew her back a little as I loomed over the Karen.

"Shut up!" I cut the evil cow off mid-rant. "Secondly, Sophie is, as Summer has already told you, at the top of her class. I'd wager she's probably got a higher IQ in her left big toe than you have in your entire bleach-blonde head!" Now Sophie was smiling, and the people in The Sanctuary were laughing. I even spotted a few phones out and recording, though I didn't know when they'd started.

"Thirdly, the manager you just insulted and harangued is a close personal friend of mine, so think yourself lucky I'm not throwing you bodily out into the street for insulting her and swearing at her just now! Fourthly, the piece you're looking at is, as you were just informed, solid gold and ruby. It sounds as though you'd be better with cheap, painted tin pieces to go with your cheap, painted face! Fifthly, we have the right to refuse service to anyone for any reason, and you've already provided more than enough just cause. So get out and don't come back: You're banned."

"I want to talk to the owner!" the woman shrieked like a harridan, at which I developed the biggest shit-eating grin ever.

"You just did," I informed her, watching her face go white in shock. "Now fuck off, bitch!"

The woman stammered something but I didn't hear, since she was drowned out by the cheering from The Sanctuary. She turned and scurried out, then I stepped over to Sophie.

"Are you OK?" I asked her, glad to see her nod and grin.

"I'm fine, thanks," she replied. "Summer already told me not to worry, but that was awesome, boss!"

"Bloody brilliant!" Summer chimed in, at which I was swarmed with congratulatory hugs and handshakes from everyone who had been watching. Apparently, one of the customers had heard the woman being horrible and had started filming in case it turned nasty, so we had video from just before I came out of my office. We all watched it again, everyone laughing and cheering as I tore into the evil bitch. I thought

I caught sight of the young woman from the shopping centre car park stairs, though I lost sight of her in the group. I had to stop myself cringing at being the centre of attention like this, though I was really glad I'd stood up to her as I had. Sophie thanked me again after the re-watch, then everyone went back to what they'd been doing.

For me, that meant getting something for lunch before I went back to work. I had been eating at The Sanctuary for most meals recently, but I fancied something different today. It had been ages since I had had some junk food, so I decided to head over to the burger place nearby. I let Summer know I was popping out, then stepped out into the fresh air. It was overcast but fortunately not raining – at least not yet, though this *was* Yorkshire so it probably would at some point. I was feeling pretty good about myself, now that I was away from all the fuss, so I had a little bounce in my step as I made my way towards the famous crowned logo.

I strode through the door, inhaling the heavenly scent of fried food and grilled meat. I placed my order and was waiting patiently, when I heard a particularly unwelcome sound.

"You're a very rude man, you know that?" It was the Karen from the shop, standing behind me with her arms crossed and tapping her foot. "I don't know how you have the nerve to come out in decent society. If you ever talk to me like that again, I'll have you arrested! As it is, I don't think you deserve to be served here." She looked over my shoulder, once again sounding the battle cry of the urban Karen. "I want to speak to the manager!"

I turned to the server at the desk. "It's OK," I told him. "You're better off not getting involved. Just get your manager for her, it's safer."

"Don't you speak about me as though I'm not here, or crazy!" she yelled, once again drawing eyes like a car crash on the motorway. "How dare you treat me like that! I'll have you know I'm the head of the PTA at my son's school!"

"Lucky them," I replied dryly, unable to stop myself.

"Excuse me," came the voice from behind me. I looked over my shoulder and 'Karen' looked past me to see a young man with 'Manager' on his nametag, which read Steve. "My server tells me you're being rude and disruptive. I think you should leave."

"He certainly is!" blurted Karen immediately. "He should be banned completely!" She glared at me triumphantly with her hands on her hips and tossing her hair back, totally assured of her own superiority.

"Actually, I was talking to you," Steve said, making her jaw drop. "Please leave, you're disrupting my customers' meals."

There were a few cheers and a smattering of applause as once again, she was forced to leave with her tail between her legs. I turned to see Steve smile at me.

"Sorry about that," he apologised to me, though I waved him off since it clearly wasn't his fault. "Please sir, how about some free onion rings as compensation?"

Yup, today was shaping up to be a *really* good day!

Chapter 25

My lunch tasted especially good, particularly the onion rings, and I finished off my milkshake with a satisfied sigh. Now I just had to hope our expedition against the Order went as well as my recent anti-bitch exercise. I spent the afternoon helping around the shop, restocking shelves and generally making myself useful. I could tell by the laughter whenever the video was shared and re-watched, each time making me cringe inwardly. I was subjected to a number of high fives, to the point where my hand started getting a little sore by the end of it all. I particularly enjoyed the shine in Angelica's eyes after she'd watched it.

I made a mental note to get someone to forward the video to my phone, so I could play it again for her just before our date. You never knew when a little extra good will or hero-worship might just carry you the final mile. I shook off the distracting images that started running through my head, a combination of memories and fantasies, and went back to training in the new battle magic I was finding. One idea I had come up with was again based on Christopher Paolini's writing. I had looked up ways of causing precision damage, rather than 'area of effect' magick. After all, as Eragon's teacher told him in Paolini's book, it only needed the right pressure at the right points to kill someone.

I had used an anatomy textbook to find the most vulnerable spots, such as certain blood vessels or nerves, that could cause instant incapacitation or death. Aiming at those meant far less expenditure of energy per technique, so I could attack more people at a greater distance with much higher effectiveness. If I kept working on it, eventually I might be able to take out huge groups with only a thought. It wasn't the most pleasant idea but given my vision in Aaru, I needed to consider fighting a war against a powerful army. The very thought of killing lots of people made my stomach churn, but I had been chosen by Isis to inherit her power. I had to live up to the responsibilities which came with it (damn you, Spiderman!).

As the week progressed, I received a message from Sovereign to say she'd struck out on all the sites on her side of the US. Apparently, despite my request to check out Alcatraz, Cheveyo was working his way there. He felt all the sacred sites I'd found deserved the same level of respect, and I supposed I could see his point from the perspective of their spiritual significance to his heritage. However, that wasn't why I'd been looking them up and he knew it. The longer it took to locate the Order, the more time they had to recruit new members, plus fortify their base both physically and magickally.

Still, it also gave *us* more time to prepare. Since many of the fresher bodies had been used by the voodoo team for the assault on Edinburgh, there were a great deal fewer available to use for the American assault. Only the corpses of those who had died recently. As a result, Seirina's contribution would be far more important this time. Sovereign had already spoken to her, so they asked if I'd be willing to get Seirina to New Orleans to assist. Of course, I told them I was more than happy to help, since we needed as many reinforcements as we could get. I also told them I'd try and work out a defence against the anti-zombie ward the Order had used in Edinburgh, otherwise all their work would be for naught once again.

I texted Seirina, arranging to take her on Friday afternoon at five p.m. That would still be morning in New Orleans, so she'd have her full working week here before she left. I used the rest of the week to continue practising, plus I wanted to work on my own ideas I'd come up with over the last few weeks. I felt they might come in useful for the fight, and certainly later on.

Some of the magicks I found in my books required a name to focus on, so I tried some of them out to see if I could get them to work just on a description. 'Black-haired vampire in a green shirt' might not be quite as specific as a true name, but I found it could be a reasonable enough focus if enough power was used. One of the ideas I'd had, however, was to try and focus such magick without any name at all. I worked on that, plus the other idea I'd had, gradually making progress as the days went by. Thanks to the wards, I had to wait until I was away from the shop to practice. Even then it was only on dummies I rigged up using old clothes, though that was better than crippling my allies in my pursuit of an arsenal.

When Friday rolled around, by the time it got to five o'clock I was ready for a break. I had been trying to use only my own energy for my training, since I needed as much stored power in Seren as possible when the fight arrived. I also didn't want to exhaust Paladin, nor become used to relying on him every time. I found the more I practised, the longer I could maintain my energy and the more efficient I became in its use. It was like a muscle and the more training I gave it, the stronger it became. I was already powerful, as Isis had told me, but this constant striving with new and varied abilities was developing things even further.

I teleported to Seirina's driveway, still able to get inside the wards since she hadn't blocked me out. I strolled up to the front door, enjoying the crunch of the gravel under my feet. I knocked on the door, smiling as I imagined the consternation on Mrs Wilson's face. She was used to being alerted to arrivals by the gate intercom, so a knock at the door would totally throw her off her game. I heard her hurrying down the hall and I composed my face to a polite mock surprise, head tilted slightly to the right and eyebrows raised. As the door opened I smiled at her gasp, then chuckled as she launched right into scolding me.

"Mr Maddox!" she cried out. "Ms Crow told me you were coming but I didn't hear the intercom! I was totally unprepared!"

"That's because I didn't use it," I reassured her. "I bypassed it. Sorry to surprise you like this."

"I suppose I should be used to it by now," she said, sighing. "Still, I'd become accustomed to the quiet and normality again after you all went your own ways. Come in, come in, she's all packed and ready for you to take her to America."

"Thank you, Mrs Wilson," I said, walking into the house and down the familiar hallway. "I take it she's in the study?"

"As usual," she replied, closing the door and trailing after me. I paused at the study door while she bustled past me into the kitchen to resume her day. I knocked on the study door, knowing better by now than to just walk in, only opening it once I heard Seirina's acknowledgement.

"Come in, Gavan," she said cheerfully, so I obeyed.

"Hi Seirina," I said as I walked across the room. "How are you doing? Been enjoying the peace and quiet?"

"Very much so," she replied. "Though I was surprised by how much I missed the company to begin with. It's amazing how you can get used to something you never expected, then miss it when it's gone even though it annoyed you at first."

"I know," I agreed. "I really miss having Mrs Wilson looking after us since I went home, though I *am* enjoying my own peace and quiet again, the same as you."

Does that mean you've also missed me? Iyrin said in my mind, climbing up the branch to stare at me through the glass. *Though I have enjoyed observing your antics over the last few weeks. You've certainly become stronger with all your training, and your emotions are delicious!*

I cringed slightly on hearing its voice, then further as it spoke of feeding off of my emotions again. I hated the fact that we were still connected, that it continued to watch my life and feed on me like a parasite. I was careful to control and hide that thought, since I remembered how it had reacted the last time I'd called it that.

"Anyway," I said, shivering again and looking over at Seirina. "Let's get you over to New Orleans so you can start building our forces again. I'm just glad there are so many cemeteries over there, otherwise you'd run out of subjects to work with far too quickly to be of any use. I'm just hoping my thought regarding the new location of the Order is right, because if it is you'll have plenty of raw materials to draw on during the battle."

"Well we can't just rely on that," she said, standing up and stepping around her desk. "So let's go. Get my bags, will you?"

"Yeth, mithtreth!" I joked, lurching across the floor like the hangman in *Robin Hood, Men in Tights.*

"Oh stop it, you daft bugger!" she said, though I could tell she was struggling not to laugh. I laughed anyway, which broke her composure and made her join the chuckle. Iyrin made a disgusted noise and turned away, climbing down its branch back into the depths of the terrarium.

I grabbed Seirina's bags and she came over and put her hand on my shoulder. Since I'd been over to Sovereign's landing zone a couple of times, I was going to teleport us this time. Just before I did, however, my phone dinged with a message. I put the bags down and pulled it out, looking down to see a notification of a photo. I opened it to see a completely different scene from where I'd taken Seirina last time, with a note saying, "This area's clear, the other is too busy right now".

Since it was a new area, I had no idea what we were heading into. It *looked* like a garden, though I had no clue what might be behind the camera. I decided to stick with a portal again, opening it a few feet into the open area shown in the picture to ensure I didn't hit anything or wind up stepping out into a koi pond.

"Oh, I do so love the warmth of New Orleans!" Seirina said as she stepped through the portal and stretched. I followed her through, lugging her bags like a valet. I got one step beyond the portal, let it close and simply dropped everything to the grass.

"Him still gat da fayah!" came Sovereign's voice from behind us.

We spun in unison to see the obeah regarding us with her usual cheery expression. Seirina chuckled while I simply sighed, rolled my eyes and shook my head.

"Yes, well, *him* still has work to do and a business to run," I said peevishly. Both of them chuckled again, so I abruptly teleported back to my office.

Within a couple of minutes I received another ping on my phone, this time from Seirina. Her message chided me over my lack of manners, then told me she'd contact me if she needed anything. It was wonderful to feel needed, to be treated with such respect. I snorted to myself. I decided people were becoming somewhat blasé about me and my abilities, familiarity breeding contempt and all. Still, I wasn't really wanting people to cower and creep whenever I walked into a room. It would be nice to have a *little* more respect though.

I was the chosen of Isis, after all. Maybe once I took out Elrulin and they saw my power during the battle, maybe then everyone would start to understand exactly what I was capable of. I had the new magicks I'd been working on, the new techniques, and even the extra idea I'd had. Hopefully it would all be enough, along with our allies, to finish the Order once and for all.

Chapter 26

I was driving myself harder and harder as the days went on, striving to forget about hearing from Cheveyo. The waiting was becoming a nagging pull at the back of my mind, an itch I just couldn't scratch. I felt like something was crawling over my skin each time I checked my email and found nothing there. The more I thought about it, the more certain I became of the *rightness* of my discovery. Alcatraz just made too much sense for the Order to have selected anywhere else as their new base of operations.

After another week of not hearing from him, I sent Cheveyo a text message asking where he was in his investigation. He sent back only two words: Getting there. His laconic disdain for my concerns irritated the ever-loving shit out of me. I fired back another message asking for more details, since he could have been at San Francisco in a matter of hours and on Alcatraz soon after. I knew he wanted to pay his respects at *all* the spiritual sites I'd discovered, but he could do that by saying a prayer in just a few minutes. That should mean he could still be at the west coast in a couple of days. Instead it had been weeks and he still wasn't there.

My itch was turning into a more significant concern: Had Cheveyo been coerced or even full-on recruited by the Order, and *that* was why he was stalling?

His response made sense from either the perspective of paying his respects, or with the view of him simply trying to delay things. Instead of just saying a prayer, he was participating in a full ceremonial remembrance at each location. That meant he was only able to see one or at most two sites per day, so with the number I'd found in the Rockies he had weeks' worth of ceremonies before he even smelled the ocean.

I continued working out my irritation with my training, honing my anger to a fine edge. The problem with that was a blade that sharp could be just as lethal to the one wielding it as to its intended target. I had to be careful not to let my anger and hatred of the Order, plus my chafing at the delay, cause me to overdo things and hurt myself. I also had to make sure to maintain the rightness of my cause, not let the negative emotions I was feeling turn into pure aggression I couldn't control.

Although most, if not all, of the Order members would be deserving of death, there would still likely be at least some who had been coerced in some way. I *had* to maintain the same clarity I had in Edinburgh, give the members the same chance to surrender. I didn't want to become an indiscriminate killer, devoid of any consideration for my enemy merely by dint of the fact that it took longer than I wanted to get the information I needed. That was the risk in having this kind of power. You became so capable of making things happen, you took it as a personal affront when things didn't go your way. Then you lost your composure but instead of just punching a pillow, you could destroy an entire city because you were having a frustrated temper tantrum. (There was a Godzilla joke in there somewhere, I was sure of it.)

I decided to take some time to work on meditation techniques, try to calm myself and work on my composure. I was never much for sitting around contemplating my navel, as my father always called it, but it might just help bring my equilibrium back enough so I didn't fly off the handle next time I communicated with Cheveyo. I took a day at home, relaxing after I'd been for my morning run. I made a pot of chilli, boxing it up for future use and storing it in the freezer once it was cold. I baked some bread, even made a pizza from scratch for dinner. In between, for an hour here or there when dough was rising or the chilli was simmering, I worked on my breathing.

By the evening, my flat smelled wonderful and I was just as frustrated as I had been. I just wasn't cut out to sit on my ass and twiddle my thumbs. The only difference was now I was frustrated at my inaction today, rather than Cheveyo's inaction over the last few weeks. I decided

I'd give him one more week, and if he hadn't got back to me I'd go to San Francisco and check things out myself. I didn't care if it pissed him off; my concerns were bigger than the ego of just one man. Yes, I realised it sounded ironic, but this wasn't about my ego. It was about protecting all those the Order might hurt in the future, plus getting justice for all those they had already hurt up to now.

I remembered how things had gone when I first got back from Aaru. I had confirmed the existence of the Veil for the Order, told them it was no longer available for them to use, given them the box it came in, even told them it had unlocked my magick. OK, so I hadn't told them the full extent of my abilities; but that was beside the point. I'd done all they had asked of me except actually delivering the Veil to them, though I had explained why (kind of). I hadn't made them pay for anything, only keeping the advance which had contractually belonged to me for completing the search as commissioned.

Still, that hadn't been enough for them, so Elrulin had demanded his meeting. He *still* hadn't been satisfied, locking Angelica up and torturing her for more information about me. I'd only gotten involved with the Order again because of their actions. If they'd simply accepted the Veil was no longer accessible to them, Elrulin could have gone on gathering power and looking for other ways to get back to Aaru. As ever, they had been their own worst enemy and quite literally created their nemesis – me.

That may sound arrogant but given Elrulin's origins, there was no one else in our line-up who was equipped to deal with him. Lucian would have been able to, but he had already proven, by helping Elrulin and then lying to me about cutting himself off from contact with the Order, that he was totally unconcerned with taking Elrulin to task. Also, since Isis had already intimated I was supposed to be facing trials of my power, and Danu had said the same, it was quite clear I needed to do this. I was under no illusion, fully aware that my power could be taken from me as easily as it had been given, plus I had seen some of what was to come in my visions in Aaru. If I ran from the Order, I had no chance in the battles to come.

I sincerely hoped I wouldn't have to sacrifice friends and allies from Earth for the sake of Aaru, since they should fight their own battles.

Then again, wasn't this battle theirs as well? Elrulin was one of their people, banished to here for crimes there. If they were going to use us as their dumping ground, which they'd done at least twice as evidenced by Lucian and Elrulin, they should help us out when their garbage caused more problems. If they weren't willing to help us, should I be bothered about helping them?

However, they *could* argue they had *already* helped us out by unlocking and training me to use my power. If I couldn't handle one Aaruan, I wouldn't be much use to them in a war. This was essentially a training exercise to see if I actually could hold my own in a fight. Edinburgh certainly wouldn't be viewed as any kind of realistic test, since the fight had lasted only a few minutes and I'd had enough allies to make sure I hadn't had to do much myself. That, in turn, meant I still needed to prove myself, hence the requirement to face the final Order stronghold without Aaruan assistance.

This was why I preferred training over meditating – the arguing back and forth just made my head hurt.

I took some headache pills and sat down to eat my pizza, accompanied by a couple of bottles of good cider. I decided on something fun for the evening, so I started watching the *John Wick* films again. Man, I could really use that guy for our fight. Give him a few pencils and just stand back! I relaxed on the sofa, feeding some of the bits of meat from the pizza to Gauvain and petting Paladin's head. I really did enjoy having them with me now, as they provided companionship without complications. If things did go well with Angelica, I'd have to consider how that might work. She got on OK with the guys; heck, they'd even given me their approval at various times. This place was, however, a little cramped for two adults, a big hawk, and a huge dog.

Given the income we'd have if we combined everything, we'd be able to get a bigger place. Still, that was definitely jumping the gun. It might be a good idea to have the date first, *then* think about moving in together. Just because things had gone well once, didn't mean they'd go the same way the second time around. There had been several situations involved that wouldn't happen again, both because she couldn't get into my mind without permission anymore and because I had no intention of letting her be captured and tortured again.

Man, life really did get complicated when you had to factor in other people.

The next morning, after my usual exercise and shower, I teleported to the shop to find the twins just finishing their shift. They tended to prefer the night shifts since most of the customers were magickal, so they didn't have to hide behind a glamour. It was giving them a huge sense of freedom and allowing them to develop more as individuals, though they still thought almost exactly the same way. However, since they could be *seen* as separate from each other, they could *interact* separately, which was something they hadn't been able to do when they were forced to use the glamour. Even Elrulin had treated them as a single organism, referring to them rather insultingly as 'Gemini'.

I was reminded of my idea to thank and help them, on which I had been making progress. I now knew it would be possible but it would take time and energy, neither of which I had sufficient of to spare right now. That didn't, however, mean I couldn't at least make the offer so they could think about it. What I was going to propose would be such a significant change to their lives, they deserved a chance to ponder the pros and cons and review all the ramifications, before making a decision. I called them into my office before they left to go upstairs.

"Hey, Gabby, hi, Izzy," I said cheerfully. "Can I have a quick word before you go, please? Don't worry, it's nothing bad, I promise."

"Sure, Gavan," Izzy said.

"No problem, boss," Gabby added.

They went into the office as I held the door for them, sitting down in the same chair my old psychiatric nurse, Frank, had used when I had my last meeting with him. I only hoped this meeting went a little better.

"I wanted you both to know how much I appreciate all you've done for me," I told them as I sat down. "You rescued me and Angelica from the Order's cells, you trusted me, and you helped pull our resistance force together. You assisted with scanning people who surrendered in Edinburgh, and last but not least, you were pivotal in helping set up and run The Sanctuary.

"I've been working on something to show you just what it has all meant to me. I've done research on feasibility, process, and precedents, all of which has proven that what I am about to say *is* in fact possible.

However it's a huge decision, so I'd never even dream of proceeding without your full understanding and agreement. Plus, since it *is* such a momentous idea, you should have time to consider it before making any decision. I would only proceed when we had the time to do it right, so after the Order is finished, but I wanted to tell you now so you could mull it over.

"I wanted to offer you the option of being separated, of each having your own body."

Their jaws dropped and they stared at me.

Chapter 27

"Are you..." Izzy whispered, swallowing hard. "Are you serious?"

"You're really offering to separate us?" Gabby added softly.

"Yes," I replied, fully prepared to go slow to allow them to wrap their heads around my momentous proposition. "Obviously, given how extensively you're joined together, separating you is no small undertaking, but I'm confident it *is* possible."

"Holy shit!" exclaimed Gabby, clearly awed by my thoughts.

"Bloody hell!" echoed Izzy.

"If we were separated, would we still..." Gabby trailed off, clearly wanting to ask something but seemingly unsure how.

"Would our minds still join as they do now?" Izzy finished, enunciating the concern Gabby had failed to express. Her sister looked gratefully at her for a moment, then both sets of eyes looked back at me.

"It would be a physical separation only," I clarified, understanding their trepidation at the thought of their minds being unable to link as they had their entire lives. "The process wouldn't affect your telepathy in any way. In fact, I wouldn't even need to affect anything above your shoulders, since your heads and necks are already apart from each other."

I sat back in my chair and crossed my left ankle over my right knee. I watched their faces, feeling the telepathic current of their thoughts flowing back and forth. I didn't intrude, even to listen, since this was such an intensely personal issue for them. Given how close they had been their entire lives, quite literally inside each other's skins, I doubted anyone could possibly comprehend the momentous change my offer represented for them. After a quarter of an hour, I broke the silence.

"Look, this is a huge decision," I said kindly. "Like I told you, I'm not proposing to do it before the Order's final stronghold is destroyed and Elrulin is dealt with. Why don't you take some time, think it through, talk it over between yourselves? I'm happy to answer any questions you might have, but I don't think this is something you should rush into."

"Would it be reversible?" Izzy asked, surprising me.

"Or would we even be able to join and separate as we wanted?" Gabby added, adding a dimension I'd never even considered.

"As far as reversing it goes," I said carefully, thinking it through as I spoke. "I don't see why not, though it would take the same time, effort and energy to reverse as it does to achieve in the first place. Making it so you could join and split at will is, I'm afraid, beyond my capabilities. It would entail a level of magic between the two of you that I couldn't even begin to understand, let alone gift you. I'm sorry." I could see why they might want both options, but unfortunately they were going to have to choose one or the other.

"Don't apologise," Gabby reassured me.

"That's pretty much what we expected," Izzy said.

"We just wanted to clarify exactly what the situation would be if we accepted," Gabby continued.

"Though we definitely need to talk it over more, consider every angle," Izzy added.

"Well why don't you head upstairs, get something to eat and some sleep," I advised. "Then you can talk about it some more. Like I said, don't make any snap decisions. You also both need to agree, whichever way you decide, since this will affect you both equally. I won't do anything unless you're both in agreement." I stood up and walked around the desk, offering them my hand to help them up.

They looked up at me with almost slavish gratitude for a moment, then put their hand in mine and stood up. I walked them to the door, opening it for them and gesturing for them to walk through.

"Still a gentleman," Izzy observed, smiling.

"And so much more besides," Gabby added, nodding to me in thanks as they walked out.

I spent the rest of the morning buried in a book on veterinary medicine, learning about different animals to use for my transmogrifications. I didn't try making any of the shifts yet, since I didn't want to make any mistakes and end up stuck. I also didn't want to waste the energy when I could be storing it for future use.

There were only minimal differences between carnivores such as canines and felines. Ruminants such as horses and cows had more significant differences, as I had already mentioned to Danu during my training. Birds and reptiles varied even more significantly, yet still seemed possible with practice. I didn't look at insects or arachnids since I wasn't sure how far the conversion in mass was possible. I'd have to discuss it with Danu next time I was in Aaru.

I grabbed a tuna salad from The Sanctuary for lunch, then went back to my office to continue boning up on animal anatomy. Given my suspicion regarding the location of the Order, I also looked online for some information on aquatic mammal anatomy. The idea was good, but the differences were even more pronounced. A dolphin, which would have been my ideal choice, had such significant differences regarding its brain structure it would take a huge amount of skill and practice to achieve. The echolocation structure in its brain, known as the melon, didn't have a comparable part in the human brain. That meant constructing whole new areas of the most complex organ in the body, something I didn't really have the time or energy to learn right now. I bookmarked the site with the information for future study, however.

The next couple of days were more of the same, along with getting increasingly tense as my date with Angelica drew closer. It was only just over a week away now, and my mind was playing best- and worst-case scenarios out in excruciating detail every time I closed my eyes. I was fluctuating between needing to get a room at The Grand right after dessert, and not even reaching dessert before getting slapped in the face and abandoned. I was going through whole tubes of Tums each day now, otherwise my stomach felt like it was trying to burn its way out through my chest.

I tried using my breathing exercises to help calm me but ended up hyperventilating instead. Then I started going for an extra run in the evening to try and tire myself out so I could sleep better, but that didn't work either. My body ended up exhausted but my mind kept spinning, so I would wind up lying in bed too tired to move but staring at the ceiling unable to sleep. I was only managing around four hours of sleep a night, broken up into half hour slots, and having to fortify myself with energy from Paladin since I didn't want to drain Seren.

Even my regular intake of Cafegeddon wasn't helping much. I was drinking about six cups a day now, which had the effect of making my left eye twitch and my hands shake but was about as much use in keeping me awake as a fart in a hurricane. I decided to give the coffee a miss, see if that might at least let me sleep, but I just got a migraine from the caffeine withdrawal.

I made the decision to leave off studying for a while, too. I elected to do some more physical training, both my katas and with Muharar. Finally, after everything else, I found a way to quiet my mind. I extended my kata sessions to almost five hours per day, with another three of sword work. Even when I *did* get unwanted mental images, I was able to put them into my training and use them for focus.

My body started to become more honed than my regular running had kept it. My body fat dropped to about two percent, and my muscles and surface veins were so defined I could have auditioned for the next Marvel movie. I worried my changes would mean my new suit wouldn't fit properly any more but fortunately, when I tried it, it hung even better than before.

At least something good had come out of my anxiety, the silver lining and all that. I would maybe even have to keep my activity level up after all this. The improved fitness would hopefully stand me in good stead for the fight against the Order, and the muscles would certainly impress Angelica. One thing I *had* noticed around the shop was the attractive woman from the shopping centre car park. She'd been in several times over the last week, confirming it *had* been her when the Karen was here, though she had tended to speak to Summer or other members of staff. It wasn't that she was avoiding me per se, more that she just always seemed to be where I wasn't.

She always smiled at me when she saw me, though she never came over to talk. Surely if she was interested she'd want to find out more about me, yet she always kept her distance. Or was she trying to find out what I was like from my staff, explore a little before she made a decision as to whether or not to take the next step?

To be honest, an extra woman in my life was the very *last* thing I needed right now. I already had too much oestrogen and not enough testosterone floating around my shop, even *with* the new guys on staff, and I had my date with Angelica coming up. Still, if a pretty girl wanted to hang around the shop, the worst that would happen would be more men coming in to try and chat to her. That meant more customers, which meant more income for everyone. If she was still hanging around after the Order was dealt with, I might try talking to her. Depending on how things went with Angie, I could either ask the girl out or simply offer her a job.

From the way the guys around looked at her, she'd be a definite draw. Anyone interested in an attractive woman would be falling over themselves to be around her, whether male or female. I'd certainly be able to tease Summer about her, threaten to stir things up with Emily, though I knew in real life there was absolutely no chance in hell of those two splitting up. Mind you, it would still be fun to wind them up about her.

As we reached the weekend and I still hadn't heard from Cheveyo, I spoke to Seirina about their 'recruiting' efforts. They had a sizeable number of 'volunteers' already, thanks in part to the significant number of cemeteries in the area, but they weren't letting up. I congratulated them and wished them luck, then told them I was planning on checking America out myself if Cheveyo didn't let me know soon.

They would have preferred more time to increase their numbers but agreed it was necessary. We couldn't keep on in this holding pattern, we needed to get on with the fight. The Order needed to be finished so we could all go on with our lives. I wished them luck again, then hung up. I left my office, smiling at Sophie who was manning the counter again today. She beamed back, her confidence significantly increased since the Karen episode, then I felt my pocket buzz as a message came in. I looked at my phone, finally seeing the information from Cheveyo I'd been waiting for. He'd made it to the coast and found exactly what I'd expected.

Alcatraz *was* the target. It was time to make our move.

Chapter 28

According to Cheveyo's message, the tourist boat trips to Alcatraz had been suspended due to 'maintenance and repairs' currently underway on the island. Yeah, right, more like 'entrenching and expanding' I thought to myself with a snort. Cheveyo reported picking up an aura around the old prison. Also, by using a pair of binoculars on the pier set up for tourists to use for a quarter, he caught sight of a troll walking on the roof of the lighthouse building.

That was quite enough to confirm the accuracy of my guess, at least in my mind. I forwarded his comments to the other faction leaders and Seirina, stating my opinion regarding its implications. By the end of the morning, every one of them had replied to say they fully concurred and were gathering their forces again. The plan was to make our move on Friday, just as dusk hit the island.

I exulted in the thought of finally putting this chapter of my life to rest once and for all. I was also eager to share the news with everyone else, since most of the magickal world had suffered from the Order's abuses at one time or another. I went into The Sanctuary and called out for attention.

"Hey, can I just make a quick announcement, please?" I shouted over the hubbub. The chatter died away as all eyes turned towards this unexpected interruption. Once the noise level had dropped, I continued. "I've just had confirmation that we've identified the Order's new headquarters across the pond," I announced, to cheers from my listeners. "The various liaisons from the magickal communities are currently gathering anyone who wants to fight, so if you're interested please let them know. The plan is to hit them this Friday as dusk falls over the area, so they'll be winding down for the weekend."

There were a few more ragged cheers scattered through a round of applause, though I noticed one glaring anomaly: Angie was staring at me stony-faced, ignoring the celebration going on around her. For a moment, I was completely confused as to why she was so annoyed – didn't she *want* the Order destroyed? Then something crept into the back of my mind, making my eyes widen, my jaw slacken, and the sweat start breaking out across my forehead.

"Oh, shit!" I said, which echoed around the room in the sudden hush which had developed as people saw my changed expression. "Our date!"

"Oh, so you remembered," she said dryly, crossing her arms. "*So* glad I do at least register somewhere in your priorities!"

"Oh, Angie, I'm sorry!" I said sincerely, stepping over to her and taking her hands which forced her to uncross her arms. "Of *course* you register! I've been looking forward to our date for weeks. Hell, I was so keen to make a good impression I even let Summer and Emily take me shopping for suitable clothes!"

Everyone else burst out laughing when I said that; even Angie cracked a slight smile. The fact that my face stayed so earnest (frank had his turn already) made her realise I was actually serious. She finally relaxed enough to give me a full grin.

"Well, at least it's for a good cause," she said, at which I finally started breathing again. "I suppose it's not like you cancelled last minute and said you were washing your hair or something."

Although her tone was light, one look at her eyes showed me the levity didn't quite reach them. She was putting on a good show but deep down, I could tell she was still angry about me cancelling on her. I made a mental note to ring The Grand and cancel our reservation, though hopefully I could just move it to the week after. I'd leave the time off as it was since I'd be away fighting and I was sure Angelica wouldn't want to be here, on the receiving end of everyone's sympathy for our cancelled plans.

I didn't just have a funny feeling, I had a ringing, resounding absolute *certainty* that this was going to come back and bite me very hard in the ass. Probably with poisonous fangs six inches long, and barbs to keep them embedded. Who, me, worried? Oh no, of course not!

That being said, I had to get ready for our upcoming battle. As much as I wanted to have my date with Angie, if I could end the Order we could have as many dates as we wanted for the rest of our lives. Which, given our magickal heritage (however new mine might be), could be a very long time. I let go of Angie's hands and tried to step in for a hug but as soon as I released her, she spun on her heel and stalked away to the kitchen.

The murmuring quietened slightly as she went, surging again as the door swung shut behind her. Judging by the looks coming my way, everyone else had some ideas on just how severely screwed I was. I looked around and shrugged, lifting my hands to shoulder level with the palms up as if to ask the universe what I'd done wrong. Then, to the sound of muted chuckles, I turned around and walked back to my office.

I slumped heavily into my chair, almost bottoming out the hydraulic cushioning as I did, then dropped my head back onto the rest and sighed up at the ceiling. Gauvain jumped across onto the chair next to my head, his chest feathers smothering my nose and forcing me to sit up so I could breathe.

You know you were correct in your assignation of importance to the various calls on your attention, he told me, making me sigh again in reluctant agreement.

"Doesn't make me feel any better, bud," I told him tiredly. "Ever since I got my power unlocked, it's been almost non-stop learning, fighting and planning. I *finally* get two glorious days with Angie, then her memory gets stolen by some Stygian Blade shit-stain and I'm back to square boned – or, more accurately, bone*less* – all over again!" I thumped my fist on the leather writing surface as I finished, having transitioned from despondent to enraged as I was talking.

Easy! G told me, flapping his wings to keep steady as the vibrations travelled back up my arm and into the chair. *You know, if you're going to take your frustrations out on something at work, maybe you should make yourself a little workout room with a heavy bag to hit. Otherwise all this lovely furniture will end up as so much kindling before too long.*

"That's actually not such a bad idea," I replied thoughtfully. "I could make a room large enough for everyone, the equipment reinforced to make it strong enough for even vampires and weres to use safely. We could even put in a ring to enable people to organise fights in a controlled environment, whether for dominance if they're weres (do they actually do that?) or to settle grudges before they turn bloody. I'll have to create an exception in the wards around the ring, or all the combatants will get is zapped without any satisfaction."

You are growing, he replied, sitting up straighter. *Turning your own frustration into a way to help others – I'm proud of you.*

"Thanks, G," I said, genuinely grateful for his ever-present support. "The idea is also a solid business expansion plan, but I'm glad you focused more on the charitable aspect." He chuckled in my head and I grinned along with him, lifted out of my doldrums by my truest friend yet again.

I made a note on my memo pad of the workout room idea, then ran through some of the new abilities and techniques I'd been working on. I needed to be as slick as possible if I was going to be going up against Elrulin. When I'd done as much as I felt prudent for one afternoon – before I started depleting Seren beyond Paladin's rate of replenishment – I took us all home. I needed to be somewhere that was…away from here.

Even the sound of Angie's voice filtering through the door from the shop was painful, and it was getting to the point where I just couldn't focus properly anymore. I had been so eager for our date, then I'd gone and buggered it all up by planning the assault on Alcatraz for the same night. If I couldn't rectify things with Angie after the Order was no longer a threat, I'd be unbe*liev*ably pissed off at myself. Them too, but that went without saying.

I threw myself face down on the sofa once we'd teleported home and screamed into the cushion. I was so angry with myself and the universe in general, the only thing to do was order junk food and watch mindless TV. I went into the kitchen and grabbed the take-out menus from the fridge, carrying them back to the couch to thumb through. I wasn't sure quite what I wanted, I just knew I wanted lots of it. I could always have cold leftovers for the next few days.

With that in mind, I picked up the phone and started dialling. I called several different places, wanting to cover all the bases. I ordered special chow mein, chicken wings in OK sauce, salt and pepper squid, a large meat supreme pizza, goat curry with rice and peas, Jamaican patties, a huge beef burrito, and three tubs of ice cream. Thank the gods the shop was doing so well, otherwise I'd have bankrupted myself to pay for it all!

I cleared off the living room table and grabbed a cider out of the fridge, deciding to watch my way through the *Resident Evil* films so I wouldn't have to make any other decisions regarding viewing material for the rest of the night. The food arrived over a period of about half an hour and I kept the first dishes warm in the oven until it was all present and correct. Then I spread my feast out on the table, pressed play, and set to with gusto.

Gauvain picked at some of the various meats, and Paladin just watched in amazement, as I did serious damage to the smorgasbord in front of me. By the time the first film finished I was definitely slowing down, then my stomach full light blinked on about halfway through the second. I belched loudly, which gave me just enough room to finish the chicken wing I was eating with G's help. I then reclined and loosened my belt with a satisfied sigh. OK, so I'd need to live on two salad leaves and a slice of tomato for the next few days, but damned if I didn't feel better for my blow-out.

After the second film finished, I forced myself to get up and clear away the remnants of my gluttony. Some went into the freezer, some the fridge, and I picked up a can of Tango while I was there. I had a new thought and reached down inside myself for the energy from everything I'd eaten. After a couple of tries I was able to transfer most of the energy into Seren, which thankfully removed the over-full feeling from my midriff. Not quite as good as harvesting from the trees around Lucian's pyramid, but definitely enjoyable and another option for future energy harvesting – eat too much and store the excess.

I drank my soda while I watched the news – hooray for the twenty-four-hour news channels – then went to bed. I lay there for a bit, still beating myself up for my scheduling snafu, while I looked for shapes in the random swirls on the ceiling. Then I turned onto my side and closed my eyes, trying to drift off to sleep. After failing dismally for a couple of hours, I got up and went into the lounge. I put the third film in the series on and sat down to watch it, then promptly fell asleep about five minutes in.

Oh well, that's what Blu-ray was for.

Chapter 29

The next morning, having been somewhat disorientated by waking up on the couch to the sounds of gunfire and explosions (the film had obviously kept restarting after it sat at the menu screen for a while), I dragged myself into the kitchen to make coffee. I winced at the sight of the accumulated take-out containers, then again as I remembered there were even more in the fridge and freezer. I was slightly cheered by recalling my new trick of transferring the extra energy to Seren, so at least I wouldn't have to go into battle against the Order looking like the Stay-Puft Marshmallow Man from *Ghostbusters*. However, the thought of eating that much even for a good cause made me feel slightly nauseated. I guess one just had to be in the mood.

I looked at Seren in the light of the slanted sunbeams pouring in through the kitchen window. The six pointed asterism blazed brightly, but I was now also able to subtly discern the image of the wings of Isis deep within, even though no energy was being put in (Pal was still asleep, having commandeered my bed as soon as I deserted it for the sofa last night). I had thought it was starting to approach a reasonable percentage of filling recently, however it had shown me just how mistaken I was. It seemed to have some kind of layering structure, maybe due to its crystalline nature, and as it had seemed to reach around fifteen percent (or so I thought) it had moved the energy to a different 'level' within itself. It was like a computer creating files within files within files, which simply proved to me that even the enormous quantities of power already stored within it were only a fraction of a percent of its total capacity.

I had definitely been woefully low in my estimation at Master Harfi's shop (the jeweller in Aaru who had created Seren for me). If this stone were filled completely and then broken, it would make Hiroshima, Nagasaki, Chernobyl, and Tunguska all combined look like the world's tiniest firecracker next to the birth of a new galaxy. My early-morning, pre-caffeine mind couldn't even begin to grasp the levels of power involved.

I turned to more practical matters, pouring myself a cup of coffee now the pot was beginning to fill, and drinking half of it in two big swallows. The slight scorch aided the wake-up punch, prompting me to head to the bedroom to get dressed for my run. Gauvain was just stretching as I went through the door, saying *Good morning, Gavan,* and shaking out his feathers in preparation for the day. Paladin, on the other hand, didn't stir himself until my pyjama shorts hit him full in the face in a scrunched up ball. Then his tail started thumping as he yawned hugely – a sight that would terrify anyone who didn't know him. His mouth was big enough to take my entire head in one bite, and his teeth looked fearsome enough to rival any monster movie wolf. I was truly glad he was on *my* side.

"Everyone ready for a jog?" I asked them, having laced up my sneakers with my traditional runner's double knot.

Are you sure you can still run, considering the impressive feast you consumed last evening? G asked jokingly, making me groan and rub my stomach dramatically.

"Ugh, don't remind me," I said, dropping my head to the left and closing my eyes briefly. "If I hadn't been able to shift most of the energy from it into Seren, I'd still be stranded on the couch like a beached whale! Remind me never to do that again."

I don't see the problem, Pal chimed in. *When there's lots of food, it only makes sense to eat as much as you can. You can always regurgitate some in a hidden storage for later.*

I knew wild wolves did exactly that, hence the term 'wolfing your food down', but the thought of eating my own vomit in that way nearly made my coffee put in an unwelcome repeat appearance of its own. I didn't dignify the comment with a response, instead I simply turned and led the way to the front door. I heard them both chuckling together in our shared mental link, and I smiled at their gentle teasing which was, in all honesty, well deserved after last night's gluttony.

G landed on my shoulder as I paused to unlock the door, and Pal leant against my hip eagerly. As soon as there was enough room, he pushed past me into the hall and danced back and forth like an excited puppy. Thankfully, after a few startled encounters, my neighbours were now somewhat used to the sight of my overgrown companions, though none were up and about just yet. Pal bounced down the stairs ahead of me, then charged off onto the grass opposite for a quick roll. Gauvain stretched his wings above his head then pushed off, flapping strongly to gain height before gliding on the early-morning thermals.

I stretched for a couple of minutes, then set off at my usual pace. I had already learned which were the oldest, most robust trees on my route, which enabled me to set a part of my mind to energy collection almost on autopilot. Other than G catching a grey squirrel for breakfast about halfway round, my run was as unremarkable as always since the Order's retreat across the great water. Pal and I met back up with Gauvain as he was finishing his breakfast, having flown the squirrel back to a tree near the apartment complex to eat. Then it was time to get more coffee, take a shower, and have a slice of toast with Marmite for breakfast, then dress for work.

I was surprised, upon my arrival in my office, to see someone had been in while I wasn't there. It was pretty well understood that my office was sacrosanct, even to the point of jokes among the staff over what kinds of deviant items and practices I enjoyed within its secret depths. It was something of a shock, therefore, to find a note set squarely in the centre of the leather writing surface. The fact that it was held in place by a cup of Cafegeddon, the steam still rising from the surface, told me who it had been and the probable contents of the unexpected missive. I braced myself for the worst with a big gulp of coffee, then headed out to face the music.

"Get. Back. In. There," came the angry voice from behind the counter. "I want a word with you!" I obediently turned around and did as directed, scurrying behind my desk as a means of taking cover from the whirlwind about to break. She might be small in stature, but I had never been in doubt regarding the size of her temper once roused. Summer strode up to my desk and planted her fists on the surface, leaning over them and thrusting her head forward threateningly.

"Did you seriously plan your attack against the Order stronghold for the same night as your date with Angelica?" she shrieked, making Gauvain add to the ear-splitting din with his own outraged cry at her pitch and volume. I lifted my hands to my ears protectively, which at least prompted her to moderate her voice somewhat, though her look was no less threatening.

"What kind of half-baked, incompetent, slack-jawed, misguided, idiotic, moronic, mentally impaired, dull-witted, fuzzy-brained, thick-skulled, fuck-faced dumbass would be so monumentally inept as to screw up the very thing he's been wanting and planning for over the last several weeks?!" She continued, elaborating colourfully on my grotesque stupidity and proceeding on to suppositions regarding my questionable heritage and how diversely unappealing it must be to have produced such a total moron.

I sat there and listened, shocked into silence by the voluminous terms she used combined with the non-stop, rapid-fire delivery. I also accepted everything she said without argument since when you got right down to it, her tirade was fuelled and justified by one inescapable fact: She was right.

She finally wound down after almost ten full minutes spent haranguing me. She sat down in a chair and stared at me from under her creased brow while trying to catch her breath.

"I know, I'm a dickhead," I replied simply, making her expression transition to surprise followed by pleased acceptance of my contrition. "I was so excited to get everything finally wrapped up with the Order, everything else went out of my head. Then, by the time I realised what a colossal fuck-up I'd caused, it was too late to change things. The faction heads were already gathering their forces for the Friday timetable, so I couldn't exactly ring them up and say, 'Oh, I'm *terribly* sorry and all that, chaps, but would you mind awfully postponing your long-awaited vengeance so I can go out with a young lady? Take in dinner and a show, and possibly have a good shag?' now could I?" Summer snickered at my upper-class British accent and the way I'd put my supposed reorganisation attempt, then sighed ruefully as she acknowledged the shit pile I'd blindly thrown myself into.

"No, I guess not," she allowed, at which I breathed a little easier knowing she wasn't going to go off into another blistering monologue. "Still, for the love of the goddess could you not just have thought for two seconds before you picked a date? I mean, holy shit, Gav, you seem to go out of your way to make life as difficult for yourself as possible sometimes, really you do."

"I know, I know!" I moaned dramatically, dropping my head onto the desk with a thump. "When I was talking to them, Friday just felt like such an important and auspicious day in my head I completely forgot to wonder *why!* It wasn't until I saw Angie's face when I announced it in The Sanctuary that I remembered, by which time it was too late."

We shared a moment of silence.

"So just out of curiosity," I continued, sitting up once. "Were you more pissed off at my stupidity, angry that I'd hurt Angie by my thoughtlessness, or upset at my ongoing self-destructiveness?" She laughed, then looked mischievously out of the corner of her eye at me.

"Yes," she said, then grinned. I laughed, since this was a running joke between us which meant 'all of the above' when someone gave you options you couldn't choose between. Plus, it was probably true that it was a close-run thing between the different choices, no doubt contributing to the prolific torrent of abuse I'd been subjected to.

"Yeah, yeah, I get it," I said, holding up my hands in surrender. "So what do I do to put it right? Chocolates, flowers, both, more?" I begged for the wisdom of her feminine perspective but this time, much to my dismay, she shook her head.

"Any of that would be too little, too late," she advised me regretfully. "Plus, it would make it look as though you could do what you wanted, then throw out some trinket or bauble and expect everything to be OK. It would make her feel unimportant and cheap, plus it sets a bad precedent for the future – if you still have one, which remains to be seen."

I nodded glumly, resting my elbows on the desk and dropping my head onto my hands. All I could do, apparently, was apologise and throw myself on the dubious mercy of the court. Then I would have to wait to see if I would be favoured with a reprieve and commuted sentence – or be condemned to death.

I sighed, then stood up and walked around the desk, holding my hand out to Summer to help her up and lead her out.

Time to face the firing squad.

Chapter 30

Apparently I had braced myself in vain since, much to my dismay, Angelica was conspicuous by her absence that morning. I snuck a look at the rota and saw she had rearranged her shifts this week to cover the nights with the twins. She was still off on Friday and over the weekend, but that meant I wouldn't see her again until the following week – unless I came in early, I considered, my Machiavellian streak rearing it's sneaky head.

Satisfied I now had a plan of attack for that aspect of my life, for once, I got on with my new routine of helping around the shop in the morning and preparing for the upcoming fight in the afternoon. The new opening hours were continuing to keep both The Sanctuary and the original Dinas Affaraon doing well. Summer and I had come up with a range of t-shirts aimed at the supernatural community, though they also seemed to be doing surprisingly well with some of the more 'fantasy' inclined youths of Yorkshire. Summer had suggested them after seeing something similar in some book she was reading, then we'd had fun coming up with our own original versions.

There were slogans such as 'Get a Taste for the Natural World – Start Lickin' a Wiccan!'; 'Get a Taste of Religion – Lick a Witch!'; 'Show your Love for Animals – Get Wild with a Were!'; and 'Love History – Bang a Fang!'. We'd laughed for ages coming up with the different rhyming pairs, though we hadn't been sure quite how well they'd do. We only ordered twenty-five of each, with Summer getting one of each for her and Emily as soon as they arrived.

To my surprise and delight, they'd sold like crazy. The staff now viewed them as the *de rigueur* 'uniform' shirts, each having a full set and exclusively wearing them for work. Then I'd had to invest in lanyards with the store logo on to identify real staff members, as the supernatural patrons all jumped on the bandwagon. The first order had run out just from staff purchases, so I'd ordered a thousand of each logo in assorted sizes and colours. Looking at the stock, I'd have to order more soon.

Another idea I'd had was to put up a suggestion box in the shop, so anyone could request items to be kept in regular stock. Every week I now emptied the box and went through the ideas, then put the best and most popular on a sheet by the register. Anyone making a purchase could then put a tick next to their favourite option. That would then become either a regular item if I thought it was worthwhile, or a temporary 'special offer' to see how well it sold. If it proved more popular than expected, it got added to regular stock; if it was just a 'flash in the pan', it was either a one-off or got placed on the list of rotating 'special items' that got featured for a week at a time depending on how poor the uptake was.

Once I'd done the stock review, smiling the whole time as I registered the levels of turnover, I did a general walk-around since I'd been shutting myself away much of the time recently. I touched base with all of the staff who were working today, checking if there were any concerns and complimenting them on how well we were doing. It was nice to see how smoothly people were getting on together, their drives to develop the shop coinciding with their desires to earn more money and lubricating their interactions.

It meant they had a real reason to work out any issues between themselves as quickly and smoothly as possible, so they had created a scheme whereby any disagreements got aired and analysed in a group setting that any one of them could convene. Then their issues got cleared up and everyone felt that this council-style resolution was equitable and fair, rather than biased from a single-person analysis.

Once I'd done my little impromptu review, I decided to have lunch and mingle with the customers in The Sanctuary. I didn't want to get the reputation for being aloof and inaccessible, otherwise everyone in the magickal community would start getting the wrong idea about me. I had no intention of my power making me into the next Elrulin, feared for what I might do if someone upset me. I wanted to be the opposite: The one people came to if they had a problem, the last port of call for the desperate among the various subcultures.

I smiled and waved at a few familiar faces as I enjoyed my chicken salad, relishing the ripple of chatter surrounding each of the recipients of my attention. It seemed my fame was growing, leading to interest from those who hadn't yet met me. That was another reason to be around – I'd rather people knew the truth about me instead of rumours starting and then getting horrendously distorted.

Once I'd finished my meal, I decided to try and take my mind off Angie by looking into the legends surrounding some of the Native American tribes. I'd only really been interested in finding the potential locations of the Order's new headquarters, so I'd skipped over the more esoteric legends in my reading. I hadn't even *started* examining the other book I'd got from Mr Davis. Now that we had the location it would be worth knowing if any legends from the area, or from other tribes seeing as they'd have power in the good ol' US of A, might be relevant or even just useful.

I pulled the Native American legends volume from my shelf and looked to see if there was an index of some kind. There wasn't, unfortunately, though I did discover that the contents page showed each chapter was regarding a single specific tribe. I leafed through to the section on the Ohlone people, who historically lived in the San Francisco Bay area. There wasn't much there, though I did discover that one of their legends related to the son of Coyote, named Kaknu, who closely resembled a peregrine falcon. I glanced at the door, thinking of G sitting out in the shop and basking in the adoration of the customers and staff. There was no way in *hell* I was going to tell him about this, or he'd never let me live it down.

I thought of Cheveyo next, someone I hadn't really managed to get to know very well thus far. I texted Seirina and asked her what tribe he hailed from, to which she replied that he was a member of the Algonquin tribe. Out of a desire to understand more about him, I turned to their chapter in the book. I discovered that the windigo I'd been attacked by was one of their legends, which must explain why Cheveyo had looked so angry and disgusted when he heard about it. He must have realised it implied one of his own tribe had been either blackmailed, suborned, or seduced by the Order.

I grabbed my phone and sent him a text. I asked if he had any idea of who might have been flipped by them, plus any clue as to how or why. I continued reading, realising he may or may not get back to me and even if he did, it might be hours or days. Imagine my surprise, therefore, when not only did I hear back from him quickly but it wasn't by text.

"Gavan Maddox speaking, hello?" I said, answering my phone and putting it on speaker without looking to see who was ringing.

"My uncle," came the impassioned voice, confusing the crap out of me since there was no preamble to give me any context. "My uncle was the one those bastards got the secrets from!"

"Huh, what?" I asked, looking up from the page I was reading. "Cheveyo?"

"Yes," he snapped. "Of course it's me. You sent me a text, I'm answering."

"Wait, you said your *uncle* told the Order about windigos?" I asked incredulously. "Why would he do that?"

"He didn't exactly choose it!" he snapped. "The shaman they recruited kidnapped him and *tortured* the information out of him. Then they dumped his mutilated body at the gates of the reservation! So now you know why I took so long to get you your precious Alcatraz information – we had to have his funeral. *That's* why I felt the need to take some time at every spiritual site you sent me to! You happy now? Those Order assholes tortured and killed my uncle and corrupted my tribe's legends and magicks."

"Cheveyo, I'm so sorry," I told him sincerely. "If you'd told me, of course I'd have eased off and given you time. Do you know who their shaman is?" I heard Cheveyo growl over the phone.

"He's a piece of shit Iroquois shaman called Oneidah," he told me. "Most of us have given up on the old tribal feuds and rivalries since the government shafted us and stuck us on reservations – oh, but we can own casinos so that makes *everything* OK. This prick, however, seems obsessed with his 'noble Iroquois heritage', which led to him finding out about the old bad blood between them and the Algonquins. He seems to think he's honouring his ancestors by having a mad on for every other tribe, us in particular. He's refused to share any knowledge with the few surviving shaman bloodlines, even going so far as to withdraw from our shared council."

Cheveyo's anger, sarcasm, and raw hatred flowed across the phone, yet there was something I'd seen that nagged in my mind.

"Hang on," I said, flipping back to the contents page in the book I was reading. "I thought Oneida was the name of a tribe, not one person."

"I'm impressed," Cheveyo said. "Not many people know that. The tribe was one of the five founding nations of the Iroquois confederacy. He spells his with an 'h' at the end, but it's a name that's sometimes used for boys as well as for the tribe. Regardless, he's an asshole who's always wanted a way to get more power. He wants to prove *his* tribe's magick is better than anyone else's."

"Well, one good thing about our upcoming trip to The Rock:" I said, wanting to try and give him something to focus on. "At least you get to kill that son of a bitch! I'll even help, if I can, though I promise to save the final blow for you."

"Deal!" he snapped out with such eagerness and ferocity, I sat back in my chair momentarily.

"Just don't let your desire to kill him get *you* killed," I said cautiously. "There's no point losing your head and rushing into things, otherwise you'll end up getting yourself killed and leave your vengeance for your uncle unfulfilled."

"Oh, don't worry," he said, turning deadly calm. "I'm not gonna do *anything* to put that at risk. That motherfucker is *not* getting away with what he's done."

"Well, thanks for the information," I said. "Though I'm sorry I brought up such a painful topic. I'll see you on Friday before we head to Alcatraz."

We said our goodbyes and hung up. One more mystery cleared up, however messily it opened yet another can of worms, and another ally with a powerfully personal reason to fight alongside us. At this rate I'd end up having to watch our allies more than those we were fighting, otherwise they'd put themselves in danger trying to get their revenge.

After all, didn't they always say 'before setting out for revenge, first dig *two* graves'? I was definitely going to have to keep an eye on some of the more hot-headed of my new friends.

Ah well, for now it was back to the research.

Chapter 31

Much to my chagrin I forgot to set my alarm that night, ending up sleeping in until almost nine the next morning. So much for my genius plan to get to the shop early to see Angie. I let myself off, bearing in mind the number of different considerations I was currently juggling. I was going to be seriously relieved to get this Friday's fight over and done with, and not just because of the chance to finally put an end to the threat posed by Elrulin and his organisation.

This whole shit-show had spun my life so far out of its previous comfortable rut, I knew for certain it would never find its way fully back. Not just because I had magick now, and not simply due to the radical changes my business had undergone. No, the main reason my life had been irrevocably spun off its axis was the awakening I had experienced. Not the magickal – that had been wonderful and a fulfilment of my life's dreams and efforts. No, it was the new awareness of the wider world and the peoples who inhabited it that had shifted my perspective so significantly.

I was so deep in my own thoughts about all these new experiences, I almost knocked someone over while I was on my run. I brought my attention back to the present quickly enough to apologise, and also notice the attractive smile that was rapidly obscured by a swirl of platinum blonde hair. I was left to contemplate the seductive chuckle and saucy hip swing as she jogged away from me, the light woodsy note of her perfume lingering behind her.

I almost felt guilty over the sudden tightening of my shorts, yet I still watched as her athletic stride carried her around the corner and away from my sight. I once heard a wise man remark, 'it doesn't matter where I get my appetite, as long as I eat at home'. I did note, however, that he was careful to say it out of his wife's hearing. Gauvain chuckled in my head at my tangential thought process, making me join in self-deprecatingly. I shook my head ruefully, then set off to finish my run.

After a shower and shave, I got dressed and arrived in my office by about half past ten. I went out to see everything running with its now accustomed increased activity, yet the ever-present smooth efficiency Summer had always attained had never faltered. The new staff had stepped up to her benchmark, meeting her expectations early on for fear of being on the receiving end of her whiplash tongue when they fell short. As someone who had felt that upbraiding on a number of occasions, despite being the titular boss, I knew full-well what a stimulating drive the wish to avoid her displeasure could be.

I smiled at the young man behind the counter, nodding to him but saying nothing so as not to distract him from the customer he was serving. I walked around Gauvain's perch at the end of the counter, feeling him squeeze my shoulder briefly before hopping off to survey and be admired. I went into the original kitchenette and picked up the coffee pot, pleased to note it was almost full. I got my thirty-two ounce insulated mug out of the overhead cupboard and filled it, inhaling the welcome aroma of Cafegeddon.

I luxuriated in that first mouthful for a moment, centering myself for the day. As I exited, I looked into The Sanctuary and stopped short. The same attractive young woman I had seen several times was back again, laughing with the staff, and this time I recognised her as the same woman I'd almost run into earlier. She was also the same woman from the stairwell in the town centre, back on my shopping trip with Summer and Emily. Was she stalking me or something?

I snorted in disbelief, freely acknowledging the obvious fact that she was attractive enough to gain the attention of anyone she wanted. I had no illusions regarding my own level of pulchritude: In my opinion I was, at best, a solid seven-point-five. *Maybe* an eight on a good day, when I took the time over my appearance. Hell, I might even push it to eight-and-a-half in my new suit. She, on the other hand, would be a nine-and-three-quarters when she was in her scruffiest sweats, with red eyes and a stuffy nose from the flu.

Her stalking me would be the equivalent of Gal Gadot becoming obsessed with the hunchback of Notre Dame.

OK, maybe not *quite* that severe, but you get the idea. Then again, she had been spending an inordinate amount of time here recently, along with just 'happening' to turn up in several places where I was at the time. So was she interested in me, or was she *interested* in me? Was she trying to see what sort of person I was, what sort of man I was, or what sort of boss I was? What was her end-game in all this? Did she know about my interest in Angelica? Was she put off, politely interested, or challenged?

A man could go crazy(-er) trying to figure out the inner workings of a woman's mind, and that was just for a woman he already knew reasonably well. For a stranger, it was more like trying to hit a fly by throwing another fly while riding blindfolded on a wild stallion that was driven mad by fire ants biting its testicles.

You know, just *once* I'd like to have something simple in my life. Then again, they do say nothing good comes easy, and everything worth having is worth fighting for. So did that mean my relationship with Angelica was worth having, or was it simply me chasing after something that no longer existed? Was I just chasing a memory? Would I be better off abandoning an ephemeral possibility, or should I prove my intent with immovable stoicism?

If I gave up at the first hurdle, was I even worthy of a relationship with such a woman? And by that, did I mean Angie or this enigmatic stranger? I had a headache already, and I'd been here for all of about five minutes. The only way to deal with this, I decided, was to forget about women in general for now. Outside of their fighting capabilities, I had to ignore their more... 'distracting' characteristics until Friday's battle was over and done with.

Still, maybe I'd get lucky and either get a concussion or a mind-wipe of my own. Maybe even not make it through at all. Oh joy, my ever-present and oh-so-helpful pessimism was back. I turned on my heel and went back to the office. I stepped past the semi-sentient rug, also known as Paladin, who was currently lolling halfway out of his more than ample bed. The main hazard was the pool of drool flowing off his tongue as he snored. I grabbed a few tissues from the box on my desk to dry up the puddle once I'd ensured my coffee was safely set down.

Once the floor was no longer an ice rink I slumped into my chair, bouncing on the hydraulics. I dropped my head back and closed my eyes, trying to find the calm centredness I had once enjoyed in here. It seemed as though ever since Angie had first sat down opposite me, the entire atmosphere of my own private sanctuary had vanished like early morning mist under a summer sun.

I took a deep breath, reassured that at least my coffee had remained constant, and turned on my computer. I emptied the spam folder of the usual 'dating' invites, then checked the status on a couple of eBay items I was bidding on. One was a pair of antique bookends, something to prop up some volumes on one of the less filled shelves. The other was an antique desktop set of inkwells. Both had over a week left to run, so I was holding off bidding until nearer the time. No sense advertising my interest too early and driving the price up.

That done, I started researching the current buildings on Alcatraz. I looked up the prison, used the satellite mode on Google Maps, anything I could think of to get an idea of the lay of the land. I spent the morning committing the geography of the island to memory, along with various tales of the tunnels underground. If the movie was to be believed, those were a maze of shit from all the rebuilding over the years. Shame I couldn't take Sean Connery with me as a guide. Mind you, that could be extremely distracting for the women – no, let's leave him out of this.

I could tell I was reaching the end of any worthwhile concentration, given the wandering of my mental processes. I looked up to realise my cup was empty, my bladder was full, and my stomach wanted lunch. I stretched, then stood up and picked up my mug. Once I'd washed it in the kitchenette, I made a beeline for the little boy's room. I admired my work in the fine finish as I washed my hands after completing my business, pleased the facilities were staying clean and well maintained. My mother had always said you could judge the true quality of a place by the bathrooms, and I was happy with what these said about my little corner of the world.

I decided on a hot steak-and-cheese baguette from The Sanctuary for lunch, along with some of their wonderful spicy potato wedges. My enigmatic stalker had made herself scarce, though there were plenty of others around who looked my way from time to time. If this kept up, certainly if it worsened after the coming battle, I was going to have to start eating in my office if I wanted any peace. All this attention was bad for the digestion, in my opinion.

I also needed to find some way of determining the difference between curiosity, admiration, and a number of less savoury emotions. I knew telepathy was one way, but did I really want to get used to reading anyone and everyone around me? Such invasion of privacy was distasteful in the extreme, though I felt a ripple of amusement at my childish naïveté across my link with Iyrin. That single reminder of its parasitic attachment to me helped me focus yet another reason into my desire to finish all this.

Deep inside, I held onto the glimmer of hope offered by Lucian's promise to help me break Iyrin's bond with me. I was looking forward to the prospect of privacy again, which would allow me to try and have a relationship without something 'tasting' my emotions at each point. Who any such relationship might be with remained to be seen, though if my scoresheet this week was any indication it might be with someone quite different from who I first imagined only a few days ago.

I just had to hope that all the effort I was expending to rid the magickal communities from the Order's influence and threat might at least count for something. Maybe even enough to offset my extreme klutziness by scheduling a major battle and a first date on the same night. I shook my head in disbelief at my own stupidity yet again, though whether it truly was stupidity or just latent self-destructive tendencies remained to be seen.

I bussed my dishes and went back to my office, deciding to take some time to relax. I opened my Kindle and chose to re-read *The Complete Sherlock Holmes*, enjoying the old familiar setting of the Baker Street apartment. The fighting would begin soon enough. It would be nice to take some time to remember and enjoy some of what we were fighting for.

I sat back, losing myself in the twists and turns of *A Study in Scarlet*.

Chapter 32

When Friday morning finally rolled round, I wasn't sure if I would make it through the day. Thankfully I wasn't at work (bollocks, I still hadn't managed to catch up with Angie), otherwise I'd have had everyone 'checking in' to make sure I was OK. Given I was decidedly *not* alright, as my knotted stomach was making me very aware, I was better off keeping myself to myself. I managed to force some water past the lump in my throat, then set out for my 'non-work' double-length run.

Damn it, my stride was off because of how tense I felt and I almost twisted my ankle on a stray stick from being so distracted. My run wouldn't do me any good like this, so I tried to push everything else away by falling back on my old anxiety standby: counting. I had done this when I was a child, as a way of trying to make some sense and order out of a world that seemed to have none of either. I rarely did it now, however. Still, the rhythm felt like an old, familiar sweatshirt on a cold day, and I soon noticed myself feeling looser and my stride evening out.

I counted steps, breaths, trees, cars, anything I noticed to take me out of my own head. By the time I finished my first circuit, I was running with my accustomed relaxed gait, so as I passed the door of the apartment complex I picked up the pace. Now I deliberately focused on the upcoming battle, using my anger to fuel my exertions. I barely noticed how fast I was going until I rounded a corner to see one of my more elderly neighbours coming out of the village shop up ahead. She startled at the sight of me, almost stumbling, though I was moving so quickly I managed to get to her and steady her before she fell.

"Sorry I startled you," I said, picking up an orange which had dropped from the top of her bag. "Here, don't forget this."

"Thank you," she said, then eyed me beadily. "Now, on you go. If you're here then you still have a way to go on your run. I often see you out my kitchen window when I'm making tea," she explained, in answer to my surprise at her knowledge of my habits. She must be one of those little old ladies police always pray for when they're canvassing for witnesses on those ubiquitous mystery shows. I just hoped she hadn't seen the windigo!

I smiled and nodded, then sped off again. The sheer normality of the interaction had been a nice change of pace to my life recently, allowing me to finish my run with a smile on my face. Then, as I went up the stairs behind the shambling mass of Paladin's furry dog butt, the memory of her charming innocence reminded me of all the families Elrulin had already torn apart; plus how many more would be harmed or destroyed if we didn't stop him tonight. The smile faded away from my lips and I went to get my shower.

The hot water went some way to restoring my equanimity, the fresh pot of Cafegeddon ready and waiting afterwards completing the process. I knew today was going to be a rollercoaster of emotions, though hopefully I could level it out as much as possible. Since I didn't have my date to prepare for, I tried to get my mind in order by getting my home in order. I cleaned, tidied, washed, even sorted out the omnipresent kitchen junk drawer that almost everyone seems to have. I barely ate anything for lunch, just grabbing a leftover slice of pizza that I found lurking in the back of the fridge. Gauvain also refused anything, not wanting to be weighed down for the fight.

As it drew close to the time I'd set for us to head to San Francisco, I got myself ready. I put on jeans and a t-shirt, older but still perfectly serviceable, since I had a funny feeling my outfit was going to suffer during the fighting. I buckled Muharar onto my left hip and put a pair of skeleton karambits into a sheath at the small of my back. I'd ordered them ages ago as something to practise with when doing my katas, and they were vicious little hooked blades with a ring for my index and little finger on each hand.

They could be used with the blade either at the thumb side or by the little finger, my preference being for the latter, and turned a punch into a flesh-ripping nightmare capable of opening major blood vessels and severing tendons. They weren't magically attuned like my sword, but they'd still be amazingly useful if the fighting got to the hand-to-hand stage.

I had Gauvain on my left shoulder and Paladin sitting by my right side as I stood waiting for the text from Cheveyo, the one with the picture I needed to teleport to him. Then we could bring all our forces directly to us through portals I would open, much as I had done on the Yorkshire Moors. The muted *beep* from my phone came right on time, showing me the inside of a vacant warehouse. I teleported there, checking to see it was deserted but for myself and Cheveyo. The door was open and the sight and sound of the docks told me he'd found or hired somewhere as close to Alcatraz as he could on the mainland.

Thankfully, the warehouse gave us cover for the vampires (not that they were anywhere near as sensitive as most supposed, as I had previously learned) as well as a measure of secrecy to gather our forces.

"G, while I'm getting everyone here, why don't you do a little aerial reconnaissance of the island for us," I said, stroking my friend. "Stay as high as you can while still being able to see, though. I don't want you triggering some defensive ward or even being attacked if they notice you. See if you can pick out a good spot for us to land on, as well as any obvious defences they've set up or changes they've made."

Of course, he replied. *It will be a pleasure to have a more physical role this time. The last two incursions have had me watching through your eyes, incapable of any direct participation. I relish the chance to play a more practical part.*

He leapt into the air, beating his wings strongly and rising up into the sky. Despite his size, he was soon lost among the seagulls and other birds as his height caused him to look smaller and – hopefully – unnoticeable by anyone who might be watching. My heart swelled with pride once again at being bonded to such an amazing creature, and I felt his gratitude, appreciation, and love washing back across our link as he acknowledged my thought. I tried to keep a part of my mind set aside to monitor what he was seeing but within a few minutes, he told me to stop. He rather snippily informed me he was more than capable of looking around without supervision, and he would let me know if there was anything worthy of my attention.

I apologised, though admittedly I sent him a little burst of the irritation I felt at being treated as a hindrance, then turned back to Cheveyo. I complimented him on his selection of location, both for its surveillance and concealment capabilities, then we started contacting the various groups who were waiting to join us. He sent messages to the shaman council and Sovereign, I contacted the weres, vampires, and Wiccans. As the replies came in, I opened portals into the warehouse for the different factions to arrive through.

Eligos arrived by his own means, needing no help from me to get where he needed to. He informed me his forces were awaiting his orders, though thankfully he hadn't brought them here to avoid overcrowding the location. I was even more thankful that since we didn't need multiple telepaths for this fight, Iyrin could stay safely in its glass-walled home in Seirina's study. I could tell by the vibrations across our link that it would nonetheless be paying close attention, ready to feed off any emotions the upcoming battle might generate.

Despite its size, the warehouse rapidly became crowded with the number of people who had joined us to exterminate this blight on the magickal world. There were even more weres than there had been for the Edinburgh assault, including wolves, felines, and bears. There were at least ten times as many vampires, most of whom were American and all of whom were – at least, so Dominic said – over four centuries old. The Wiccan contingent consisted of dozens of covens from across Europe and the US, though I was less than enthusiastic about seeing the ever-cheerful Seb again. Fortunately, he took one look around at the accumulated mass of humanity and stalked outside. He stood, arms crossed and brow furrowed, staring across the bay at our target.

I could kind of understand, since the crowd was beginning to feel oppressive for me as well, even though I was glad we had so many to help us take the fight to the Order. I, however, didn't have the option of being moody and taciturn since I was expected to lead this whole insane *mishegas*. Yes, OK, I know that's a redundancy. Kind of like 'stupid idiot' or 'crazy nutjob'. Still, it fit with how I was feeling so I refuse to apologise. Finally the only group left to come were the obeahs, along with Seirina, and their resurrected, rancid, rambling, rotting regiment. Yeah, yeah, the nerves were setting off my alliteration thing again.

Just as I was about to open their portal, Gauvain suddenly notified me about something out of place he had picked up on. Since I wasn't exactly relishing having a bunch of corpses standing around, I texted them to stand by and I went to stand outside next to (oh joy) Seb. According to the satellite pictures on Google Maps, the east end of the island had a paved or concrete-covered area labelled as the parade ground. At the very tip, it looked like there was a bunch of bushes or trees. Gauvain told me there had been a change from the images we had seen during our research, namely the appearance of a dragon.

Fortunately not a flesh and bone dragon, instead a beautifully carved wooden sculpture. When G showed me the image of what he had seen, it jogged a memory of something I'd read in passing when I had been doing some earlier research. Apparently a local artist near Bolton Castle had carved the twenty-foot-long dragon from a fallen ash tree, where it had become an additional tourist attraction in the area. It seemed Elrulin had either bought or, more likely, stolen it and brought it with him as a spoil of war. Funny, I thought the victor got the spoils. I guess Elrulin was still cheating, taking whatever he wanted whenever he chose.

I swore aloud, my irritation at yet more evidence of Elrulin's selfish high-handedness prompting my unguarded outburst.

"Hey, I was just standing out here minding my own business," Seb complained, rounding on me from his vantage point overlooking the bay. "You're the one who disturbed *me*, so why the hell am *I* the bastard?"

"Huh?" I said, momentarily lost. Then I realised he had overheard my name-calling and thought I'd directed it at him. "No, sorry, I was referring to Elrulin not you. Gauvain, my hawk friend, has been conducting some overhead surveillance for us and he's spotted something on the island. Elrulin stole the ash dragon sculpture from near Bolton Castle and now he's got it, sat in pride of place on the parade ground like some kind of trophy."

"Fucking people," he swore. "Always thinking they can do whatever they want. The damned sculptor should never have desecrated the poor tree in the first place, then that asshole thinks he can just take it from its home and drag it halfway across the world just because he wants it!"

Seb was getting worked up yet again at the high-handedness of humans over the environment, then suddenly his eyes locked on some point in the distance and an almost scary grin stole across his mouth.

"Wait, a *wooden dragon*?" he mused, suddenly uncharacteristically gleeful. "Do you think you could help me and some of my colleagues with an idea I've just had? Between your power and our affinity with nature, we just might be able to gain a powerful ally and piss Elrulin off at the same time."

Ooh, this sounded interesting.

Chapter 33

Seb turned away and went into the warehouse, walking with a spring in his step I had never seen from him before. Given the way he'd spoken, I had a sneaking suspicion of what his plan was. I had a supplementary idea of my own to both enhance his scheme and also, I hoped, give him something to smile about for a change. I started making some preparations, based on my guess of Seb's brainwave, assisted by Gauvain who agreed with and fully supported my idea. I also remembered to set up the portal for the obeahs and their stinky squadron to come through, hoping we wouldn't have to suffer their oppressive odour for too long.

"Mr Maddox?" came a voice from behind me, as I stood gazing absently out over the water. "Sebastian asked me to let you know he's ready."

"Thank you," I replied, turning and following the young lady who'd spoken. I didn't recognise her, so assumed she must be one of the multitude of new additions. She led me across to where the group of Wiccans were gathered, forming a series of seven concentric circles around a central individual. Seb was the man in the middle, sitting cross-legged on the floor with his eyes closed. The young lady I'd followed cleared her throat, at which Seb opened his eyes and looked over at me.

"This will definitely work," he said, sounding a little strained by maintaining his focus. "Fortunately the dragon was carved from a tree near my own home, so our vibrations are closely attuned. Far more so than the cock-sucker who stole it. We just need you to add some power.

We're trying to bring the dragon to a semblance of life, so I can then direct it to fight on your side. That way we can actually help in the battle, rather than just standing by to heal anyone who might or might not need it."

"That sounds great," I said. "But won't it take a lot of focus? Would it not be better to give it a life of its own so it could fight without all of you having to power and direct it?"

The subtle murmuring from the circled Wiccans faltered and gradually ceased as they realised what I was proposing.

"Umm, the level of power that would take is way beyond us," Seb said, suddenly looking at me with a new fear in his eyes. Most of the new members of his group looked mildly amused, no doubt thinking me hopelessly naïve and uninitiated for my idea. Some of the returning members were whispering amongst themselves, however, with the tales they were sharing rapidly spreading amongst the newbies.

"I think you underestimate yourselves," I told them, pleased to see my subtle praise of their abilities making many of them sit up straighter and prouder. "You believe plants are aware and have a degree of consciousness, correct?"

"Of course," Seb agreed, taking a deep breath to prepare for one of his infamous rants. I was quick to jump in and cut him off before he could get going, smothering a grin as I saw a couple of grins or sighs of relief as I did.

"Great, so all we need to do is enhance that," I elaborated. "I was thinking about it outside, basing my idea on my guess of what you had planned. I'm going to join you in the centre, Seb, and if all of you can focus on me, I'll then focus on the dragon. I'll rest my hands on your shoulders and use that connection to link the dragon to you, if that's OK, Seb?"

All of them nodded, Seb giving another of his uncharacteristic smiles. The atmosphere became charged with excited expectation as I stepped carefully through the circles to join him in the middle. I knelt down behind Seb *seiza* style, just as I would in a dojo, then laid my hands on his shoulders as I had said. I closed my eyes, linking to Gauvain to see the dragon through his vantage point, and also sensing Seb through my palms.

I was inundated by a wash of power as the Wiccans started chanting again, focusing their attention on me this time rather than Seb as they had before. I reached into Seren, the amount in the stone making the Wiccans' contributions seem like a squirt gun in a monsoon (not that I was going to tell *them* that). I reached towards the sculpture, feeling for the spark of life residing in the wood. I used Seb's certainty, combined with my own ideas based on film representations such as *Day of the Triffids* and Audrey Two from *Little Shop of Horrors*, to guide and enhance that spark into a unique consciousness. I created a link, formed from my knowledge of my own bond to Gauvain, pairing the dragon with Seb.

I heard Seb gasp as the dragon accepted and strengthened the bonding, both of them exploring the joining with joy and love. I poured power into the dragon, giving it life and shaping its development. There were a few abilities Seb would discover as they got to know each other, plus several that would become apparent during the battle. I had already come up with a name while I was outside, aiming for something based around an appellation meaning light. I had settled on Lukasz, so used that to coalesce the dragon's new life and awareness and anchor it into the form we were creating for it. I heard Seb repeat the name, accepting and approving it, and thus cementing it for the new being.

I withdrew from the link, lifting my hand from Seb's shoulders and holding them up to stop the chanting. Seb let out a joyous whoop almost simultaneously, scrambling to his feet and dashing for the door. Everyone trailed him out to the dock, following his eager stare across the bay towards Alcatraz Island. We all heard a roar echoing over the water, then a flurry of movement could be seen at the eastern end of the island.

A figure leapt into the air, opening wings that shone green in the rays of the setting sun. It circled up, then headed towards us. Several of the non-Wiccans seemed to be utterly confused as to what was happening, only having come out of the warehouse from a sense of curiosity at the mad rush. They cried out in fear at seeing a dragon flying our way, many of them diving for the door to get back inside, though the Wiccans let out such a cheer it seemed to reassure most of them. Seb shouted out the fledgeling dragon's name and reached up with both his arms as if to catch him. I smiled to see Gauvain keeping pace with Lukasz and held my breath, hoping to see the ability I'd tried to give our new baby manifest itself.

As Lukasz drew nearer, the green of his wings was revealed to be leaves, arranged along branches in the same way as a bird's wing was structured with bones and feathers. I'd guided that formation since I had become extremely familiar with the anatomy of an avian limb thanks to my time with Gauvain. At least seeing him spread his wings out to preen so often had finally paid off! Lukasz's tail had spikes at the end similar to a stegosaurus, though his looked to be giant thorns rather than bone like a dinosaur. His teeth, easily seen as he roared his joy into the evening air, were similarly thorns and looked to be needle sharp. I'd wanted the leaves on his wings, as that would allow him to use sunlight for energy, just as a tree would, so he would be self-sustaining.

As Lukasz drew closer, even the Wiccans began to be slightly apprehensive. Clearly they were wondering how and where their new friend would land, since they didn't know what I'd done as we breathed life into the sculpture. Just as even I began doubting, I let out the breath I'd been holding in a rush of relief. Lukasz shrank as he covered the last twenty feet to Seb, condensing down to roughly the size of an adult chameleon (just under two feet long). He landed on Seb's left shoulder with his back legs, folding his wings to his back and then dropping his front legs onto Seb's right shoulder with his body around the back of Seb's neck. Lukasz's tail wrapped Seb's neck loosely, the thorns at the end folding flat to prevent stabbing his new bond-mate. His scales were the exact brown of ash tree bark, perfectly in keeping with his origins, though they seemed to soften where they rubbed against his new friend.

Seb turned to stare at me, his right hand rising to rest on Lukasz's head, his eyes brimming with tears of wonder and gratitude. His mouth worked to form words but nothing came out, clearly overwhelmed by the storm of emotions caused by the new bond. I well-remembered how powerful those were from my bonding to G, who alighted on my shoulder as I thought back to that special moment. He rubbed his head against my cheek and I felt his love and happiness mirror my own across our own special bond.

Suddenly a new voice appeared in my mind, sounding totally different from the deep voice I had expected from a dragon. It sounded like a combination of branches rubbing with overtones of leaves rustling, higher pitched and softer than I thought it would be having seen how large and formidable Lukasz appeared in full form.

Thank you for your wonderful gift, he said, blinking his pale green eyes at me. *We're both overwhelmed by your generosity, though Seb seems to be having a little trouble expressing it.*

I heard Lukasz chuckle and saw Seb turn to look at his face, the biggest smile I'd ever seen from Seb lighting him up like a lantern.

"You're most welcome," I told them both. "Though don't forget to thank the other Wiccans. It would have been much more difficult without their help and support." Seb immediately nodded to his gathered compatriots, though Lukasz kept his gaze firmly on me.

You're very kind but I know the truth, he said, narrowing his thoughts so only I would hear him. *You provided the power, the skill, and the knowledge. Without you, their efforts would probably have been able to make the sculpture I was born from move, but I would have become no more than a marionette. They would have quickly become exhausted, at which point I would have lapsed back into immobility once again without ever knowing more.*

They don't need to ever know that, I told him just as subtly, making sure Seb wasn't aware of our exchange. I appreciated the acknowledgement, however unnecessary, but I didn't want Lukasz's awareness of my true abilities passing on to Seb. He agreed silently with a subtle wink, then tucked his head under Seb's chin. Seb looked like a child who'd had a dozen birthdays, Christmases, *Hanukkahs*, *Bar Mitzvahs*, and graduations all come at once, his previous miserable reticence buried in the elation of his new experience. For the sake of the other Wiccans, as much as for the new pairing, I hoped this joy lasted for the rest of his life.

I gently guided Seb back inside, since he was utterly entranced by Lukasz and completely taken up by admiring him. Thankfully everyone else followed, either to admire the new arrival or simply out of prudence, since Lukasz's awakening and flight would undoubtedly have alerted the Order to our presence and shown them where we were. I was just as concerned over the revelation of our presence to our enemy, though the lift Lukasz had given our forces was more than worth it.

Still, there was no benefit to be gained by any further delay so as everyone re-joined their various groups, I went up a set of rickety old metal stairs against one wall. The stairs led to an equally rusted catwalk halfway up the warehouse. I banged on the metal railing with my keys, creating a ringing peal to draw everyone's attention.

"Well, as wonderful as our new ally's arrival is," I called out, once the noise had abated. "I think any chance of a surprise attack is certainly out the window now." I waited for the chuckles to die down before I delivered the final attack order.

"So everyone get your shit together," I yelled, raising my fist. "It's time to get this party started!

"We attack in five!"

Chapter 34

Yeah, fine, so I sounded like a cheese-ball. The point was to get them all fired up and raring to go. We all knew this was going to be tough, and there was always a chance of not coming back, but we'd made the decision to put an end to the Order for the sake of the entire magickal world. It was time to put up or shut up, fish or cut bait, put our money where our mouths were, step up to the plate, put our game faces on, rally the troops, shit or get off the pot... OK, you get the idea.

While I'd been outside, I had adjusted my vision into the magickal spectrum as I'd learned back in Aaru and assessed the island. As expected, the Order – or more precisely, Elrulin – had created wards to completely cover the prison and its environs. That was why I'd said five minutes: I had a plan to bring down the wards. It was overblown, dramatic, reckless, and foolhardy, but if it worked it would be amazingly cool. I sent Gauvain back out to keep an eye on the island while I made my preparations.

I *had* to bring the wards down, otherwise our zombie army would be incapacitated just as quickly as it had been in Edinburgh. Still, at least I now had an idea of how their wards were constructed. I'd studied them at the UK bases when we were looking for any information on the location of this new headquarters, so I knew I'd be able to bring them down. It was just a case of finding the most expedient method, which I'd already had an idea about.

I knew their wards would be aimed at keeping us away, so they'd probably be focused at ground level. I had seen they'd formed a bubble to try to avoid any means of access, however, which had given me my idea. If there was a weak point, it would be up at the top of the dome, so that was where I was going to try my luck. My hope was that I'd be able to slice through the wards using Muharar, much as I had with the lock on Alcina's cell, and the shock of rupturing them plus a little extra push would enable me to bring them down completely. It was a total Hail Mary but if I didn't give this everything I had, I knew I'd never forgive myself if we failed.

I got everyone to establish a clear space by the main loading door of the warehouse, which was where I'd open the portal if I was successful. Then, taking a fresh look at the view from Gauvain's overhead surveillance, I took a deep breath and teleported. As planned, I came out far above the island and started to drop. I drew Muharar and altered my vision to see exactly where the border of the wards was, then focused my power along my blade.

I had already practiced using my telekinesis to levitate myself – something I'd thought of when looking down from the top of Lucian's pyramid and envisioning being thrown off by a pissed off devil. I was therefore able to control my fall and at the right moment, I swung my sword with all my strength.

There was a huge flash and a *crack* like a rubber band snapping, then I was spinning somersaults in the wake of Muharar's momentum. I slowed the rotation and arrested the rate of my fall before I pancaked, then I made the decision to ham it up as much as I could. I held my sword out at arm's length to my right, just above shoulder level, the blade horizontal and pointing diagonally forward across my body. My left fist was balled up and used to brace my landing. My right leg was angled at ninety degrees and my left was under me so I landed on that knee, in a full-on Iron Man pose.

"Superhero landing!" I yelled at the top of my voice, so elated with the success of my gambit I couldn't resist quoting Deadpool, then I stood up and threw my arms wide. I ripped through space to open a huge portal behind me, from the loading dock of the warehouse to Alcatraz Island, then heard the cheer of the assembled warriors as they saw my triumphant pose. I didn't care about the noise, since the ear-splitting crack of the wards shattering had pretty much given away any chance of a surprise sneak attack.

As planned, the zombie horde was the first wave through. The two trolls that had been patrolling the parade ground, having been driven to the floor by the magickal backlash from my less-than-subtle entrance, were just getting up when the tidal wave of pus and putrescence poured over them. Their size gave them an advantage, and they'd just begun to fight free of the horde when Lukasz flew over my head. As he passed me and soared up into the air, he rapidly grew back to his full size. His roar froze the trolls, making them look from where the sculpture had been (and where all that remained was the carved knight's leg from its mouth) up to where Lukasz hung above them in the lights from the prison.

I watched expectantly, knowing fire was a bad idea for a *wooden* dragon, yet wondering just how he was planning to attack. He reared back, opened his mouth, and unleashed a lethal torrent of thorns similar to those in his tail. They shredded the trolls' flesh, pinning their ventilated corpses to the concrete. I winced for a moment at the sheer unadulterated violence and lethality, then shrugged. They were knowingly supporting Elrulin, so they deserved what they got.

In the time it had taken for Lukasz to obliterate the first line of defence, the alarm – which must have been raised by the ear-splitting noise of my destruction of their defensive spells – had drawn Order members from all around the prison. They came streaming out from every entrance I could see, plus some I couldn't.

Some of the larger and more monstrous creatures were jumping straight down from the building where the lighthouse was, shaking the ground as they landed. I sincerely hoped they were sending most of their forces to meet us here, because if this was just the first level of their defence, we were in much deeper shit than I'd realised.

I was just about to charge into the fray when Seirina stepped through the portal, her eyes glowing green as she directed her skeletal assassins. She laid her hand on my shoulder and held me back, prompting me to look at her. She shook her head gently.

"You need to hang back," she said. "I know you want to rush in and protect everyone but remember, they're all here to take their own revenge on the Order for everything they've suffered. It wouldn't be fair for you to rob them of that. Besides, we need you to assist where you're needed, not just barrel in and get caught up."

"Very sensible," came another voice from the portal. "As the commander, it's now time to oversee from the back, rather than lead from the front. That way you can maintain a wider perspective and redistribute your forces where they will be of greatest benefit." Eligos stepped up to my other side as he spoke.

While Seirina, Eligos, and I were talking, the rest of the alliance members were streaming around us and heading towards the Order's monstrosities. The more fighters who came through the portal, the more Order members poured out of the prison to face them. The numbers were reasonably even to begin with, though gradually the battle started to swing in the Order's favour. I saw a whole squad of skeletons reduced to piles of bones by a single troll landing on them from the wall above. A wolf went down with a broken leg. Order vampires were feeding with abandon on Wiccans, obeahs, and shamans. I was casting lightning, fire, even plasma, but I couldn't do as much as I wanted for fear of hitting our own forces.

Even Lukasz was restricted by the close proximity of the two armies, though he continued to spit thorns from his mouth and release razor-edged leaves from his wings whenever he saw an enemy far enough from our forces to be safe. I prepared again to charge in when Eligos raised his hand to stop me once more. He then snapped his fingers and I felt something crawling up my spine like trails of ice. I realised he must have called his legendary legions to fight on our side, as promised, though I was almost as afraid of them as I was of the Order monstrosities.

I hadn't seen them up to this point, as he had only brought them where they were needed for the fights against the two locations he and Iyrin had assaulted. I saw their movements out of the corner of my eye; whenever I tried to focus on any one fighter, however, they seemed to shimmer like something underwater.

They seemed to radiate fear, making it almost impossible to stare at them for too long, though the Order warriors were either immune or protected somehow. As a result, even Eligos began to seem at least slightly concerned as his soldiers' numbers began to be significantly adversely affected. Next thing I knew he drew his own sword, which looked to be made of some material so black it actively sucked light *in*, then charged into the melee.

I was starting to become concerned by the daunting variety of enemies, especially bearing in mind the sheer *number* of each that the Order seemed to have pulled together. I couldn't believe there were this many people – beings, creatures, monsters, whatever – who were willing to be used to gain someone *else* power and prestige. I knew at least some had to have been coerced but still, not enough were standing aside to make a difference. When I saw an Order were, in hybrid man/feline form, come racing in and begin hamstringing many of our fighters, I couldn't hold back any longer.

The Order member had to be a were cheetah, since that was the only explanation for its speed, and we didn't have anyone who seemed able to keep up – not even the vampires. However I had been concerned over the possibility of Elrulin fighting in his new vampire body, while using magick to further enhance his speed, so I had come up with a technique to counteract it. Since temporal fields were so difficult to form, the heat of battle wasn't really the best situation to try. I'd therefore bound a very specific field form to a crystal I'd strung onto my necklace. That would enable me to activate it with a thought, bringing its oh-so-special properties into force.

I'd managed to create a field that fitted to my body, only hovering about a quarter of an inch from my skin, and moving with me like armour. Since the field was so small, I had been able to establish a significant temporal distortion effect. It gave me an effective time differential of forty to one. That meant that for every ten seconds in the world, I had four *hundred* inside the field. That, in turn, meant that instead of a top speed of maybe eighteen to twenty miles an hour at a flat-out sprint, I could move through the world at nearly *eight hundred miles per hour!*

The Order fighters were stunned to see a blur heading towards them silently at first, until suddenly the sonic boom of a body breaking Mach 1 reached them. The shock wave knocked several of the lighter fighters flying and had the were cheetah crouching down, flattening its ears to its head. At this speed, Muharar simply wasn't practical any longer as the weight would pull me off balance too easily. I yanked my karambits out of their sheath, fitting them onto my hands with the vicious hooked blades on the little finger side of my fists facing away from me, and charged into the fray.

It was time to start levelling the playing field.

Chapter 35

Much to my chagrin, I quickly discovered having super-speed wasn't all it was cracked up to be. I'm sure lots of people have watched *The Flash* and thought how cool it would be, but unfortunately it came with significant problems. To begin with I had to make sure I didn't over-anticipate an enemy's movements, since their actions were now almost glacial by comparison. Second, trying to attack at speed could be more hazardous than you might think – a fact I discovered when I nearly ripped my arm out of its socket by trying to do a 'slash-and-run' on a troll's stomach.

Fortunately, I quickly discovered slowing down allowed their flesh time to adapt to my time distortion within the slight margin from my skin. I just had to move at what to me was a sedate pace, though to them it was no doubt still just a blur. I spent the next few minutes disabling the Order's more lethal fighters – starting with the were-cheetah – and pulling several of our fighters away from attacks which might otherwise have proven crippling if not outright fatal.

Gauvain stayed mostly up high, directing me to Order members who were sneaking up on any of our fighters or trying to get behind us. He occasionally dove steeply, raking his claws across some unfortunate monster's eyes to blind them at a crucial moment before wheeling back up to surveil again. Paladin, meanwhile, was having the time of his life by trailing in my wake and savaging those unlucky individuals who were writhing in pain on the ground, the recipients of my hyper-accelerated blades.

Once the majority of their warriors were dealt with, I re-sheathed my karambits in the small of my back and discontinued the temporal field to prevent wasting the power it took to maintain it. I also wanted to be able to talk to our forces to plan the next step, which was impossible going forty times the speed of everyone else. It made me realise just how implausible the idea of *The Flash* really was, since his metabolism was permanently accelerated. Trying to talk to anyone else would be like trying to decipher a tape playing one syllable every three hours or something, while moving slow enough to not give himself away (bearing in mind he can apparently move at speeds far in excess of the speed of light) would be so tortuous it would likely drive him mad the first day he had his abilities.

Sorry DC, I just made it untenable for myself to believe in one of your most popular and beloved superheroes. Two, in fact, since I was sure Superman would have it just as bad. Man, there goes my childhood. I now had visions of having to throw out two-thirds of my cherished comic collection. Ah well, I'd always have *Calvin and Hobbes*.

Some of the looks I received once I deactivated my 'super-speed' were frankly terrified. Others were so obviously carnally appraising I blushed, and they ran the full gamut from one to the other. Fortunately the vast majority were simply approving, though when I saw the devastation I had unleashed I tended to veer more towards terrified, even of my own abilities. If I was capable of such total carnage already, what might I become in a couple of centuries if unchecked?

Yet who would even be *capable* of holding me accountable, bearing in mind I had been 'powered up' to become the Chosen of Isis for some apocalyptic battle? It seemed my own conscience would be my only leash. Maybe that 'control valve' Isis had bestowed on me might have been a good idea after all, though I wasn't going to let anyone deep enough into my mind ever again to recreate it now.

Our wounded retreated across the parade ground, where I created a new portal to take them back to the warehouse. There, the Wiccans who weren't so 'combat oriented' were waiting to administer first aid, magickal healing, and comfort. Seb, among others, was staying at the front. He was acting more as a liaison to Lukasz to direct him where he would be the most beneficial, so as such he was worth at least a dozen of our less capable, more conventional fighters such as some of the younger werewolves.

I had a private word with Seb regarding the best way for him to benefit us in the next stage of our assault, whereupon we agreed he would remain outside with Lukasz on overwatch. Probably from the top of the lighthouse. His new friend could easily carry him up there, from which vantage point they could spot any Order members who were trying to either flee or flank us. We arranged that any member waving a white handkerchief or tissue would have been reviewed and accepted as having been coerced in some way, so would be allowed to leave safely through the portal to the warehouse after the battle.

To that end, I began scanning those few who had stood aside or even turned against their fellows. I quickly found out the Order had resorted more to threats against family since arriving on this side of the Atlantic. That was no doubt due to not having had time enough to accumulate sufficient blackmail material to make the more subtle forms of persuasion possible. Apparently we'd have some cleaning up to do, even after we'd 'purified' Alcatraz.

"So now that the Order's cannon-fodder has been dealt with," Dominic said, dropping the body of some poor unfortunate to the floor. "Can we assume you'll no longer be needing us? That you can handle the indoor portion of the festivities solo?" I tilted my head to the right and gave him the most dry, old-fashioned look I could muster.

"My name is Maddox," I drawled. "Not Wick. And I have a couple of knives, not a gun with a 'Hollywood bottomless magazine'." My reference drew several chuckles and, surprisingly, several relieved expressions. I furrowed my brow questioningly at Kazemde, who was one of those looking reassured by my apparent fallibility and dependence.

"Having witnessed you, quite literally, 'cutting loose' just now," he explained by way of reply, "I think many of us are comforted to hear you admit your ongoing humanity." There were a couple of chuckles at his turn of phrase and widespread head nodding. I understood their trepidation, even if I would have preferred it not to be there.

"Come on," I said, tipping my head left and spreading my hands. "You've all seen magick before, all experienced power. Why am *I* suddenly being cast as Baba Yaga?"

"Because you are so new to your power," came the deep and unexpected voice of Eligos. He stepped into view, wiping off his sword before re-sheathing it. "Yet in the short time you have had it, you have surpassed everyone here in terms of ability. On top of that, you have already achieved that which no-one else had managed in over two centuries. Clearly, you are far beyond an 'ordinary' magick user. In fact, we don't even know what *kind* of magick user you are."

"I was advised not to pigeon-hole myself with a label," I said. "I was told humans' need to have a name for everything could be seriously limiting, so to simply be me."

"Well, it's nice to hear you still consider yourself to be human and fallible," quipped Seirina, her eyes finally back to normal. "So who passed on such notable wisdom, if I might ask?"

"Umm, well," I stammered, knowing the reaction my words would generate. "That would be Isis and Danu."

"Oh," deadpanned Seirina, crossing her arms and continuing for everyone else's benefit since she already knew all this. "So the goddess of magick and the goddess of knowledge. Clearly you just had routine, everyday teachers then." I shrugged for everyone else, though I narrowed my eyes at her since I knew what she was doing and why. She was deliberately building my rep for our allies while warning any Order members in earshot just who it was they were facing.

"I never said they were my teachers," I warned, at which there were a few gasps at the implication of being taught by such luminaries. "Still, a good teacher doesn't necessarily mean a remarkable student you know."

"Precisely the issue," chimed in Aurora, much to my surprise. "You were able, apparently, to learn enough for them to send you home with their blessing. And, according to Seirina, for them to accept you as the Chosen of Isis." I glared at the enchantress; after this, we were going to have words about confidentiality. Though there was no un-ringing the bell now the cat was out the bag drinking the spilled milk – and yes, I know that's a dizzying mash-up of phraseology.

"Look, this is all fascinating," I said, sighing. "We need to finish this before these fuckers escape and set up somewhere else all over again. Inside the prison, it's going to be much closer quarters with the cream of the Order's members. That's going to include the last of the Stygian

Blade, so I'll understand if anyone wants to back out. I need the most powerful and accomplished fighters for this – I can't afford any dead weight."

"You can be assured that the vampires are more than capable," stated Dominic. "We also have a score to settle with Elrulin. He took over a vampire, so we want to know how. More importantly, we need to know that it won't happen again."

"Suits me," I said, glad to have their speed and strength along. "The rest of you have three minutes to get back through the portal to the warehouse. After that, I'm closing it until this is done."

There was a surge of bodies towards the shimmering gateway, almost everyone other than the vampires choosing to view their fight as finished. The few non-vampires who stayed had already exhibited a recklessness that spoke of a deeper-than-average hatred and anger at the Order. They came from all factions, though the look in each of their eyes was identical. Cheveyo, in particular, was shifting from foot to foot restlessly, clearly eager to get to the shaman who had tortured and murdered his uncle.

We regarded each other with the deathly calm of like-minded fury, though I also stroked Paladin's head and called G down from his overflight. Since Lukasz would be watching with Seb, Gauvain's surveillance would no longer be required. However, as we'd be inside and out of sight, he would be staying with them to act as my liaison to them for the remainder of the fight.

As soon as the last few stragglers were through to the warehouse, I finally dropped the portal. Only then did I realise, despite it not taking *much* to keep open, the drain was still noticeable. It was just as nice to terminate the strain as it would be to take off a backpack at the end of a long hike, even one that wasn't especially overloaded.

I looked around at the gathered alliance members who had remained, nodding to them in thanks for their continued support while acknowledging their own deeply personal reasons for doing so. There were deep breaths taken, shoulders squared, and Paladin shook himself and bared his teeth in the direction of the nearest prison door.

G ruffled his feathers, *skree'd* at the evening sky, then pushed off my shoulder to join Seb and Lukasz. He wished me well, then settled down to merely observe so as not to distract me unless needed. Then I started walking towards the prison door, hearing the others fall into step behind me.

Time to end this.

Chapter 36

As we neared the door to the prison, I was surprised to see Eligos waiting there for us. I raised an eyebrow as we approached.

"I thought you'd gone back to the warehouse," I remarked, deliberately sounding offhand and unconcerned, though I was secretly glad to still have him here. He was a powerful fighter in his own right, plus his ability to summon his forces was a great secret weapon to be heading in with.

"I agreed to aid you until this enterprise reached its *successful* conclusion," he explained, frowning. "I missed that clause when I agreed to fulfil my favour to Lucian. We had been speaking of my simply providing aid, then he specified until the end of your undertaking. Then, as we made our agreement, he threw in the word 'successful' and I missed it initially. It registered just as we sealed our agreement with a handshake, though by then it was too late. I therefore have a vested interest in your achieving a positive resolution to this endeavour."

As glad as I was to hear of Eligos' obligation to not only assist us, but to actually help us *win,* I felt a shiver run down my spine all the same. All my concerns over making a deal with the Devil came flooding back and I started going over every word of our own bargain in my head. I recalled how I had listened so carefully at the time, since I had already had reservations, then my relief as he had phrased things so I only had to *attempt* to provide my assistance. Even then, it had been conditional on our *successful* resolution of my issues with Elrulin.

I suddenly understood his reasoning for obligating Eligos as he had: It would, in turn, obligate me to stand witness for him to Isis. The stories of his convoluted specifications in his contracts were clearly *under*stated, if anything. My mind suddenly pictured Crowley, from *Supernatural*, sitting down to read a contract scroll that went onto the floor and across the room, so I had to struggle to keep my face composed as befitted the discussion we were having. Eligos and Lucian had both expressed their disdain for my mental segues, so I didn't need to give him more ammunition. I dragged my attention back to what Eligos was saying before he started in on my 'human lack of attention span'.

"To that end," Eligos continued. "You need to understand the shortcomings in your mental defences. If you face Elrulin with your current level of defensive ineptitude, he will access your thoughts with ridiculous ease and you will be defeated almost before you begin."

I desperately tried to hide my excitement. My main reason for wanting to keep on Lucian's good side was to learn how to better defend my mind, most particularly from one specific, creepy, skeletal bastard who'd established an unwanted mental link with me. I composed my face into calm interest to try my best to mask the surge of adrenaline flooding my system.

"Your oversight is a simple one made by most humans," he explained. "You create your defence by visualising a wall. While effective for anyone attempting a head-on assault, any more subtle and experienced attempt would simply come from another direction."

"So, use an image of a fully surrounded mind," I replied, immediately catching on to what he was telling me. "Like a cube?"

"I generally advise a sphere," Eligos replied. "While a cube is acceptable, a sphere leaves no edges or flat surfaces to attack. The curved surface also makes attacks less likely to detect your presence at all, since the probe would simply slide off your mental defences." I nodded in understanding and immediately upgraded my protective approach. I saw Eligos' expression change as he lost his access to my mind, first a slight irritation followed by a grudging approval at my success.

I couldn't believe I had agreed to help Lucian in exchange for a three-second piece of advice. That asshole was the master of the unequal bargain. Mind you, now I had him over a barrel – he had nothing to trade now, so I had an out from being his conversion representative to Isis. Still, I shouldn't get ahead of myself – it might be a good idea to finish our current mission first. I thanked Eligos for his tip, then squared my shoulders and headed for the door.

As I reached for the door, I felt a buzzing sensation under my palm that made me pause. I reached out with my magickal senses and immediately drew my hand back. Someone had clearly been watching *Home Alone* and taking notes: The handle of the door was electrified. I scanned for anything else but happily, they'd left off the head-level blowtorch when they set this up. I booted the door to avoid touching the handle, though I completely missed the fact that the door opened *outwards*. All I got was a jarring thud up my leg and a bunch of snickering from everyone gathered behind me.

"OK, *ow*," I said, rubbing my knee. "Look, it always works in the movies."

"Yeah, well the movies always ignore basic fire safety," said Dominic. "This is an institution, so all the doors have to open *out* so they can be pushed open by people running in a panic."

"Oh, here we go," said one of the other vampires, rolling his eyes so hard his whole head went backward until he was looking up at the sky. "Every time he gets near a building, he goes off on his whole architectural lecture thing. Just because you were a building inspector once, will you *please* not start telling us everything wrong as we walk in here? Otherwise I'm gonna get so bored I'll fall asleep before we get to the fighting."

The rest of the vampires and the others who'd stayed all chuckled, while Dominic pursed his lips and I saw the flexion of his jaw muscles as he ground his teeth. I cleared my throat and used my magick to rip the door out of the frame, creating a shower of sparks as the wire to the handle was snapped. It looked dramatic but all I cared about was getting inside without getting fried – or bored to death by Dominic spouting depressingly mundane building code violation stories. Paladin bounded past me into the prison and I chased him inside, scanning quickly to ensure there wasn't anyone – or any*thing* – waiting next to the doorway to pounce.

We sped through the labyrinth of corridors and rooms, taking out groups of Order members as we went. At one point Eligos broke away to clear a side branch, joining back up with us a few minutes later with blood dripping off his sword. Paladin stuck by my side, working in concert with me like a well-oiled machine to add to my lethality. We had a few weres in animal form jump down on us from upper balconies as we went through one of the cell blocks, and two of the largest trolls I'd ever seen (and the smelliest) waited for us as we reached the cafeteria.

Given the additional space, I drew Muharar and spun it in a circle to my right side. The vampires attacked the troll on the right *en masse*, burying it under sheer weight of numbers and ripping into it as it hit the floor. The other reached for me and I jumped to my left, swinging Muharar upward which took both its hands off at the wrists with a single swipe. As it reared back and shrieked in pain, I drove Muharar directly through the roof of its mouth diagonally up into its brain. The shriek immediately cut off as the creature dropped like a puppet with cut strings.

I placed my foot on its face to try and pull my blade out, finding the troll's skull was gripping surprisingly tightly. I gave a firm yank and my sword finally came free, though I was less than pleased with its subsequent direction. The heavy conical spike on the hilt made incredibly rapid contact with my testicles, dropping me to my knees as I gasped for breath and tried to stop myself from throwing up. Once again I managed to reduce the rest of my team to tears of mirth, though I did at least get a few sympathetic groans this time along with one guy crossing his own legs protectively. Paladin came over and slobbered all over my face, which did nothing to help my lack of dignity just then.

I coughed a few times then took several deep breaths, finally getting control of my reflexive reaction. I pushed myself back to my feet by leaning on my sword, thankful the magickal nature of the blade protected it from the contact with the concrete floor. One of the American female vampires came over to me, clearly desperately trying not to laugh. She put her hand on my shoulder and leant in.

"I was considering asking you out after this," she said in a strangled voice. "But clearly you're going to need some 'down time'."

"I'm flattered," I said, coughing slightly. "I'm fine now, but I'm actually already interested in someone else." I was so out of it, I didn't even pick up on the obvious joking tone, though I quickly caught up as she continued.

"Well, I guess you can simply 'play ball' when you get home then," she said, bursting out laughing along with the rest. I wanted to roll my eyes at being taken in, but I just didn't have the energy right then.

"Hey, leave the guy alone," called someone else through the laughter. "At least give him time to 'batter up'."

"Maybe his girl's a lumberjack," called out another. "Then she wouldn't mind about his 'wood' being 'chopped down'."

"All of you can b–" I stopped quickly, since what I was about to say was definitely the wrong word when surrounded by vampires. "Bugger off," I finished, to further chuckles.

"If you have all quite finished with your childish humour at Gavan's expense," Eligos intoned. "Can we resume our mission, please?"

"Yes, please," I said, eager to turn the attention away from myself and back where it belonged.

Everyone else seemed looser for a little laughter, though I just wished it could have been at someone else's expense. I lifted Muharar and took one final deep breath, channelling some energy from Seren into my nether regions to dull the throbbing (not the welcome kind Angelica had caused, either), then set off through the mess hall once again. Everyone followed suit and fortunately, no more Order members popped up from behind the food service area. Once we made it out the other side, there were more cells along with corridors leading off in multiple directions.

Suddenly a group of humans in the signature Stygian Blade jackets appeared in front of us, stepping out from various doorways with hands glowing in an array of colours. A sickeningly familiar voice sounded from a door up ahead, making my skin crawl even before I saw his smug, supercilious face.

"Well, well, if it isn't geeky little Gavan. So you finally got yourself a tiny iota of power and now you think you can stand against The Order of the Nine Seals? You still have no idea about real magick or just how insignificant you are, do you?"

"Heffernan," I observed tiredly, sighing in resignation. "Why am I not surprised to see you slithering out from this particular rock? Uncurled your nose-hairs yet after that 'shocking' encounter in Tibet?"

"That's *DOCTOR* to you, you talentless little shit," he snapped back, as I'd known he would. Sometimes it was nice to see old friends, though it could be just as good to see old rivals. I shuffled my grip on Muharar and grinned evilly.

I was *really* going to enjoy this.

Chapter 37

"Take them down, but the pompous shit in the back is mine," I said to my assembled warriors, though it didn't seem to be quite as intimidating to the gathering of Stygian Blade agents as I'd hoped. Several of them actually had trouble maintaining their magickal focus due to laughing so hard – though that was somewhat unfortunate for them, as it gave us the opportunity to attack before they could regroup. Seven of them had their throats ripped out in the first three seconds, after which the remaining assholes seemed to lose their humour fairly quickly.

I threw up a hasty shield in time to deflect their various assaults, though from what I felt I suddenly realised just how powerful Aaruans were compared to human magick users. If these were the most powerful members of the Order, it was no wonder Elrulin found it so easy to dominate them. I barely detected a ripple in my block from their combined spells, though I did find it exceedingly satisfying to watch the smile slide off Heffernan's face like warm oil off his greasy hair.

I smiled evilly at him, at which he paled further before turning tail and running. I *pushed* my shield at the remaining Blade members, watching gleefully as it made their next attacks rebound on them. Four or five of them were immediately blasted into walls and knocked unconscious, at which my allies pounced on them and proceeded to tie them up securely. A couple more were merely disoriented, which still allowed for restraints to be applied without resistance.

To be honest, I was actually quite surprised at just how many sets of restraints they had with them until one of the vampires explained.

"It's easier to keep them fresh if they're still alive, and it's easier to keep them alive if they're tied up," said the female vampire who'd laughed at my testicular misfortune, though the wink she gave me left me unsure whether she was joking or not. Dominic had informed me previously that modern vampires used willing blood donors nowadays, often running blood-banks and only taking a small percentage of the total donations to live on. The rest went to supply hospitals and clinics, though back in the UK it was all to the NHS. It was apparently much easier to make a real profit over this side of the Atlantic, though the English contingent also worked with pharmaceutical companies and private healthcare providers to keep themselves flush.

"Fine, just keep them quiet and out of the way," I deadpanned, relieved to see the shock on her face when she thought I might be accepting of them taking victims to feed on. My subtle wink had her struggling to keep a straight face so as not to give things away to their prisoners, to the point where she had to turn away from their view and bite her lips. Those who were conscious by that point squirmed and even whimpered slightly at the possibility of being eaten, though I didn't really care how scared they were since I felt they actually deserved to be used as blood-bags.

By my estimation there were still six Blade operatives plus Heffernan out there, along with Elrulin and any other monstrosities he still had tucked away. Cheveyo had already told me he had found and killed the shaman on the way here, though he would stick with us despite already having obtained his vengeance. Still, if the Blade agents we'd just defeated were any indication, I really didn't have anything to worry about magickally at this point. Elrulin was quite evidently the only one on my level, thanks to Isis' power bump from her Veil, so now it was just the 'brute force and ignorance' crowd I needed to be concerned with – though if truth be told, even they weren't exactly a threat.

Muscles vs. magick wasn't any kind of level playing field, so I finally understood why Eligos and others had all told me this wasn't the major undertaking I thought it was. I still had to deal with Elrulin, who wouldn't be any kind of a push-over, but I was starting to feel much happier about our chances. It was also telling to see the expressions from some of my allies at quite how easily I'd taken down the Stygian Blade members we'd just encountered. A couple of them were looking at me almost fearfully again, though I rather enjoyed feeling more secure about further fights.

I left my allies dealing with our captives and charged ahead into the prison again. I glanced over to see Eligos was easily keeping pace with me, his sword drawn and his teeth bared in feral glee as he ran. I could hear a few other sets of footsteps trailing behind us, so I used a little of my stored power to pour on the speed. I didn't use my super-speed field again as I'd have left everyone in the dust, which wouldn't be the most sensible idea. Despite my earlier reassurance regarding my levels of ability compared to the Stygian Blade, knowing my luck I'd come across all of them plus Elrulin together as soon as I tried to go solo. I'd seen way too many movies to think going solo was a good idea. I wasn't some ditzy blonde with a big rack, after all.

We finally came to the other end of the prison and I blasted the door in front of us rather than risk another electrified handle. We emerged from the building into the walled area that Google Maps had labelled as the 'prisoner gardens' when I was doing my research. Seated at the far end, on a huge, ornate wooden throne (chair was far too prosaic a term for it) was Elrulin, still clad in his stolen vampiric meat-suit. Heffernan stood to his left, and the remains of the Stygian Blade were arrayed in a line abreast about ten feet in front of him, including our hapless mole whom Eligos had captured back before the first assaults.

I made a sweeping motion with my arm, reaching out to grip each of them magickally which threw them all bodily into the wall and knocked them all unconscious. I hoped Iyrin felt the jolt through his puppet, since the little creep deserved it for establishing the unwanted link to me. Elrulin then turned slightly to gesture forward with his left hand, motioning Heffernan towards us while propping his left ankle on his right knee.

"Here's your chance to prove yourself and take your revenge," he said, at which the dumbass doctor looked significantly alarmed. Heffernan quickly tried to disguise his consternation in a determined mien, though I wasn't fooled. He stepped forward, shaking his hands out as if to try and loosen up for a fight, so I matched his advance while struggling to keep the inappropriate grin off my face. I sheathed Muharar, wanting to do this more up close and personal given our past history. I also mentally instructed Paladin to stay back out of the way, so he sat by the door we had entered through.

"You're gonna pay for what you did in Tibet, you prick," Ciarán swore at me.

I raised a quizzical eyebrow and shrugged, though I remained silent.

I wondered what I was supposed to be paying for most: Getting the Veil before him, knocking him out, or making him face-plant by tying his laces together? The lack of response to his threat clearly irritated him, if the tightening around Heffernan's eyes and the thinning lips were an accurate telegraphing of his fury. I brushed my hair back from my forehead, then swept some specks of dust off my shoulders.

As I dropped my hands, I subtly activated my temporal field and slowed my movements to a crawl to avoid making it too obvious. I wanted to watch him get more and more frustrated as I either deflected or outright avoided his attacks, before finally beating that supercilious look so hard off of his face he'd never be able to use it again. He seemed to remember the altercation we'd had outside Dinas Affaraon, way back when this all started, as he refrained from simply wading in with his fists flying. Instead he raised both hands, forming a crackling ball of electricity which he raised over his head and hurled at me.

I had to move with deliberately considered slowness to make it look like I was struggling to avoid his attack. I swayed to my left, raising my right arm to allow the ball to pass by me. Since there were some of my allies behind me, I latched onto it telekinetically and swung it around behind my back to head sideways into the garden wall, frying a tendril of ivy that was climbing up the stonework. Doctor Dumbass followed it up with a fireball that was just as (in-)effective, followed by another arcball that went the same way as the first.

I quickly realised my speed-field was as needed as an aqualung in the middle of the desert, so I deactivated it while I waited for the self-important dickweed to catch his breath. I stood there, polishing my nails on my shirt, watching him gasp with his hands on his knees. He'd clearly put everything he had into those three attacks, which made me understand just how little power he really had. When he finally stood back up and saw how unconcerned I was, he lost all semblance of composure and charged me like a demented wrestler.

I grabbed his wrist as he neared me, swinging him around in the same path his electro-balls had followed and launching him towards the wall with an extra telekinetic push to make sure he hit hard enough to knock himself out cold. I did a quick Michael Jackson spin, finishing with the hand in the air pose, then faced Elrulin again with a huge, unconcerned grin on my face. I felt him reach for my mind as he had once before, though this time he skated off my defence like Bambi on ice. He raised an eyebrow at my advanced defences, though he still didn't seem concerned enough to even uncross his legs at this point.

"I see someone has educated you somewhat since our last encounter," he drawled, steepling his fingers in a clear expression of his perceived superiority. I shrugged unconcernedly, wanting to demonstrate how little I cared about Elrulin now despite feeling a fluttering in my stomach at the thought of having to face him again. Given his vampiric body I was slightly concerned about the possibility of him trying to sink his teeth into my neck again, so I prepared myself to reactivate my time field at a moment's notice.

Eligos and the vampires all shuffled themselves around me, ready to fight our final enemy, but I turned and motioned them away.

"Guys, I appreciate the sentiment and all your help thus far," I told them. "But I need to do this last step on my own. You can hang back by the door in case I fail – there's only the one way out, since this is the prison garden, so he's not going to get out any other way. For now, though, I have several scores to settle with this scum-sucking bottom-feeder."

My name-calling finally elicited a reaction from the Aaruan as he uncrossed his legs and gripped the carved wooden arms of his throne. He leant forward and scowled deeply, narrowing his eyes at me as the rest of my allies backed away and cleared the field for our battle. He pushed himself upright and stepped towards me, so I rolled my head on my neck and shook my arms loose. I managed to get a satisfying *crack* as I brought my head back around, then dropped my right leg back half a step and brought my hands up into basic guard position.

"Alright, you parasitic shithead," I riffed, deliberately insulting him to try to throw him off balance. "It's time we finish this. You happy with your current meat sack, or you wanna trade up before we do this?" Inexplicably, his face tightened in the greatest expression of rage I'd ever seen from him. He flared his nostrils and bared his teeth. I just had time to activate my super-speed as he lunged at me, his vampiric body lending him a speed and strength that would have otherwise completely overpowered me in moments.

The fight was on.

Chapter 38

I was expecting this to be a definite struggle compared to the fights I'd had with the Order members thus far, even more so due to the fact that Elrulin had been sitting back relaxing and conserving his energies while I had used mine to even reach him. Thankfully my stores in Seren were still significant, though I was prepared to burn through them all if needed; I was absolutely *not* going to let this asshole get away. As my temporal field snapped into place I saw him slow from a blur to a glacier in my perspective, so I moved just enough to make it look like a lucky escape as his vampire claws went past my ribs. While his back was turned I whipped Muharar out and fell into a ready stance so that when he turned, Elrulin was facing my sword.

I felt him reach for my mind, though the temporal field further disrupted his attempts on top of my upgraded mental armour (*thank you, Eligos*, I thought, wondering idly what kind of fruit basket he'd prefer). The extra time I now had allowed me to analyse Elrulin's attacks, both physical and mental, in a way I hadn't been able to before. I was surprised to note just how rudimentary his physical style was, clearly having mostly been gleaned from the minds of his various hosts. I realised he'd never *needed* to learn any kind of martial arts, since his mental capabilities would have instantly overpowered his victims up to now, rendering the physical side moot.

That's not to say he wasn't still a threat, since his current vampiric host had endowed him with a significant speed and strength advantage over most people. It was the disabling of his mental attacks which was most crippling for him, allowing me to focus on simply keeping him at bay and waiting for him to tire himself out. I saw his eyes tighten in frustration, then flick towards the heap of Stygian Blade members piled against the wall where they'd been knocked senseless. He was clearly planning on getting to them and using their souls for more energy, which I absolutely couldn't allow. Not that it would help him overcome the speed differential I now had, nor was I especially well disposed towards those who had voluntarily been party to the darker side of Elrulin's business. I merely had no intention of permitting him to draw this out any longer than necessary.

To that end, I dashed full speed to get between him and them, even that small distance creating a slight pop as I broke the sound barrier again (that was still so cool!). Elrulin actually stepped back, staggered by my suddenly vastly superior speed, and his whole face changed as he finally realised quite how wide and deep a pile of shit he could potentially be in right now.

Clearly, since he had been here on Earth after his banishment from Aaru at the hands of Isis and the Council, Lucian must have been the only individual he thought of as being on the same level as himself. Now, since he knew Isis had helped me infuse the power of her Veil into myself, he was suddenly faced with someone who knew who and what he was. As a result, I was on at least a level playing field when it came to power, and he knew I really didn't like him very much.

That last point was the crux, since Lucian was in a comparable position with regard to knowledge and power but didn't really care about stopping him. Lucian had (or so he *said*, though recent revelations cast doubt on his assertion) cut ties and kicked Elrulin to the curb, though hadn't cared enough about protecting humanity to do any more than that. I most certainly *did* care about humanity, several members in particular, which put us most decidedly at odds and him in a position he'd never before experienced.

Plus, there was the added wrinkle of Aaruans merely resorting to banishment from their realm as a punishment. I had no intention of allowing this giant turd-stain to terrorise some other poor group, so I was planning to finish things once and for all. I had already planned to take his energy the same way as I had with Fiona, storing it in Seren to use for the future, and I could see the realisation of my terminal intent wash over his face.

For the first time, I saw something akin to fear in his eyes. They widened, darting around to look for an exit, and his jaw went slack. Unfortunately for him, he'd planned his location well to only allow a single point of access. His intent had clearly been to trap *me* but it had rebounded on him, since my allies – including Eligos – were arrayed in front of the door, watching the fight. It surprised me that he didn't simply abandon his vampire body and get the hell out of there in an incorporeal form, since that would enable him to be immune to physical attacks and not be restricted by the walls. However, he remained stubbornly encased in his latest stolen meat-suit.

Not that I was complaining, don't get me wrong, since I would have far rather gotten it over and done with immediately than he float off to cause havoc again somewhere else later. It was just another curious incident in the weirdness that had become my life lately.

He charged at me, claws bared, as if trying to get close enough to rip my face off, though I had a sneaking suspicion he might be feinting to get me to move so he could reach the pile of Blade operatives. Instead, I stood my ground and simply dipped Muharar so the blade was pointed directly at his chest. Now if he didn't stop, he'd impale himself and save me the effort.

He pulled up short, clearly infuriated by the failure of his gambit, and proceeded to glare at me impotently. I had to resist the temptation to laugh, since he was still a dangerous adversary and I didn't want him to turn on my allies, but the relief I felt at finding myself so easily able to compete with him was immense.

I had been working myself up into a fearful stew at the thought of facing him, terrified he would ravage my mind and vastly overpower me. Still, my trepidation had done me a huge favour, since I had based my preparations on that level of fear. As a result, I had made *myself* so overpowered compared to *him* that I could now compete physically with him without even breaking a sweat. Also, thanks to Eligos' little tip, my mind was more secure than ever and seemed utterly immune to his probes.

Still, I couldn't quite suppress my happiness completely, a huge shit-eating grin breaking out across my face. The sight of it seemed to infuriate Elrulin even more, the grinding of his teeth reaching me clearly. I raised Muharar into a ready stance again, then dared to take my left hand off the hilt and give Elrulin a little finger wave just to taunt him. I used the movement to also deactivate my speed field momentarily, so I could talk to him.

"Still sticking with the same suit?" I enquired, both to irritate him and to satisfy my own curiosity. "It's clearly not as superior as you'd hoped, otherwise you would've kicked my ass by now. So why stick with a failed idea?"

"Because you fucked everything up, and now I've got no choice, you stupid hairless ape! You interfering, primitive, moronic piece of shit!" he swore. My eyebrows shot up in surprise at his vehement admission. I could see a similar emotion mirrored in Eligos' expression over Elrulin's shoulder, though I didn't dare take my attention off my enemy for more than a split second.

"Huh?" I responded eloquently. "What did *I* do?"

"Because of you, I needed to find a host that could better withstand and channel my immense power," he said, actually stamping his foot like a spoiled child not getting his way. He even crossed his arms and sank his chin to his chest as he continued his whining, getting louder and angrier as he continued. "Because of *you*, Isis infused her Veil into a talentless primate. *Because of you*, I got blasted by Isis' power and had to fight in a way I never had before to hold onto my host body. *BECAUSE OF YOU, I ended up fused to this vampiric asshole and now I can't get out!*"

As he shrieked his last comment, he turned towards me and I instinctively reactivated my speed field. I was just in time to slip past his claws as he dove for me, rage distorting the vampire's once handsome features. I stumbled slightly on a loose stone, though my speed allowed me to recover in time to slash at Elrulin as he passed me. Due to my lack of poise I was only able to gash his arm instead of the decapitation I was going for, though the pain was clearly something Elrulin wasn't used to experiencing.

He screamed and quickly backpedalled, scrambling away towards his putative throne. He gripped his arm, a look of utter terror on his face as he seemed to understand his precarious predicament. For the first time in his many centuries of existence, he was in truly mortal danger. He could no longer simply flee his shell when danger threatened, and he had finally come up against someone who wasn't going to either join him or run and hide from his organisation. Not only that but the man he had tried to threaten and use was now in a position to destroy him, having already taken apart the organisation he had spent so long building.

I advanced as slowly as I could towards him, my speed field meaning that I had to move like a comical slow motion parody if I wanted my advance to have any kind of gravitas. I supposed I could have disarmed it, though I remembered the old adage that an animal is never more dangerous than when wounded and cornered. Elrulin quite literally had nothing left to lose, so I had no intention of getting careless when victory was so close.

I stopped around a dozen feet away from him, holding Muharar in between us in a grip that was suddenly much sweatier than I had expected. I felt my heart racing, though I didn't even want to try and calculate the rate multiplied by my forty times speed field. I could feel my adrenaline spiking, which had my mind racing down its usual inane tangents. I was watching every little twitch on Elrulin's face, every subtle movement of his arms that could indicate when and how he might attack.

His eyes darted across to where Eligos and the rest of my allies were still guarding the door, then over to a section of the wall where the top had started to crumble. I could almost hear his thoughts of trying to use his vampire speed and strength to jump and climb his way out of this walled-in enclosure. I tensed my legs, preparing to rush after him and cut him off before he could escape. I wasn't going to go through all this just for this walking diaper-stain to squeeze out of some overlooked bolt-hole or secret door.

I had already spotted the sewer entrance, having been primed to check for it after watching Connery and Cage in *The Rock*, though as far as I had seen it was welded closed. Just as I looked away for a split second, Elrulin made his escape attempt.

I was after him before he took his second step, lifting my sword and swinging at his legs. My blade bit deep into the back of his left leg, hamstringing him and sending him tumbling head over heels until he wound up in a heap. He was still at least twenty feet from the wall, his gaze fixed on his hoped-for escape route.

I deactivated my speed field and stepped over to him, my allies suddenly inching forward so they didn't miss these final moments. I raised my sword, driving through Elrulin's back as he attempted to crawl to the wall and pinning him to the concrete. I put my left knee into his back and my right hand on the back of his head, keeping him pinned with my left hand on my sword's hilt. As everyone watched, I drained Elrulin's energy and funnelled it into Seren. Isis' wings flared, as if in victory, as I finally ended the threat the magickal world had been living under for over two hundred and fifty years.

Once I had emptied the body of energy, I stood up and yanked Muharar out of Elrulin's back to raise the blade high in the air. The lights from the prison building flashed on the blade briefly, before I swung it down and cut deep into the neck. Unfortunately, unlike in the movies, the neck isn't quite as easy to cut through in one smooth move as people think. I had been careful with my swing, remembering how I had used Muharar to cut through the cell lock to free Alcina, so I hadn't used my full strength. Still, better than burying the blade into the concrete or damaging it (though with the protection I had forged into it, thanks to the techniques I'd learned from Master Harfi, I wasn't sure it *could* be damaged in such a mundane way). I was forced to take a second swing to finish the job, the momentum sending Elrulin's head bouncing across the garden to wind up under Eligos' foot.

Finally, it was over.

Chapter 39

Eligos took his foot off of Elrulin's head, gave me a swift look that seemed to be one part thankful, one part relief, and a soupçon of glee, then disappeared. I had a funny feeling his next stop would be Lucian's pyramid to inform him of the success of our venture, and thus the completion of his obligation. That meant Lucian would, in turn, no doubt soon be contacting me regarding my side of *our* agreement. I'd deal with that when it happened but for now, I just wanted to take a breath and savour the first time since Angelica walked into my shop and my life that I could truly relax without the threat of some mysterious asshole lurking somewhere in the background.

I knew Seirina was going to be upset at missing the grand finale, so I decided I'd take the head back as a trophy for her. I stepped wearily over to where the head still rested, with Dominic and the rest still staring at it, feeling the accumulated fatigue of several months of continuous tension and stress come rushing in as the adrenaline finally began to ebb. I felt my back twinge as I bent over to grab the head by its hair, groaning like an old man as I straightened up. I narrowed my eyes at several of the vampires as they smirked at my tired noises, elevating my middle finger of the head-holding hand in their direction which elicited several chuckles.

I turned my back on them and unceremoniously ripped open a portal back to the warehouse, then remembered something and looked over at the Stygian Blade assholes, including Heffernan, over by the wall. I saw three of the vampires head over to them, dragging them to their feet and herding them towards the portal. While they did, I called Gauvain from his perch on the lighthouse. He, in turn, let Seb and Lukasz know it was all over, so Lukasz brought them to join us to head back.

We were greeted by cheers as we stepped through into the warehouse, which redoubled in intensity as I tiredly held my battle trophy up for all to see. Spontaneous applause broke out and those of us who had just returned were almost bruised by everyone patting us on our backs.

Several people spat on the head. I immediately wiped it off and stared angrily at those responsible, at which everyone quickly got the message that defiling my trophy would not go down well. I sidled out of the limelight, edged over to the stairs I had used as my platform to deliver my stirring attack speech and sat down. I set the head on the floor between my feet, rested my elbows on my knees and hung my head in exhaustion.

The come-down from the adrenaline high was like being hit with a whole sack-full of fatigue, and I wasn't sure I had the energy to partake in the well-deserved celebrations that were currently revving up. I had to fend off some well-meaning dog kisses from Paladin, though he quickly sat beside me and just leant against my shoulder.

I was about to use some of the energy in Seren to refresh myself when I remembered where the latest infusion had come from. I suddenly viewed my main energy store with a new-found distaste which I hoped would fade with time, since I really didn't want to waste everything in there. Hopefully it was just my fatigue talking, though I still refrained from using it just now.

I felt a hand on my shoulder and looked up to see Seirina standing over me, looking surprisingly irritated. I had no idea why she was annoyed at first, then I looked down at the head and understood.

"Hey, so I guess I won?" I said, aiming for humorous but falling far short and just sounding exhausted. Despite my failed attempt, Seirina finally smiled.

"Even though I didn't get to witness the final blow," she said grudgingly, "I guess you did OK."

"Just OK?" I said, coming up off the stairs and then swaying slightly before grabbing the rail. "I thought I did slightly better than OK." I crossed my arms in a huff, putting my foot on Elrulin's head like a victorious hunter. "I didn't see anyone else stepping up to kick his ass. I thought that might at least rate a 'thank you'."

"Oh, stop pouting," she said. "Fine, fine, you did a good job." She chuckled, then grabbed me for a tight hug. "I can't believe it's finally over after all this time! So when are you going to get things going with Angie again?"

I shifted uncomfortably, which didn't go unnoticed by Seirina.

"*Gavan*," she said, sounding like my mother back when I was a child, catching me making mud pies. "What did you do?"

"Look, it wasn't my fault," I said, then realised it actually was so I couldn't really back that one up. "Yeah, OK, so it *was* my fault, but I didn't exactly *mean* to screw it up like this."

"What. Did. You. *DO?*" she raged, one eye going green and one red as *both* her abilities flared up. It was at this point I realised I might actually be even more screwed than I thought.

"I kinda asked her out and then *brmblfr thsnt,*" I trailed off, at which the green faded and the red flared in both eyes even brighter.

"AND THEN *WHAT?*" she stormed, getting so loud the nearby celebratory festivities died down. People started looking over at us, the silence spreading like ripples in a pond until the entire warehouse was silent and staring at us.

"I planned the attack for the same night," I said quietly, though loud enough for Seirina to hear – and, apparently, enough allies nearby for the story to start spreading across the warehouse in the same way the silence had just moments before. Some looked at me sympathetically, some in disgust, and the majority looked to be struggling to hold in the chuckles. Personally I came down on the side of disgust, so I couldn't really feel aggrieved at any of them.

"Oh, you dim-witted, inconsiderate, thick-headed moron!" Seirina said, her sentiment clearly echoed by everyone else if the nods were anything to go by.

"Yeah, that's pretty much what I thought too," I admitted, owning up to my own stupidity. "I've been beating myself up ever since, but I haven't been able to track her down to apologise and reorganise things. She's rearranged her schedule to completely avoid me. I swear, though, my top priority is going to be to arrange a new date. Hey, I booked a chef's tasting menu dinner at a five-star hotel for our date – it's not like I was cheaping out!"

I finally looked to be getting some sympathy, along with a few admiring glances when people heard my plans. "I just got excited by the idea of finally finishing the fight with The Order, so I arranged for tonight's excursion before I remembered quite *why* it was an important night."

"OK, that's actually a pretty nice date idea," she said, her eyes thankfully fading back to normal at last. "You're still a bonehead, but at least you're a well-intentioned bonehead."

Paladin, having been patted by pretty much everyone in the warehouse by now since our return, came over and pushed his head under my hand. Gauvain flew over from his perch on the stair railing to land on my shoulder, rubbing his cheek on my head and scowling at Seirina.

"Oh, tone it down," she said, looking straight at G. "You and I *both* know how badly he screwed up, so stop acting like his protector."

I am truly sorry, Gavan, G told me. *She is correct. You really are a knobhead.* I burst out laughing at his incongruous name-calling. It was so out of character I almost asked him to repeat himself to confirm he'd said what he'd said, then I reconsidered. He really didn't need more opportunities to insult me. He'd clearly sent his thoughts to Seirina as well, since she was laughing right along with me.

"Your only option is to throw yourself on her mercy, beg for her forgiveness, and try to arrange another date," she advised me. "I'd definitely stick with the tasting menu idea, though. That's a solid gold winner." Several of the women nearby nodded, making me happy that at least my idea was a winner even if *I* was a total loser.

"My first priority when I get back is to arrange a new date for our date," I said. "I just have to try and track her down without acting like a total stalker. That's not really the right vibe to put out to a woman you want to have a relationship with, at least last time I checked." There were a few more chuckles at my observation, and finally a lessening of Seirina's 'angry mother/schoolteacher' vibe.

"Probably a solid starting point," she agreed, to a fresh round of chuckles from everyone else. "Just don't be so subtle it takes you a month to talk to her."

"Yeah, yeah," I said, waving off her concern. Then I bent down and grabbed my grisly trophy. "Here, since you weren't there for the actual moment, I thought you might like a little memento." She gripped the head by the hair and swung it down beside her.

"While I might appreciate the thought," she said. "I'd go with flowers or chocolates or jewellery for Angelica. You know, something a little more conventional and traditional, at least at first." I wasn't the only one to laugh at the obviousness of her comment.

"No, really?" I asked sarcastically. "I was planning on breaking out the handcuffs and ball-gag at dinner. Why, you think that's too much?" Now it was Seirina's turn to roll her eyes at *my* comment.

"OK, fine, so you're not a completely inept idiot," she replied. "Just remember, I'm here if you need any help or advice."

"Thanks, but I'd rather do this without enchantress interference if you don't mind," I said with a shrug.

"Yeah, you said that once before," she remarked. "Then you went and booked our major fight for the same evening as your all-important second first date, so forgive me if I'm not overly confident in your seduction skills." I winced at both the painful accuracy and the awkward embarrassment of her observation.

"Harsh, but fair," I allowed. "Look, come to The Sanctuary and talk to her if you really want to. Besides, I've spent so much time at your house, I'd like you to see my shop. Plus the extra features I've added." I turned and projected my voice around the warehouse. "That goes for everyone, by the way. My shop has full warding, so it's a very safe space, and The Sanctuary has a great menu."

With that, I began opening the return portals for our allies and everyone headed for home. The Stygian Blade agents were taken by the vampires, though I didn't see Heffernan among them. He must have slipped away in the celebration and made his escape, the slimy bastard. I made a mental note to track him down and pay him back for his hand in this, especially when I recalled what he'd done to my sister – feeding her to Elrulin as his way into the Stygian Blade. That one earned him a special place at the permanent head of my personal shit list.

At last, only Seirina and I were left, the obeahs having thankfully taken their undead forces with them to return to their resting places. I offered Seirina my arm and teleported us to her home, rather than using a portal, then I headed back to my place with Pal and G. I was ready for a good night's sleep, then I'd *finally* try and track down my elusive ex-but-hopefully-soon-to-be-new girlfriend. I made myself a toasted cheese and bacon sandwich, watched a couple of episodes of *Grimm* to wind down from all the excitement of the evening, and then took my plate into the kitchen to wash it up.

I took a quick shower to wash the sweat off, then flaked out for the rest of the night.

Chapter 40

I woke the following afternoon with a sense of lightness I hadn't felt since that day, all those weeks ago, when Angelica had first walked into my shop to set me on this road. The Order was seemingly finished at last, I had my magick, my shop had its new additions and was doing better than ever. Now if only I could straighten out my personal life, everything would be right in my world.

I almost felt like I was floating a foot off the ground when I went for my run, Paladin and Gauvain catching my mood and having a great time as I went. Pal was bouncing around like a puppy seeing toys for the first time, while G was surpassing himself with his aerobatic loops and wheeling.

Although I wasn't due to go into work, which was a good thing since the battle had eaten up the night here due to the time difference, I was excited to go and make sure everyone was aware of our victory. I showered and shaved, then dressed casually in comfortable jeans and a soft, white shirt.

G hopped onto my shoulder while Pal leant heavily against my leg, then I teleported us to my office at the shop. I breathed deeply, closing my eyes and luxuriating in the familiar smells of leather, books, and polish, smiling again as I thought of being able to enjoy all this without the looming threat of Elrulin hanging over my head.

I stepped around Paladin, who'd already flung himself into his bed and settled in for a nap, shaking my head indulgently as I walked to the office door. I swung it open, nodding to Sophie who happened to be behind the counter again today.

"Hey, Sophie," I greeted her, surprised to see her looking worried when she saw me. "Is everything OK? That 'Karen' hasn't come back, has she?"

"Oh, no," she said, looking over her shoulder fleetingly. "I just wasn't expecting to see you. You're not down as working this weekend, so I didn't think you'd be back in until Tuesday."

"I know, I just wanted to let everyone know the good news," I reassured her. "We did it! We finally ended the Order, so people can relax and stop worrying about them." I made a mental note to talk to Cheveyo about possible leftovers in the US at some point, then focused back on Sophie.

"Oh, that's wonderful!" she exclaimed, finally showing some of the excitement I had expected to see, though she still seemed anxious about something. "Are you OK? Was anyone seriously hurt?"

"Unfortunately, yes," I said. "It's impossible to wage war without casualties, though we were lucky that the Wiccans were ready to heal our wounded so quickly. We were able to minimise the fatalities on our side, and everyone else was healed by the time we left."

I was walking around the counter as I spoke, though Sophie stepped with me and seemed to be trying to keep herself between me and The Sanctuary as I went. I stopped moving, raised an eyebrow at her and crossed my arms.

"OK, spill," I said. "What's up? Did you have a rave in here last night and not have time to finish the clean-up or something? You look like a kid whose parents came home a day early." Sophie ducked her head and slid her eyes away from me, at which my anxiety ratcheted up several notches. I had been joking with her, but now, thanks to her telling body language, I knew something was definitely wrong.

"No, nothing like that," she said, but still refused to meet my gaze.

"Then what?" I asked, looking around to try and spot any problems. As I did, my eyes slid over her shoulder and I finally saw into The Sanctuary. There were no signs of any disasters, everyone was settled and chatting, and business looked to be humming along fine. Then a chill washed over me and my vision tunnelled as I finally caught sight of what Sophie had clearly been trying to shield me from.

Angelica was stood near the kitchen with her arms around one of the young Sanctuary staff, whose name was James if my memory served me correctly, and as I looked on their lips met. I felt my stomach drop away like I'd stepped out of a plane, and it felt like I couldn't breathe. I knew she had been angry with me, but I hadn't expected this.

Then again, I was still working on emotional attachment one-point-oh, from when she'd first come in and then been a damsel in distress. She, on the other hand, was working on reset software since her memory wipe. As far as *she* was concerned, we'd only met at Edinburgh. Then we'd shared a couple of meals at Seirina's and I'd given her a job. We'd flirted back and forth, shared some jokes, but nothing more.

I'd asked her out then double-booked the date, probably making her feel less than valued when I'd picked the other appointment over her, even though that other appointment had wider ramifications. Even I could freely admit she had every right to accept another invitation, since we had no commitment of any kind as far as she knew, although my emotions didn't seem to be quite as understanding as my intellect. Plus, I knew she'd been filled in on some of what we'd had by the twins, so she wasn't completely naïve to my feelings or our history. Sophie clearly realised I'd seen, since she followed my eye-line, as she stepped over to me and rested her hand on my arm.

"Oh, Gavan, I'm so sorry," she said, sighing. "I was hoping they might have separated before you saw her. I heard he asked her out to a concert once your date with her got cancelled."

"As long as she's happy…" I managed to force out past the giant lump in my throat. My head was spinning and I thought I might pass out, so I put a hand on the counter and took some deep breaths. I closed my eyes for a moment, turning away from Sophie since I didn't feel like accepting anyone's sympathy right then. I opened my eyes again, looking around at the solid comfort of my shop, and forced my feelings down deep. It might hurt now, but I knew it would get better eventually – though quite how long that might take was anyone's guess.

"You're a great guy, Gav," Sophie said, sighing again. "I'm sure you'll find someone else really quickly, and I know we'll all be here to support you. Just give it time."

As much as I knew she meant well, platitudes weren't really what I needed right then. What I needed was to beat the living shit out of something, burn it to the ground, and salt the earth. I could feel Gauvain and Paladin responding to my distress across our link, then I heard scrabbling at the office door as Pal tried to get to me. I turned and gave Sophie a brief smile, though it felt like my face cramped as I did. I went back into my personal sanctuary where I grabbed Pal, caught G as he flew over to me, and ripped us away from there.

I must have let my emotions guide me, since my mind wasn't in any kind of fit state to rule my decisions, and I found myself standing outside the one place I might actually get some meaningful discussion about what had happened: Seirina's home. I walked up to the front door and rang the bell tiredly, a genuine smile forcing its way past my lips as I heard Mrs Wilson hurrying down the corridor. Paladin went around the house to lay on the lawn while Gauvain flew up to perch in the big oak tree.

"Mr Maddox!" she exclaimed as she opened the door, putting her right hand to her chest. "I'm really going to have to get used to you popping in without using the gate. Is everything alright? Ms Crow told me you managed to finish the Order last night, so I thought you'd be out celebrating today."

"I was getting ready to," I said ruefully. "Then I kind of took a solid punch to the nethers that took away my inclination. Is Seirina free?"

"Oh dear," she replied, struggling to keep a straight face. "That doesn't sound like much fun. Of course, flower, she's in her study." She stood back to let me in, closing the door behind me and then edging past to go ahead and announce me as I knew she would.

"Ms Crow," she said, opening the door after knocking perfunctorily. "Mr Maddox is here, asking to see you."

"Gavan?" Seirina said, clearly just as confused as to why I'd shown up as Mrs Wilson was. "Get in here. What the hell happened?" she continued when she saw me. She stood up and walked around her desk towards me, and I heard the leaves rustle as Iyrin reared its creepy skeletal head as well. Seirina's eyes glowed scarlet, so I knew she was using her enchantress side to assess me, which meant she'd figure out what had happened in short order. I stepped over to the chairs in front of her desk and slumped heavily into one, hearing her sigh as she 'read' me.

"Oh, Gavan," she said, resting her hand on my shoulder.

"Don't, please," I said. "I can't take sympathy right now. I'm more in the 'tear it all down and burn it to ashes' phase at the moment. Know anyone who needs a loose cannon pointing their way just now?" I was only half joking, since the catharsis would probably feel good right about now, though it probably wasn't the best solution to my current situation. Seirina rolled her eyes and shook her head, not falling for it for a second.

"No, and you shouldn't be going around looking for a fight right now anyway," she cautioned. "With your emotions like this, you're as liable to hurt yourself as you are anyone else. Magick gets notoriously twitchy around severe emotion, so you might experience a power surge or a complete power outage. Even if you *can* control your abilities right now, your aim is likely to be just as erratic. Even teleporting here was a massive risk, and I certainly wouldn't recommend you do it again for a while."

I am surprised to hear of your distress, Iyrin remarked, apparently communicating to both of us since Seirina twitched and looked over at the terrarium. *I don't feel anything from you at all.*

One tiny corner of my mind registered its consternation and felt satisfaction that my mental defences were now effective, though the majority of my focus was still on my wounded emotional state. I ignored the watcher and looked at Seirina, hoping she might have some words of wisdom to get me through this. My hope, however, was destined to be as successful as my dating life.

"So what do I do?" I asked her, sitting forward in the chair in my eagerness for her advice.

"You give it time," she replied simply, at which point I huffed and slumped back in my seat.

"Some enchantress," I muttered mulishly. "I thought you were supposed to be all insightful, be able to sort this all out for me."

"Don't blame me for your incompetence," she said, crossing her arms and tapping her foot. "You're the one who fucked up your date by organising the fight for the same night."

"Yeah, but I didn't expect her to go out with someone else that fast!" I objected angrily.

"Wait, she's seeing someone else?" she asked, raising her eyebrows and dropping her arms. "What... who... when... how?"

"You missed out where, why, and which," I observed bitterly. "The 'who' is one of the guys working in The Sanctuary. 'When' was last night; 'where' was apparently a concert; the 'how' I'm guessing was he asked and actually followed through; and 'why' is no doubt because I fucked up so spectacularly."

Seirina walked back around her desk and sat down heavily in her chair.

"Well, *that* wasn't what I expected!" she said.

"Yeah, no shit Sherlock!" I replied.

Chapter 41

"OK, I'll let that one slide because you're upset right now," Seirina said, resting her left forearm on the desk in front of her and stabbing her right index finger onto the surface. "Just don't push it. Don't forget, this *is* ultimately your fault for leaving things so long and then double-booking your date night."

I am still curious as to why I feel nothing of your distress, Iyrin remarked. *Who taught you how to block me, and why?*

"Eligos," I remarked bluntly, taking a perverse pleasure in seeing it flinch at the sound of that name. I doubted I'd ever learn the reason *why* it was afraid of Eligos, I was just glad it was. "And just so you know, it had nothing to do with you. That's just a happy side effect for me. He was trying to teach me how to protect my mind better, otherwise Elrulin might have been able to overpower me mentally during our battle."

I see, it responded, sounding resigned. *I suppose such information was essential to your success, though it's still irritating. I was rather enjoying your emotional upheavals.*

I shuddered at the implication of its parasitic feeding practices. I closed my eyes and felt for the link it had created, finding it still present. It led to my mental wall, then beyond it, like a wire clamped by a metal sheet. Now that I focused on it, I could sense Iyrin at the other end, though its vibrations stopped at my defences. I focused on my wall at the point the link touched it, imagining my border as a set of wire cutters and clamping down hard. The link shivered, then suddenly snapped. My end dissolved while Iyrin's end flew away like a cable under tension, so I opened my eyes to see it flinch as the backlash reached it.

"Well, *that* makes me feel a little better," I said smugly, grinning at Seirina. "If the little fucker gets too much for you, just let me know. I just managed to sever our connection completely, so I'm sure I could teach you, too. And I will if you harm her in any way at all, or so much as *look* at anyone else I care about the wrong way." I addressed my last comment directly to Iyrin, surprised to see it flinch from me in the same way it had when Eligos spoke to it.

I guessed starvation was the reason it disliked Eligos, which meant now *I* was included in the rarefied group of individuals who could defy it with impunity. So much for my earlier doubts, but this was one time I was actually glad to have been wrong. Silver linings, I guess.

"Really?" she asked, at which Iyrin's skull spun to look at her so fast I almost laughed.

"Absolutely," I answered, looking at the terrarium with an evil grin. It turned its back on me and descended out of sight. I heaved a sigh of relief and relaxed my guard for the first time since Eligos had helped me upgrade. I'd been maintaining it in the hopes it would protect me from Iyrin, but I hadn't been sure until I got here. Yet again, the scales balanced themselves with a loss and gain in kind of equal measure. (Not really, but I'd take what I could get!)

"So now I can think and feel without someone – or more to the point, some*thing* – looking over my proverbial shoulder," I continued, sighing and sitting back in my chair. "Just what am I supposed to do about this new genital thwart?"

Seirina sprayed the sip of tea she had just taken over her desk, then fought to cough, laugh, and breathe at the same time.

"Holy crap!" she swore, once she finally managed to inhale. "Warn a person when you're going to say something like that! What the hell is a 'genital thwart', and is it as unpleasant as it sounds?"

"It's the PC, gender-neutral version of a cock block," I informed her, laughing at her evident distress. "At least I'm doing my best to laugh at my shit-sandwich of a situation. But getting back to my question, *what do I do?*"

"There's not a lot you *can* do right now," she said, tilting her head to her left and furrowing her brow slightly. "You have to let their relationship play out as it will, unless you're going to try and deliberately sabotage them. That runs the risk of turning them against you and driving them closer together, though, or at *best* splitting them up and making at least one of them hate you. Relationships are a treacherous enough prospect at the best of times. Injecting that sort of dynamic is like playing with lit matches, while standing in a pool of gasoline, with your pockets full of dynamite that's old and sweating."

"So, what you're saying is, it's doable?" I quipped, immediately holding my hands up and trying to wave off her look of indignant fury. "Kidding, I swear! Well, sort of. I mean, I know it's a bad idea, I just can't help wishing..." I trailed off and slumped down. Seirina sighed and nodded.

"I know, sweetie, really I do," she said. "I saw how you two were together before Edinburgh, and I know for a *fact* how much you loved her." When she said that, it jogged a memory of her talking to me at breakfast one morning with her eyes glowing red.

"Wait, that day when you threatened me with your enchantress abilities," I said, my mind racing through the thought process as I was talking. "You were actually trying to seduce me, weren't you? Then when it failed, it was proof I was really in love with Angie, which is why you nodded to her and she smiled so hugely!"

"I'm impressed," she told me. "You worked that out very well. Yes, only true love can defend you against an enchantress' seductive powers. The question you have to ask yourself now is, do you love her enough to let her be happy with someone else? Can you see her every day at work and tolerate her being with another man in front of you, if that is what she wants?"

"A daily dose of a root canal crossed with someone trying to dig out my heart with a rusty spoon? Sounds like great fun," I said, shrugging as she rolled her eyes at my not-so-subtle sarcasm. "Look, I know it's going to suck beyond all conceivable levels, but yes. I *do* love her that much, and if he makes her happy, then so be it. If he hurts her, however..."

Seirina raised her eyebrows and nodded in understanding.

"Yeah, I can only imagine the degrees of pain and suffering you'd rain down on him in that scenario," she acknowledged. "In fact, I'd expect nothing less from someone with your abilities. However, there's something you need to understand before you start down that road. It might *feel* like you're doing the right thing by defending her honour in that way, but karma is a tricky thing. If the guy hasn't done anything to you, and he hasn't truly done anything *evil*, you'd be exacting punishment out of proportion to his actions.

"After all, relationships have a natural flow and life expectancy. They may not all work out how we plan, but that doesn't mean anyone necessarily did anything wrong. Sometimes people grow apart as they learn more about each other, discovering they're not as compatible as they thought at first. Sometimes their lives just lead them in different directions, and they simply can't stay together if they want to live their lives the way they choose to.

"Whatever the reason, all you can do is let things develop as *they* make them happen. By all means be there for her if they fail, just don't help them along to that point."

I nodded, wanting to reassure her that I understood and wouldn't go off half-, full-, or any other degree of cocked.

"I know, I know," I agreed, albeit reluctantly and despite my better judgement. Hey, I could still *fantasise* about ripping the guy's spleen out through his ass, even if I knew I couldn't actually *do* it.

"I wish you sounded a little more convincing, but I'll take what I can get," Seirina said wryly.

"Yeah, sorry," I replied, shrugging. "That's about as much as I've got in me right now."

"Look, I know this isn't what you want to hear," she continued. "But you just have to give it time."

"Oh joy, more platitudes," I deadpanned, prompting pursed lips and a head shake from Seirina. "Look, I'm not trying to be an asshole. I know you're trying to help. It's just all those sayings are well-known, so I don't need someone to say them for me. I've already had a dose from Sophie at the shop, so I was hoping for something a little more insightful or helpful from you. Especially since you're an enchantress."

"Hey, those abilities just help with seducing someone to bend them to my will," she explained. "They don't make me any better than anyone else at dealing with rejection or a broken heart."

"Great," I grumped. "Well, then, thanks for just about nothing, I guess. No, really," I continued, as her mouth opened ready to deliver what would no doubt be a blistering tirade about my ingratitude. "I appreciate you listening to me, and I know there isn't really anything more anyone can do. I'm just feeling sorry for myself right now.

"Look, I'll leave you alone to get back to your weekend. I'm gonna go home and curl up on my couch, lick my wounds, and wallow for a couple of days. I'll see you later." As I finished, I stood up and headed for the door.

"Gav, look," she said, getting up to follow me. I ignored her, opened the study door and made my way through the kitchen to the back door. I said goodbye to Mrs Wilson as I went, then went out into the garden and called Paladin and Gauvain as I reached the grass.

The second G hit my shoulder and Pal was close enough to touch, I ripped us away from the garden to land in the living room of my apartment. Neither of them said anything, though I could feel their love and support washing through our connections. I was glad they were there, even if they had no more idea of how to help than Seirina did. I threw myself onto the sofa, grabbed the TV remote, and switched on Judge Judy. Maybe I could make myself feel better by watching people even more stupid than me.

G had already flown over to his perch, while Paladin clambered onto the couch with me and lay with his front legs and head in my lap. I put my hand on his head and started rubbing his ears, finally smiling as he groaned in pleasure. I kicked off my shoes and put my feet up on the coffee table, resting my head back against the cushion to stare up at the ceiling.

How was it, just when I was apparently the hero of the entire magickal world for destroying Elrulin and his bunch of cockamamie, power-hungry assholes, my own world was coming crashing down around my ears? Where was karma when it came to reward time, huh? How come it only seemed to come around to bite you in the ass when you were ready for the good times to start? The fickle bitch was nowhere to be found when things were already shit, and you were waiting for your luck to finally pay off. I closed my eyes, listening to Judge Judy laying the smack down as I drifted off to sleep with one final thought:

Fuck this shit.

Chapter 42

I spent the rest of the weekend moping around. I couldn't be bothered to cook, so I just ordered pizza and lounged around in my sweats. I didn't even go out for my run on Sunday, instead ordering a breakfast sandwich from Uber Eats and hibernating on the sofa again. Thankfully, Gauvain was quite happy to fly out the window and hunt for himself, so I didn't even have to sort him out any food. The only time I got up was to get another drink from the fridge or to let the takeaway driver up.

When Monday finally rolled around, I forced myself to lace up my running shoes and go outside. I knew if I didn't go to work today, I'd just keep hiding. Every day would get harder to go back, and more tempting to stay cocooned in my little corner of the world. I trudged round my three miles, feeling a little achy after having missed a day but glad to get some fresh air again. I stretched a bit longer than normal at the end, working out the kinks, then went up to get my shower. I shaved, managing to nick myself three times in my distraction, then got dressed. Thankfully I could heal myself, otherwise I'd look like I'd walked through a slaughterhouse to get to work.

I didn't have the energy or focus to teleport to the shop, so I grabbed my keys and walked down the stairs to the car. Gauvain took his usual front seat perch, while Pal spread himself out in the load area. I'd put a flat beanbag in there for him, though he'd never had a chance to try it out since we didn't really use the car much anymore. He sent me his silent approval as I fastened my seatbelt, leading to my first partial smile in a couple of days. I turned the key in the ignition and set off for the shop.

I meandered my way through the Monday morning traffic, quite happy to let rush hour procrastinate for me. Finally, inevitably, I managed to navigate the treacherous waters of the Yorkshire roadways to arrive at my shop and pull into my accustomed parking spot. As I turned off the engine, I realised the downside to my cunning plan. Namely, I had to walk in through the front door in full view of the staff.

I contemplated teleporting into my office from outside, although I'd still have to go out to the shop if I wanted my coffee. I knew there was no way in hell I could forgo my morning caffeine, unless I wanted to make it to lunch-time over the bloodied and twisted corpses of my workers, so I might as well get it over with now. There was no point trying to be inconspicuous while I had Paladin and Gauvain with me, so I took a few deep breaths and then braced myself to walk in with my head held high.

Thankfully, the only person in the shop was one of the new guys. His name, if memory served, was Michael, and he had joined us only a couple of weeks ago. He was the nephew once removed or something of one of the Wiccans in Aurora's coven, though he himself hadn't shown any aptitude thus far. Still, he was at least aware of the magickal world, so he was glad to work somewhere that kept him in touch with it.

He was already using every opportunity to pore over any books he could get his hands on to try to awaken some kind of talent or ability, and I'd promised him I'd try and help once the Order was dealt with. I just hoped he would give me a bit of a breather before he expected me to start, since I really didn't think my current frame of mind would be especially conducive to his efforts.

To my great relief, he seemed to be aware of my situation, though he didn't get all mushy about it. Instead, I was the recipient of a surprisingly mature manly nod and a ready-made pot of Cafegeddon. I gave him the requisite return head bob, went into my office, and locked the door behind me. Paladin was already comfortably ensconced in his bed, while G stood on his perch and looked at me.

Well, now what? he asked, sympathetically but practically. *You can't exactly hide in here all day, every day; not if you want to continue to run the shop as the boss. People are going to want to congratulate you on defeating the Order, and you need to be seen to celebrate with them. Right now you're the hero of the magickal community, so you need to focus on that as much as possible. You need to be seen and approachable, and you need to show everyone you're as happy as they are that Elrulin and his cronies are gone. And, as painful as it may be, you need to try to be OK with Angelica and her new beau.*

"I know," I groaned, dropping into my chair and putting my head back to stare up at the ceiling. "But can I at least do all that shit when I've had a full mug of coffee?"

G chuckled, though I felt his love and support flow across our bond as I sighed with my eyes closed. I relaxed in the familiar environment of my sanctuary for a few minutes, then took a long pull at my mug while my computer booted up. I spent the next couple of hours going through the records from the weekend, then my coffee decided to make a break for freedom so I was forced out of hibernation if I didn't want to soil my jeans.

I unlocked my office door as quietly as I could, taking a breath before opening it as normally as possible. I walked directly to the staff toilet, glad no-one tried to talk to me on the way since my bladder wasn't going to allow me to stop and chat. When I came out, however, I realised people had become aware of my presence. The cheers and applause took me by complete surprise, and I found myself blushing like a schoolgirl on her first date. People were reaching out to shake my hand like I was a movie star or an astronaut, women were kissing my cheeks so often I was going to need make-up remover.

Even Angelica was there, cheering along with everyone else, though she didn't kiss my cheek. I smiled and thanked everyone, gradually edging my way back to my office until I finally made it back after taking almost half an hour to walk a mere five yards. At least I'd made it through my first meeting with Angie intact, so hopefully I could simply move on with my life now. However painful it might be for me, however much I might wish it were otherwise, she had made her choice. If she was happy, that was as much as I could hope for, and I would just have to do my best to follow Seirina's advice to let her relationship flow naturally.

I sat back behind my desk with a totally unexpected smile, switching my computer from the accounts and stock program to my emails. There were the usual offers of women in my area looking for a date, penis enlargement and sexual prowess enhancers, plus I had apparently won a five thousand pound gift card if I just signed up to a message service that would send me six messages at one pound fifty each. Once all that dross was cleared out, there was a message from my dad checking in to see how I was doing. I wasn't quite sure how to answer that, given my wonderful personal life success and the fact that he'd never believed in magick.

I played it safe and just told him the business was doing well, leaving everything else out for safety's sake. I *might* be able to explain the rest face to face like I had with Frank – though I remembered how well *that* effort went – but over email it would just sound like the storyline for a cheesy fantasy novel. After that was sent, I checked a couple more messages from suppliers on the business account and then closed the program.

As I sat back in my chair and stretched, I realised I hadn't ordered any more coffee in quite a while. I knew my home stock was running low, especially after I'd shared it with Seirina and the girls, and I could only imagine how hard the shop supply had been hit by all the new staff. I went online and opened up the Death Wish Coffee site, deciding it was now time to use their subscription service to save some money. I saw they now did a medium roast but I went with their dark roast Death Wish, since I didn't want to risk upsetting my formula. I also made sure I didn't forget the essential Odinforce Blend Valhalla Java, ordering several five pound bags of each.

Next I went to the Throat Punch Coffee website, spending a little time reading about their fantastic new shop in Edinburgh. I wished it had been open when we'd been up there for our assault, though I could always pop up there some time now that I didn't have to drive. Once I'd read all about that, I went to the section for buying their coffee. They had expanded their selection, though I stuck with their Indian Cherry Robusta for making my Cafegeddon blend. Again, no point messing with greatness. I did, however, decide to also order a kilo of their new Number Thirty Espresso Blend for myself, just to test.

I was able to tick that off of my mental to-do list now, though given the postage costs for the Death Wish stuff from the US, I really wished they had the big bags available over here. Mind you, perfection was hard to achieve and worth striving and paying for, so I did what I had to in order to create my version of it. Thank the gods I had my retainer from the Order and the shop was doing so well! I also decided to go onto the UK trademark website and trademark the Cafegeddon name. That way I could maybe even start selling the blend in The Sanctuary for people to take home.

I completed the application and set the process in motion, then decided to try to come up with a design for it. I ended up designing a mushroom cloud made out of coffee beans, with the name in an arc over the top. I ordered a few stickers of the design as a trial run, then looked over at the clock in surprise to see it was after four already. Time really did fly when you were having fun.

I went out to the shop, returning a couple of waves from people who looked to still be celebrating the end of Elrulin and the Order. My stomach let out a resounding rumble, reminding me I hadn't eaten anything all day, so I made my way into The Sanctuary and sat down at one of the tables. After perusing the menu for a while, I decided on a bacon cheeseburger with mushrooms, Cajun wedges, onion rings, and a portion of spicy buffalo wings. I downed my first beer fairly quickly, ordering a second while I was still only a quarter of the way through my meal.

By the time the last stripped chicken bone hit the plate, I was feeling much better about myself and my situation. It was amazing how much more philosophical one could be on a full stomach. As I paid, I saw the attractive woman who I'd noticed several times before was staring right at me. I smiled and nodded at her, just in time to see her features ripple and shift slightly. My jaw dropped as I recognised her: the Fae I'd rescued from the cells at Edinburgh, Alcina!

She smiled briefly at me before turning and walking out through the shop. I considered running after her, but I knew that, given her head start, she'd have disappeared long before I could reach her. I was sure I'd see her again, and everyone knew the Fae only revealed their purpose to you when *they* were ready. Still, at least I knew it wasn't my imagination now – I was definitely being watched.

As I made my way back to my office, I noticed someone at the counter talking to Michael. He appeared to be demanding something, while my staff member was stoically refusing to comply. As I got close enough to hear what they were saying, I realised *I* was the subject of their disagreement.

"I'm sorry, sir," Michael said, politely yet firmly. "Mr Maddox only sees people by appointment, and you clearly don't have one. If you'd care to book something, I can pencil you in next week sometime."

I smiled at his firm adherence to the rules I'd set down, though the visitor was quite clearly less impressed.

"I have to talk to him today," he demanded. "It's for his own…" He trailed off as he caught sight of me, apparently familiar with my appearance somehow. "Mr Maddox, I have to talk to you. My name is Marcus, and I represent the Council of Enlightenment here in Yorkshire. We represent all *major* magick users, and it is therefore time to discuss your membership."

For fuck's sake, not *another* group of assholes who were going to try and make me do what they wanted. I groaned inwardly but realised I may as well get this over with quickly, although this asshole had better change his tone if he wanted to walk out of here in the same condition as when he entered. I sighed and gestured to my office, letting him go first.

I really didn't need this shit right now.

Chapter 43

"So who, exactly, are the 'Council of Enlightenment'?" I asked as I walked around my desk, being sure to emphasise my air-quotes as I spoke. "And why exactly should I even care? It's not as if you were any kind of help during the fight against the Order, so why the fuck should I even give you the time of day now?" I became more animated with each sentence, finally slamming my open hands onto the leather writing surface of my desk loudly enough to startle Pal out of his sleep with a bark and make Gauvain shriek in protest.

"Now, Mr Maddox," Marcus said carefully, leaning back in his chair in the face of my anger. "I can understand you being upset at our lack of support–"

"UPSET?!" I roared, to the sound of further barking and shrieking from my friends. "You think this is me *upset*? This is me mildly irritated, slightly perturbed, vaguely put out. Believe me, if I was truly *upset* right now, you'd be a bloody smear on the wall. If I was actually *angry*, on the other hand, there'd be a smouldering crater in the middle of my shop. Trust me when I say you shouldn't make me angry. You *really* wouldn't like me when I'm angry." I smiled tightly as I paraphrased the famous line from the original angry man, generating a somewhat wavering smile from Marcus in return.

"I apologise, Mr Maddox," he said quickly. "I misspoke. Please, may we start again?"

"Very well," I replied, finally sitting down in my chair and steepling my fingers. "But I wouldn't recommend starting with a demand for me to join your 'Council'. Your lack of assistance has been noted and found offensive, so you're starting on very shaky ground." The name 'Council of Enlightenment' seemed to have infected my speech patterns with a degree of formality that wasn't my norm, although Marcus seemed to respond to it.

"So tell me," I continued. "As I asked before, what exactly is this council and why should I even care?"

"The Council is the governing body for all magick users of any significance," Marcus stated grandiosely, insulting several of my friends and allies with that one sentence alone. "We have heard of your abilities and accomplishments, and we wish to offer you the opportunity to join our ranks."

"So you're saying that Seirina Crow, a woman who has powers most would give their right *and* left arms to possess, is not a 'magick user of any significance'?" I asked casually, handing him every inch of rope he needed to hang himself with and then sitting back to watch.

"Well... that is, I mean to say..." he stammered, suddenly realising just how deep the hole he had dug for himself was. "I'm sorry, I seem to be saying everything wrong. I swear I'm not trying to upset you, but the Council has ordered me to get you to join us." I could hear the capitalisation of the name he used each time, so I took a perverse delight in not doing the same.

"And given the council's previously mentioned astounding lack of assistance – or even presence – thus far, why would I be interested in joining them?" I asked. "I have just fought an organisation which, if your council's absence is anything to go by, had you all hiding under the bed like frightened children.

"I and my allies beat them and I killed their leader, all without any help from your so-called 'magick users of any significance'. And now you come here, denigrating my allies and their abilities, and expect me to come running when you snap your fingers?" My voice remained calm, modulated, even quiet by the end of my little speech, though Marcus seemed to react even more to the inherent danger of my attitude than when I had been openly shouting. Sweat broke out across his forehead as he struggled to make his way out of the mess he'd made for himself.

"Again, I apologise for any offence," he said, swallowing convulsively. "Please, would you at least consider meeting with some of them? Listen to what the Council has to say, understand what they stand for? Maybe they can explain better than I can. Witches, wizards, warlocks, and sorcerers have traditionally stuck together for the most part, and we could help you develop your abilities in ways you've barely even begun to consider."

He leant forward as he spoke, his belief and passion for his topic coming across clearly. This was the first time since I'd met him that Marcus hadn't pissed me off inadvertently. His honest belief in the value of the council was the only thing that evinced even the slightest degree of curiosity in me, though the high-handedness of their attitude was very nearly enough to eclipse that interest.

"Didn't your parents tell you about the Council when you came into your powers?" Marcus asked, curiously. "How have you never heard of it before?"

"Clearly you don't know anything about me," I replied. "To start with, I'm what you would call 'a first'." The surprise was blatantly evident on Marcus' face. Clearly my abilities were far in excess of his expectations for a first, just as they had been for Seirina. "Yes, I thought that might surprise you. I apparently blocked my abilities when I was a child due to my disbelief when I first used magick. Then, when the Order sent me on a hunt for the Veil of Isis, my abilities were unlocked. My training was at the hands of individuals who, I am quite sure, would have your council members grovelling on the floor. So, as I'm sure you can understand, I am somewhat doubtful of what you might have to teach me."

"I had no idea," he murmured, furrowing his brow. "Your being a first would be why the Council was unaware of your family, and anything to do with Isis would certainly explain your unusual level of power. I would be intrigued to hear the full story one day," he finished, immediately holding up his hands in acknowledgement of the impertinence of his enquiry.

"So you see," I observed. "My story is somewhat different than your council realised. I suggest you go back to them and let them know what I've told you. Then maybe, if the council representative approaches me correctly next time, I'll be inclined to give them more than just the time of day."

Marcus bowed his head briefly then stood up, fully understanding his dismissal. As he walked out, I saw several staff members hovering outside my office, no doubt alerted by my earlier shouting and the noise from Paladin and Gauvain. I waved them off and they backed away to let Marcus out, though all of them watched him closely all the way to the door.

I flicked my fingers and closed the door telekinetically, sitting back in my chair to contemplate this revelation of the council's existence. It meant that there were significantly more magick users out there than I had been aware of before, though it also revealed how self-serving they apparently were when it came to protecting their own asses.

Now I understood why they said a little knowledge was a dangerous thing: The small amount of knowledge I had of the council was certainly enough to piss me off without allowing me to see any redeeming virtues they might have.

I stared up at the ceiling, puffing out a deep breath as I contemplated this newest wrinkle in my life's rich tapestry. Yeah, OK, I was feeling philosophical – fuck off. I couldn't believe how far I'd come since that day, just a few short months ago, when Angelica had walked into my shop and sent my entire life spiralling out of the rut it had been in into an entirely new dimension. Quite literally, if you considered my little sojourn in Aaru.

Magick was really real; I was the 'Chosen of Isis'; I'd been trained by the Goddess of Knowledge; I'd met the literal Devil and made a deal with him; I'd fought alongside a demon; I'd killed someone who had been terrorising the entire magickal world for over two-and-a-half centuries – I couldn't have imagined this if I'd dared to dream it. Then I'd managed to almost mentally destroy a friend when I'd revealed it all to Frank, so I'd had to wipe his mind for his own good.

That reminded me, now the Order was done and Elrulin was dead, Lucian was no doubt ready to claim his side of the deal. Still, I'd learned some things about him that made my representing him to Isis a little more problematic than I'd thought. He still treated other beings as slaves and irrelevant, he lied to me about distancing himself from Elrulin… How the hell could I stand witness for him to the Aaruan council, knowing all that?

Then there was my personal life, or lack thereof right now. I'd rescued Angie from the Order, we'd gotten together finally, then her memory got wiped. She'd come to work for me but we'd kept missing our opportunity, then I'd finally asked her out only to screw up and double book the night. Then, after all that, she'd gone out with another of my employees while I'd been out saving the entire magickal world and I was left twisting in the wind again.

On top of *that* there was Alcina. The Fae had been rescued from the magick-suppressing prison cell in Edinburgh by me, then had changed her appearance to keep popping up at various times. Now that I finally knew it was her, I had to wonder what her interest in me actually was. Was it romantic? Did she want me for something at the behest of her queen? A combination of both? Neither?

And now, on top of all that, here comes this 'Council of Enlightenment' telling me I needed to join them for some reason.

I had a headache.

Paladin got up off his bed, came over and sat next to me, resting his massive head in my lap. He looked up at me and gave a classic doggy moan/whine. Gauvain hopped onto my shoulder from his perch and nibbled my hair, both of my friends sending me their silent reassurance. I guessed they didn't really know what to say, since they both knew how I'd felt about Angie before her mind-wipe. This was kind of out of their wheelhouse in terms of advice, but at least they were letting me know they were there for me regardless.

I stroked them both, the simple action reaffirming my love for them and simultaneously calming me down. The tension gradually eased from my neck, releasing the pressure in my head, and settling my mind. I knew I had a lot to get straight, and I really doubted the effectiveness of my sanctuary this time. I needed to get away from here; there were just too many associations between Angelica, Alcina, my magick…

I shut my computer down, got up, and took myself and my friends out of the shop. I used my magick to clear the alcohol out of my system, since I didn't need a car crash on top of everything else just now. I got us all settled in the car and I put my phone into the holder, cued up my driving music playlist, turned up the volume, and just drove. I didn't know where I was going, I just needed to think.

I drove around the countryside for what felt like hours, watching as the sun drooped in the sky and the headlights started coming on. I knew I'd reached the end of a huge piece of my life, but it was barely an introduction to the real story still to come.

I pulled the car into the garage underneath my apartment building, settling it into its accustomed spot. The three of us got out, my friends remaining silent but supportive as I trudged my way up the stairs to my floor. I let us in, Paladin immediately heading to his bed and curling up while Gauvain flew to his perch.

I sat down on the sofa, my mind still whirling a million miles a second with everything that had happened and everything still to come. I honestly can't remember what I watched on TV, I just know I couldn't fall asleep no matter how hard I tried.

Eventually I did drift off, my turmoil of thoughts turning into some weird-ass dreams. I woke up with my head dangling off the sofa and Paladin licking my face. I wiped off his doggy slobber and sat up, hanging my head as I rested my elbows on my knees.

Then I took a deep breath, stood up, and made my way to the shower, stripping off as I went.

Time to see what the next instalment of my life had to offer.

Epilogue

I was sitting at my desk, going over the bookkeeping program, making a couple of notes on which lines were or weren't selling, when the phone rang. I hit the speaker button without looking away from the screen, since I didn't want to lose my place if I didn't have to.

"Dinas Affaraon, Gavan Maddox speaking," I said automatically.

"I'm disappointed," came a familiar voice, making my head snap away from what I was doing to focus fully on the call. "I didn't think I would need to prompt you to fulfil your obligations. I thought you were more honourable and conscientious than that."

A chill ran down my spine at the implication, and sweat broke out across my forehead as my mind started racing to play catch-up.

"Lucian," I said. "My apologies; I've been dealing with a few personal issues recently. And let's be honest, it's only been a couple of days."

"Be that as it may, you have a debt to be repaid," he intoned, leaving me with precisely zero doubts as to why he was calling – not that I really had any to begin with.

Clearly, the Devil wanted his due.

GAVAN MADDOX
WILL RETURN...

Acknowledgements

As ever, there are a number of people I need to thank here. Firstly, my wife Melanie for her ever-patient, long-suffering ongoing support. Without her, I'd probably still be trying to figure out my first book. She also is my perennial assistant when it comes to going through the voluminous edits I get sent.

That leads me to Keidi Keating and her team, who struggle through my atrocious grammar and punctuation to knock my story into an acceptable form.

Thirdly, to Tammy, Larry, Paige, LeAnn, and Cindy for putting up with my horrendous first draft and suggesting how to turn it into a more coherent story.

Fourthly, to Luke Watkins for reminding me about the ash dragon near Bolton Castle, and thus being the inspiration behind Lukasz.

Lastly, to all of you my readers. Thank you for sticking with me and Gavan through our adventures. Don't worry, there's more to come…

Alex Polak is a qualified doctor who lives and works in Yorkshire. He attended Harrow School and then Leeds University, where he studied medicine. He lives with his loving and supportive wife Melanie, her mother, and their two cats, Samson and Delilah. Alex previously practiced GKR karate, becoming a qualified instructor and entering several competitions. He enjoys reading, watching films, and playing computer games on several platforms, as well as swimming, cycling, and horse riding. He loves cooking - and eating! - and he and his wife spend much of their time together in the kitchen.

He has been an avid reader since childhood, reading everything from comic books to Shakespeare, Tolkien to Tom Clancy. Over recent years he has gravitated more to urban fantasy, becoming involved in several Facebook groups for different authors and finally becoming inspired to try writing for himself.

www.ingramcontent.com/pod-product-compliance
Lightning Source LLC
Chambersburg PA
CBHW031213260626
47169CB00007B/2038